If You Don't
Know Me

Also by Mary B. Morrison

The Crystal Series
Baby, You're the Best
Just Can't Let Go

If I Can't Have You Series
If I Can't Have You
I'd Rather Be With You
If You Don't Know Me

Soulmates Dissipate Series
Soulmates Dissipate
Never Again Once More
He's Just a Friend
Somebody's Gotta Be on Top
Nothing Has Ever Felt Like This
When Somebody Loves You Back
Darius Jones

The Honey Diaries Series
Sweeter Than Honey
Who's Loving You
Unconditionally Single
Darius Jones

She Ain't the One (coauthored with Carl Weber)
Maneater (anthology with Noire)
The Eternal Engagement
Justice Just Us Just Me
Who's Making Love

Mary B. Morrison, writing as HoneyB
Sexcapades
Single Husbands
Married on Mondays
The Rich Girls Club

Presented by Mary B. Morrison
Diverse Stories: From the Imaginations of Sixth Graders
(an anthology of fiction written by thirty-three 6th graders)

If You Don't Know Me

MARY B. MORRISON

Kensington Publishing Corp.
http://www.kensingtonbooks.com

DAFINA BOOKS are published by

Kensington Publishing Corp.
119 West 40th Street
New York, NY 10018

All Kensington titles, imprints, and distributed lines are available at special quantity discounts for bulk purchases for sales promotion, premiums, fund-raising, educational, or institutional use. Special book excerpts or customized printings can also be created to fit specific needs. For details, write or phone the office of the Kensington Special Sales Manager: Attn. Special Sales Department. Kensington Publishing Corp., 119 West 40th Street, New York, NY 10018. Phone: 1-800-221-2647.

Dafina and the Dafina logo Reg. U.S. Pat. & TM Off.

ISBN-13: 978-0-7582-7307-9
ISBN-10: 0-7582-7307-X
First Kensington Hardcover Edition: April 2014
First Kensington Trade Edition: February 2015
First Kensington Mass Market Edition: February 2017

eISBN-13: 978-1-61773-867-8
eISBN-10: 1-61773-867-0
First Kensington Electronic Edition: February 2015

10 9 8 7 6 5 4 3 2 1

Printed in the United States of America

Dedicated to the real men I met while in Houston, Texas, working on this series.

Souleymane Bakayoto
Harold V. Dutton Jr.
Jason Griffin
Donald Hogan
Raynard Richardson
Kevin Smith
and
Dominique McClellan

Acknowledgments

All great things must cum to a climax. That is why I'm ending my *If I Can't Have You* trilogy with an orgasmic, "Oh my God!" and not leaving you with a cliffhanger this time. As I conclude, I must thank God for blessing me with the gift to write for Kensington Publishing Corporation for fourteen consecutive years. I don't take for granted the continued success I've had in the literary industry. For my longevity, I thank you, my friends, family, and fans, for buying my books!

I'm excited about my next two projects. My new series is *Single Moms*. Get ready to meet Sandara, Alexis, Mercedes, and Devereaux. Then there is my upcoming book, *D.A.D.: A woman's guide to choosing the right one.* D.A.D. stands for "Dicks are Dumb." Don't believe me just read it.

If you want to get and keep a man, ladies, you shouldn't act like a lady (hopefully you're already that) and think like a man (realistically you'll never be one). Real women know the rela will last longer when you "act like a bitch and think like a dick."

The phenomenal people in my life lift me to higher heights. Marissa "Pynk" Monteilh is my bestest author friend and confidant. Kimberla Lawson Roby is the most consistent and caring author I know. Your support never wavers and I thank both of you for your authenticity.

My son, Jesse Bernard Byrd Jr., is absolutely outstanding. Susan Mary Malone describes my son's debut novel, *Oiseau*, as "brilliant!" I wholeheartedly agree. Jesse writes for adolescents and up. I continue to say, "God gave me the right child." Jesse's apparel, OiseauClothes.com, was promoted at an *At Risk Youth* charitable event with Tyler Perry and worn by Marlon Wayans, Chris Bosh, Jason Derulo, Kali Hawk, and a host of other celebrities. My son's fiancée, Emaan Abbass, is a beautiful woman inside and out. I couldn't have a better future daughter-in-law.

Timothy Kees, I'm extremely proud of you. I've known you since you were four years old. Now you're a branch manager at Wells Fargo, a grad student, and a homeowner. I pray for your continued blessings and success.

While doing research for this novel, I stayed at Magic Johnson's son's Hotel ICON and Hotel ZaZa, both in Houston. I had the privilege of a private tour of the Texas State Capitol in Austin and the office of State Representative Harold V. Dutton Jr. by Rep. Dutton. Thanks for the love, my love.

Dining at Corner Table, happy hour at Eddie V's, a quick stop at 51Fifteen, a burger at Avalon Diner, jazz at the Red Cat Café, and drinks at Swagger, just to name a few of the places I enjoyed while in Houston, Texas. I love a man in a suit wearing cowboy boots. Thanks to all the wonderful people I met!

Thanks to all my Facebook fans who came to support my venues across the country. To name a few, at the Decatur Book Festival: Bookworm Divas Book Club, LaLinda Hernandez, Charles Bailey, and Lawrence C. Newson (and wife).

Much love and appreciation to my unmarried

husband Richard C. Montgomery. I cannot thank you enough for your undying hospitality and unconditional friendship, man. There's nothing I wouldn't do for you.

Jack Manning, you're the best photographer! Love, love, love all your pics. The photos are beautiful, thanks to Jennifer Ferriola, and Shiedah Williams, my personal make-up artist. Shay, my hair stylist. Ashley Gray, Marissa Monteilh's make-up artist. Lindsay Rochelle Brown, make-up artist to my fans.

I am eternally grateful to Phillip Rafshoon, Jullian Kuhns, Googie Daniels, Lisa Baron, Ella D. Curry, Stephanie Perry Moore and E. Missy Daniels (Delta Sigma Theta), Pearl Woolridge, Vera Warren-Williams, Yolanda Gore, Tira McDonald (UCAAB), and Brian Smith, for your support.

To the Honorable Vanessa Gilmore, your assistance is forever greatly appreciated. Jason Griffin and Souleymane Bakayoto, thanks for your Southern hospitality. My special friend Dominique McClellan, I hope you outrun that bear in the woods. I wish you the best in your acting, modeling, and singing career. See you at the top! Chad Bailey, bartender at Ted's Montana Grill in Decatur, Georgia, you should consider modeling.

I enjoyed hanging out in Atlanta with my sisters Margie Rickerson and Regina Morrison. My nephew Roland Morrison, thanks for being my personal assistant. My nephew Devin Barrett, I'm proud of you. Welcome to the family. My niece, Eboni Perry, it was a real blast seeing you in the ATL.

My friend since third grade, Vanessa Ibanitoru, thanks for hanging. My earthly mother, Barbara Cooper, I love you. I'm eternally grateful to have lifetime friends: Felicia Polk, Vyllorya A. Evens, Marilyn Edge, Michela Burnett, Shannette Slaughter, Eve Lynne Robinson, and Carmen Polk.

My mother, Elester Noel, wish I would've known you before God called you home. My father, Joseph Henry Morrison, thanks for the everlasting wisdom. It's because of you that I keep it real. Thanks for getting it in before leaving out.

My great-aunt, Ella Beatrice Turner, and my great-uncle, Willie Frinkle, reared me and for that I am truly blessed. Didn't understand why my great-aunt was hard on me back then but I get it now. Thanks for the tough love!

Wayne, Andrea, Derrick, and Regina Morrison, Margie Rickerson, Debra Noel, and Bryan Turner are my siblings. Thanks guys, I love you! Derrick, Dannette, Angela Lewis-Morrison, and Wanda Hutchinson, I'm sure I speak for the fam when I say, "Thanks for organizing our first Morrison Family Reunion. Looking forward to 2015."

I genuinely appreciate each and every one of my Facebook family, friends, and fans, my Twitter and Instagram followers, and my McDonogh 35 Senior High alumni.

Thanks to my editor and friend, Selena James at Kensington Publishing Corporation. To Steven Zacharius, Adam Zacharius, Laurie Parkin, Karen Auerbach, Adeola Saul, Lesleigh Irish-Underwood, and everyone at Kensington, thanks for growing my literary career.

Well, what's an author without brilliant agents? I'm fortunate to have two of the best agents in the literary business, Andrew Stuart and Claudia Menza. You are appreciated. Thanks to my attorneys, Kendall Minter, Esq., and Kenneth P. Norwick, Esq.

On to the next. It's Hollywood, baby! We are still preparing for the theatrical release of *Soulmates Dissipate*, the movie. I wish I could give you a behind-the-scenes breakdown of making a movie. I'll have to blog about it at a later time. I thank everyone for working diligently on the project: Leslie Small, director/producer; Jeff Clanagan, CEO of Codeblack Entertainment; producer Dawn C Mallory; and Jesse Byrd Jr.

Wishing each of my readers peace and prosperity in abundance. Visit me online at MaryMorrison.com, sign up for my HoneyBuzz newsletter. Join my fan page on Facebook at Mary-Honey-B-Morrison, follow me on Twitter @marybmorrison and Instagram at maryhoneybmorrison.

PROLOGUE

Sindy

Real women didn't play childish games.

One lie after another, she sabotaged her marriage. For that, I was not going to feel sorry for her. All the women who thought or had said, "She's wrong for sleeping with another woman's husband," needed to keep it real, put the blame where it belonged, and attend to their guy before a confident woman like me took him from her. Scandalous females didn't get empathy from me. And they sure as hell didn't deserve to have a good man.

No, I wasn't a judge or the keeper of any woman's unscrupulous behavior. No award had "Sindy Singleton is a thirty-year-old virgin" engraved on it. I wasn't better than Madison Tyler because I valued my vagina. I was smarter.

She was the one who'd accepted his ring, then reneged on her commitment and opened her legs for a loser during her engagement. She was the one who'd agreed to a stupid bet to have sex with her best friend's ex. She was the one who got knocked up and wasn't sure who the father was. I'd never make such a despicable decision.

Surely her mother had told her that semen could slip through a crack or spill out the side of a condom. She had to know that, once a man ejaculated, sperm could wander aimlessly inside her pussy from three to five days, penetrate one of her eggs, and impregnate her.

Nine months after she'd cheated, she gave birth to a light-skinned, eight-pound, twenty-two inch, dark curly-haired boy. The paternity test documented the baby was for her husband. The kid's gigantic hands and feet resembled the other guy's.

In my days of practicing law, I knew firsthand that the right amount of money bought unimaginable favors. After viewing the sex video her fling-thing presented in court, I sensed her baby was the result of her one-night stand with him. It didn't matter what I thought about her, her husband loved that child so much he'd give a kidney, a rib, even lay down his life if it meant saving his illegitimate son.

Vowing to be faithful to the most handsome eligible bachelor in all of Houston, Texas, she stood at the altar with a fetus in her stomach knowing it might not be his. She was nasty—in a devious manner. Her conniving ways had kept him trapped in her web. One day her luck would end. I'd make sure.

In some countries, a woman like her would've been stoned to death.

His filing for divorce was his first step toward our freedom to love one another. A marriage license was a privilege, not an entitlement to make someone's life a living hell. Sure she had a cute face, big butt, and tiny waist that attracted him. From the strip clubs to the country clubs, Houston had a plethora of gorgeous women. I was in the upper echelon. In addition to my great looks, I was a wealthy single woman with no kids.

New pussy may have excited her husband but at some point all pussy was new. The difference between hers and mine? Mine wasn't used. If she'd given him mind-blowing orgasms, that might explain why he was spellbound. Despite her best efforts, her marriage was coming to an end . . . soon. Her husband had encountered a more seductive woman who was breaking his concentration.

Most men suffered from ADDD—Attention Deficit–Dick Disorder. A classy lady with a hypnotic body, friendly smile, and magnetic personality could get any man's attention. Keeping him focused was the challenge.

Men didn't need an incentive to cheat but when that jezebel gave her man a reason, his desire to fuck me was her problem, not mine.

Her husband rightfully kicked her to the curb. I intended to make sure the trifling bitch stayed there.

CHAPTER 1

Sindy

"When he walks in, you'll walk out."

"Are you sure?" Nyle asked me after the prison guard closed the door to our private glass-enclosed room.

We sat facing each other. The chill from the stainless steel chair made me sit on the edge of my seat. The rectangular-shaped metal table was cold enough to keep my favorite butter pecan ice cream from melting. Three feet of space separated us.

I stared into his crystal-blue eyes as I said, "Help me get Granville Washington back behind bars and you'll be discharged the same day he's booked. The remaining two-and-a-half of your three-year sentence will be dismissed. You'll be on a one-year probation with an officer that you'll meet face-to-face one time. After that you'll check in over the phone. A few people owe me favors. If you complete the assignment to my satisfaction, your early release is guaranteed."

Nyle sighed heavily. His neatly arched brows

drew close together. His eyes darted to the left. He blinked. When he opened his eyes, they were intensely on me. Instantly, I became motionless.

"I've already done what you've asked of me."

"Not exactly."

"Not exactly my ass." Veins protruded from his neck. His voice escalated in anger. "The outcome isn't what either of us anticipated but I did my part. Now you want me to do you another favor? Fuck the money you paid me. I want out of here today."

That wasn't happening. When we left this room, I was going home; he was headed back to his cell. I did not influence him to commit a crime. That was his choice. Helping him get out was mine.

"What if what you want now isn't what you expect later? Then what? You walk away and leave me to do all of my time?"

Precisely. In my mind, I nodded, but didn't move my head. He had nothing to lose. I did. I needed him to calm down so he could focus on what was important to me.

I softened my tone. "Fair enough. Regardless of what happens this time, I'll keep my word." Not sure if I were lying, I extended my hand and shook his. I had to tell Nyle what he needed to hear.

Getting men to do whatever I wanted—with the exception of my father—that was my strength. Loving another woman's husband was my weakness.

Better for me to pursue the man I wanted than to allow my dad to arrange for my husband the way he'd done with Siara. I missed her. Skype was nice but I hadn't seen my sister in person in twelve years. Her being sold by our father wasn't my fault but she didn't feel the same. Occasionally, she still says, "You are my big sister. You were supposed to protect me." I think our father or her husband told her not to come back to America and not to let me visit her in Paris. I wasn't sure how or when but one day we would reunite.

Trust your gut instincts. That was how I lived. My word used to be a firm commitment. Since I was a little girl, when Sindy Singleton made a promise, I kept it. Truth or lie, right or wrong, my love for Roosevelt "Chicago" Dubois was gradually overruling my senses. Lately I'd been doing what was in my best interest. When things didn't go my way, I didn't hesitate to change my mind.

This morning I'd smoothed back my long straight cinnamon hair and coiled it into a bun that sat at the nape of my neck. My cream-colored pants, which I only wore when I visited the Federal Detention Center, were loosely fitted. A simple short-sleeved matching blouse draped my hips. Comfortable leather flats clung to my feet. No lipstick. No perfume. No jewelry. My purse was in the trunk of my Bentley that I'd parked in a downtown lot a block away. My keys were secured in one of the small lockers in the lobby. My Texas driver's license was left with the guard at the security entrance.

Sitting in a room reserved for attorney/client visits, I was the attorney. Nyle Carter was my protégé. I needed this inmate's help the same as he desperately desired mine.

"Let me get this straight. *I* have to find a way to bring Granville back to prison *before* you'll get me out of here?" he lamented.

Peering through the glass door, I scanned the visitors' room. There was a handful of folks who had come to see what I called "the mentally ill and prayed up." Prison made grown men ask the Lord, Buddha, Allah, Jehovah, or whatever higher power they believed in to set them free. Forgiveness wasn't practical for repeat offenders. I wished repentance wasn't an option for them either.

A lot of the criminals I represented were guilty but the majority of them had raised their right hands and sworn on the Bible that they were innocent. I was paid to defend, not to judge. Ultimately, that was God's job.

Nyle had pleaded the Fifth on his charges and still had to do time. He'd become known to those on the inside as G-double-A. Some youngster by the name of No Chainz had given Nyle the name saying it meant "Got All the Answers." I wished that were true for me. I wouldn't be sitting in this cold room trying to convince a man to entrap another man so that I could be with the man I loved.

"I said you were to make sure he never got out."

Nyle remained quiet.

On a scale from one to ten, Nyle was handsome above average. Put a suit on him the way he used to dress prior to getting locked up and no one would believe he was forty years old when he was arrested. Not that there was a better age to be charged but with his thick blond curly hair and smooth pale skin he could easily pass for thirty.

"I paid you twenty thousand to give Granville advice that would get him convicted with two consecutive life sentences."

He slid his hand from his forehead to the nape of his neck. No response.

Nyle could benefit from a daily dose of natural vitamin D. The inmates didn't get much sunlight.

Everything was indoors, including the gym. The few windows they had were high above the basketball court. Nyle deserved to be here but didn't belong. There were some people you never envisioned behind bars. Others you knew it wasn't *if* they were going to do time. It was when and for how long?

"Why did the judge overturn the jury's decision?" I asked.

Getting myself this involved, I could risk being disbarred and losing Roosevelt if he thought I was part of the conspiracy to kill him. I was undoubtedly determined to have that man.

Secretly, I was attracted to Roosevelt well before we'd met. A schoolgirl crush, more like college, was what I had. We didn't go to the same university but I'd gone to his football games. Unlike some of the other players, Roosevelt never had a bunch of groupies tailing him. For me it was one of those situations where I liked him, but never thought we'd meet. After his engagement was announced on the news and he married Madison, I'd given up on my fantasy of being with him until his brother came to my office one day for business. Chaz suggested Numbiya and I stop by Eddie V's. Roosevelt was there. Instantly, we hit it off. Initially, I wasn't, then I was, then I wasn't saving my virginity for him but now that I knew him better, I'd decided Roosevelt—not the billionaire who had paid my father for my hand in marriage—was the one.

How long was Nyle going to hold out without answering me? I refused to say another word. If he was done, so was I.

My father was a self-made multimillionaire. If Charles Singleton owned all the gold in Fort Knox, it wouldn't be enough and it'd never make him happy. He was so driven by greed he didn't know how to enjoy life or value people. Money was his god.

I still didn't believe my mother accidentally fell down the stairs. Never saw her insurance policy but knowing my father he'd probably collected a hefty seven figures. My father told us he had our mama cremated. Her family begged for a memorial service. They had no legal rights. Jasmine Singleton had no funeral. Dysfunctional as we were, until the day Mama died and Siara was sold, we were a family. Shortly after Mama's ashes were scattered over the Gulf of Mexico, my daddy became richer. My gut told me there was no wake because there was no death. Perhaps that was my wishful belief.

The man that I wanted couldn't be bought. If I were more like my father, I'd pay Roosevelt's wife to leave him alone. If she'd refused, I'd hire a hit man.

Nyle had ten minutes. If I stood, I was leaving and not coming back.

I was thirty. Ready to walk down the aisle and eventually breastfeed Roosevelt's children. Unlike my father, I knew how to be happy. *I think.*

Tired of Madison Tyler-DuBois interfering with my getting her husband, I added her to Sindy's shit list. I was about to strip that bitch of her last name like she'd lost an all-or-nothing game of poker. It was time for her to find herself another man. The horrible things she'd done, she should've petitioned for their divorce.

Madison was responsible for her husband having been shot, then she'd taken him off the respirator hoping he'd die. God had a different plan.

Her soon-to-be ex-husband had survived. And rather than her letting him love me, she'd prefer to keep him and smother his generous forgiving spirit. Her having his baby was the last lucky charm I was going to snatch from her.

Roosevelt had no idea what to do with Madison. Keep her? Let her go? Stay for the baby? Men generally embraced the "Do as I say" philosophy. The women, "Do as I do." Neither gave a damn about how the other felt as long as the other obeyed. Madison wasn't the conforming type. Neither was I. I was a true Southern belle born and wrapped in a Republican cloak of cutthroat confidence.

I was soft, only on the outside.

Three minutes.

When I saw on the news that Roosevelt "Chicago" DuBois had been shot three times, I had to find out who wanted him dead and why. Granville pulled the trigger but that imbecile could never mastermind an execution. Right now, I was getting involved with every aspect. That was why I was sitting in this freezing room instead of being outside in the sunny eighty-degree weather.

Nyle stared at me. "Welcome back," he said.

"Same to you." I'd drifted into my own world but where had he gone?

"Granville is so dumb he's actually smart. Tell me what I need to do to walk out of here. I'll make sure it's done."

Nyle's son was in my I'm Not Locked Up nonprofit program for kids with parents in jail. His son was an amazingly brilliant child. Landry was so impressive that six months ago I accompanied him on a visit here to the Federal Detention Center to meet his father.

I had to know what kind of man could have single-parented a brilliant child then ended up behind bars. I'd learned that Nyle had an office downtown. He represented hundreds of clients for a decade. Problem was, he'd never passed the bar. His degree was real. His credentials weren't valid. How could people retain a lawyer without certifying if the attorney was legit?

I agreed. "Granville is the smartest dumbest person I've witnessed as well. Do you know how many inmates represent themselves and get off? Almost none. Hearing Granville question Chaz, watching him get Loretta arrested, seeing him present that sex tape of Madison, made me realize we cannot underestimate this guy. When he degraded Roosevelt on the stand. Made a mockery of my man. That was it. We've got to get him to state and I'm not talking about a high school championship. Prison is where Granville belongs."

"What do I need to do this time?" Nyle asked.

"Tell the guard to inform the warden that Granville Washington is attempting to kill Roosevelt again. Then—"

Shaking his head, Nyle interrupted. "How do you know this?"

"Trust me. I do. All I need you to say is Granville told you this in confidence before his release. Then you must insist that they issue a search warrant for all of his property. His apartment, his car, his mama's house, and her grave."

Leaning back, Nyle said, "Her what?"

I was the type of woman who believed in staying three steps ahead of all men. Perhaps Granville wouldn't do such a thing but the gun hadn't been found after the shooting. He either knew where it was or now that he was out of jail he had it in his possession. The guy had proven he wasn't dumb. Playpens, cemeteries, cereal boxes, diaper bags were just a few of the countless places I'd discovered where criminals had hidden weapons.

"You heard me right. Her grave. Her services are tomorrow. If Granville has that gun, he's going to get rid of it. Tell them to dig up Sarah Lee Washington, search the soil, and her coffin. Roosevelt's life is dependent on you." I'd make a few calls later today and have someone secretly videotape Sarah's funeral from beginning to end.

Roosevelt was a good man. He was the youngest vice president/general manager in the league and we were blessed to have him for our football team. After all the wrong his wife had done to him, he did all the right things for her. A man that wonderful deserved a wife like me.

I didn't disclose to Nyle the details of what the authorities would find. What my father had done, I was about to undo.

CHAPTER 2

Granville

That baby looks just like me.

I closed my eyes then pictured his head full of wavy black hair. I used to have his kind of hair until my first cut when I was one. Instantly my 'fro had gone from what Mama called "good to bad."

My son's coconut was round. His hands and feet were large like mine when I was born. Zach was twenty-two inches long and weighed eight pounds. That was no coincidence. His genitals looked like they were in 3D and they were darker than the rest of his body, the same as the baby photos of me in my iPhone.

I missed Mama. That weird sound she'd made when she took her last breath echoed in my ear. I rattled my head. Stared at her body in the coffin. Mama had told my brother and me, "Don't ever say a baby ain't yours 'cause they don't look like you. Genes go way back in every family tree. Newborn babies change a lot. One minute they look like the father, then the mother. They come out light-skinned. End up dark. Born with blue eyes that turn green or brown."

All I knew was I was no deadbeat. Why did women say they wanted a good man, then when I treated them like a queen they dogged me out? After they rode my big black dick, came all over it while screaming, "Oh my God," they couldn't stand me? Oh, they'd give it up again but refused to commit to a relationship. I wasn't a mechanical bull. I had a heart, just like a woman. It was breakable, the same as theirs.

I wanted to cry. Madison had stepped on my heart with those pretty high heels like it was a cockroach. Then she squished until my guts squirted out. How would she feel if . . . a vengeful idea came to mind.

Hey, I should start charging them chicks to ride my pine. A hundred dollars a hump. Even when I wasn't trying to be funny, I cracked myself up. Starting to slap my thigh, I stopped. This was not the place for that. Almost forgot where I was at. I scratched my knee, then thought, "You should've been a comedian for real, dude." Talking to people was cool but I loved getting dirty and operating heavy machinery. I drove my excavator with precision. Construction work was all I'd done since high school. My boss Manny praised me all the time.

If Madison didn't want me, I could deal with that. Fine. Not really. I was lying to myself hoping that would help me get over her. I loved her more now that she had my baby. There had to be a mistake that the DNA test was a match for her husband. But how could I get the baby, take my own test, and prove I'm right? Didn't want to go to jail for kidnapping or child endangerment. I wouldn't hurt Zach. He was mine and I'd take care of him.

Mama used to tell me, "You're never going to be the sharpest knife in the drawer, baby, but make sure you always have the right amount of edge." She taught me to stand up for what I believed in. One day my third grade teacher gave me a U. She claimed my story was unsatisfactory because she couldn't understand my handwriting. I pleaded my case. I had the biggest fingers in the class and that skinny no. 2 pencil was too small for me. The fat pencil was too big. It made me write under the lines. I'd stayed up all night rewriting my paragraph. The next day when I showed her the other five pages where I kept starting over and reminded her she was the one that taught me to write, write, and rewrite, she gave me a G.

I wish Mama would've seen her grandson before she died a few days ago. My son was a week old. My son. You hear me! I'm not crazy. I wanted to jump off the bench and scream, "Zach DuBois should be *Washington*. He's *my* son, y'all!"

An elbow nudged me in the side. I opened my eyes to a woman singing, "*Why should I feel discouraged . . .*" Mrs. Mae stood at the podium near the altar. A black wide-brim hat sat on top of her dark-colored wig. Pressing a white handkerchief against her red cheek, she looked at me and said, "Sarah Lee Washington was an angel on earth so I know she's one in heaven." She focused on my brother then resumed singing, "*Let not your heart be troubled . . .*"

Dressed in my best designer suit and cowboy boots, I sat on the front pew feeling guilty for what I was about to do. I needed to hear *His Eyes Are on the Sparrow.* That was Mama's favorite hymn. My aunt was uncomfortably close to my left. She was the one who'd poked me. My only brother sat to my right.

Nothing was going to bring Mama back. My mind was on my kid. Torn between the two people I loved the most, I was in my hometown of Port Arthur at my mama's funeral and my child was a hundred miles away in Houston. I wanted to see him, hold him in my arms, change his diapers, and feed him. Tell him funny stories about my childhood. Hearing his laugh would make me smile. How did his laugh sound? Could he laugh at one week? I didn't know. What I wouldn't give to have him throw up on my new suit then stare at me and grin. Did he have dimples? The sadness in my heart brought tears.

I stood. Massaging my chest, I missed my mama and my son. "This ain't right! I want my mama back," I cried.

Beaux pulled the tail of my jacket. "Dude, Mama don't want this."

He was right. I sat down. Her body was in front of me. The thing inside her body that made her tick, that made all of us tick, was gone. The mortician had done an amazing job of making that little woman look like a princess. My mama was my one and only queen. She was five-four, ninety-eight pounds. Cancer had eaten fifty pounds of her flesh. After she was diagnosed she refused chemotherapy. Didn't take radiation either. Said, "Baby, it's time for me to go be with your father."

I wiped my tears.

"It's all good, bro," my brother Beaux said patting my thigh.

What those people had to say about my family

after Mrs. Mae finished singing was for them, not for us. There was nothing anyone had said that could bring my mama back. Her ticker was gone. If I could give her mine, I would.

Glancing over my shoulder, I saw a dude back there videotaping. Guess the people at the funeral home were going to try and sell it to us later. I wasn't buying it. Had to make sure he couldn't see what was about to go down shortly.

It was too late for Mama to see her first grand-child but I still had a chance to be a father to my kid. Mama would turn over in her grave if I didn't fight for what was mine.

I didn't care about Madison texting me a copy of the results showing her husband was 99.99-plus percent the biological father. That meant there was almost a .01 percent chance the baby could be mine. Miracles happened every day.

I was beginning to hate rich folks. People with money believed they could buy whatever and whomever they wanted. I might look dumb but I'm not. All that dough Chicago had didn't keep me from walking out of the courtroom a free man. So what if I did shoot him for marrying my woman. I wasn't crazy enough to do that again. I was forty-five going on forty-six. If I had been convicted, life without the possibility of parole meant I would've died in prison.

While I sat in the front pew, my mind wandered. Guess I had that attention disorder Mama told me about. In her last days, she had it too. Most dying folks did.

It didn't matter that my ex-girlfriend Loretta hated me, especially after I'd sexed and started dating her friend Madison. During my trial, I represented myself. I was responsible for making Loretta lie under oath and do thirty days at the Federal Detention Center for perjury. A dumb person couldn't have done that.

How did I know Madison didn't pay someone to give her the results she wanted? She'd fired me from my construction job at her company after riding my wood. It wasn't my fault her pussy snatched my condom off. On her video when I came out, it was gone. That's how I knew the baby had to be mine. I didn't want to but if I had to use that tape again, I would.

Worrying about Mama and my son, I'd almost forgotten about my wrongful termination. I had to find a way to do my own paternity test. Could I file for joint custody and take her to court?

Maybe if I showed up at their house tonight, she'd hear me out. Exhaling, I knew that wouldn't work. Or . . . Loretta hated me but she hated Madison more. Maybe I could convince Loretta to help me steal baby Zach long enough to have our blood drawn and prove I'm not losing my mind. Naw, she'd probably want some more of my dick. Sure was glad Loretta didn't have my baby. Her lil girl was cute though.

First, my brother and I had to bury my mom.

Other than getting a glimpse of baby Zach through the nursery window at the hospital the day he was born, I hadn't seen him in person. I'd watched the video of his birth two hundred times before someone took it off of YouTube.

"Man, it's time," Beaux whispered in my ear. "We've got to get rid of this"—he patted his chest— "before they close the casket for the last time."

We sat on the front pew. Beaux was still claiming

the gun he had was the snub-nosed I'd used to shoot Chicago three times. Said he returned to the scene, found it stuck in one of the gutters in the swimming pool. How could that be if the man who'd just hired me to kill Chicago for two million dollars said he had the gun? Then there was a third gun that these kids found at the hotel by the pool. A news reporter alleged that might be the gun used to shoot Chicago.

I didn't know what to believe anymore. As Mama used to say, "Whoever is lying, tell the other one to shut up." That worked on Beaux and me a few times before we figured it out. Couldn't use that in my situation. I'd never get Madison and Chicago to meet me at the same time. I hoped the gun found by those kids at the hotel wasn't mine. What made that six-year-old boy shoot his twin sister in the head was probably his mama and daddy's fault for letting him play violent video games.

Kill the pedestrian, Granville. Run over the old lady, Granville. How they knew my name? I had a memory like an elephant. Yep, Mama wouldn't lie. Maybe I should change my name for those games.

Those messages were evil. My son was going to be raised the way my mama raised my brother and me. "Y'all go outside and play."

I mumbled back, "All right. When you say your last good-byes, fall into the casket, then cry like a baby. I'll cover you. Make sure you slip the gun under the lining. When you're done, look at me, then I'll hug you and help you sit on the pew until it's time for us to carry her out. Oh, and stay close to me so dude in the back won't get us on tape."

Beaux looked over his shoulder, turned back,

then nodded. We'd gone over what we were going to do for the last time. Now that the moment was here, could my brother follow through with his plan?

I hadn't gone through with mine. I still hadn't opened the briefcase, more like suitcase, that Charles Singleton gave me. Inside was supposed to be one million dollars cash, a gun, and an iPhone. There was a Facebook account for me but it wasn't under my real name. The e-mail and password weren't linked to me either. Under this "LuvinMeSumMe" account I was a girl. Chicago was my friend and I was his fan. I could track his every move as long as his locations were on. I didn't want to go back to jail for doing the same thing. Might not be so lucky next time if I represented myself again.

Charles might have hired that dude in the back taping. Can't put anything past a person who had me kidnapped from my penthouse, blindfolded me, and had his drivers bring me to his house. He'd sat in the dark telling me what I was gonna do. The money, if it was really in that briefcase, made me reconsider pulling the trigger one more time.

The pastor started closing the service by reading my mom's eulogy.

"Sarah Lee Washington was a woman of God. She had a full and fruitful life. This here is a celebration of her time on earth. She moved her family out of the projects of Port Artha and into a great neighborhood near the tracks."

The pastor wiped the sweat from his face with his cloth, then continued. "Sarah moved physically but she never stopped being neighbaly. Whateva

she could do to help othas or help out here at the
chuch she did it until her health wouldn't allow
her to do it no mo'," he said.

I think my going to jail may have killed my
mama. She was fine before then.

This pastor didn't know my mother. The preacher
that knew Mom best had gone on to glory years ago.
He'd died of cancer too. Mama was with Daddy now.
He'd died of cancer too. Seem like everyone that
lived close to the refineries in our town all their
life got some kind of cancer.

I nudged Beaux in his side with my elbow. If we
were carrying out our plan, now was the time.

"We're going to miss Sarah Lee just as much as
her family. Sarah Lee was family. She leaves with us
her two sons, Granville and Beaux Washington,
and her sister, Wilma Sims," the pastor said.

Beaux stood. I stood too. Side by side we walked
up to Mama's casket. Forcing himself to cry, my
brother fell over Mama's dead body. When he
reached into his jacket, I leaned closer.

"Hurry up, bro," I whispered as I felt a heavy
hand on my shoulder. I faked the kind of cry that
was more sound than tears.

"It's going to be okay," someone said. "Your
mother is no longer suffering."

Aunt Wilma came up just as Beaux finished covering up the gun. "Okay, boys. Sarah don' gone
home. I'm here for you now," she said. "You know
my sister don't want y'all doing this. Get yourselves
together."

My aunt was there to take charge all right. She'd
be nice until she got the long list of things she
wanted out of Mama's house—jewelry, clothes,
furniture, china, silver—all that plus more. Then

her life would return to normal and we wouldn't see her for years. If we outlived Aunt Wilma, we'd probably get all that stuff back, until we died. Then it'd be somebody else's turn to keep watch over Mama's possessions.

Mama had on a beautiful long white lace dress that Aunt Wilma had picked out from Mama's closet. She wanted to put jewelry on Mama but Beaux and I didn't want to give anyone a reason to dig up Mama's body so we insisted, no jewelry. Mama's hands were folded at her waist; her favorite white Bible with that fancy gold trim around the edges of the pages lay on her stomach right underneath her palms.

Standing tall, Beaux and I tucked the white satin liner deep into the casket. The guys from the funeral home came over. "We'll do this. That's our job."

"We want to do it," Beaux said.

When I slammed the top, the coffin slid. People in the church gasped, then somebody laughed.

What was funny? Mama almost fell down.

Beaux caught Mama's casket before it hit the floor. "Bro, you still clumsy," Beaux said laughing too. "Mama probably got a kick out of that."

I should kick him. What if the gun was on top of Mama's Bible? It was a good thing we didn't have to open the casket again. I locked it, then eyed the dude in the back. He was still taping.

The guys from the funeral home helped us carry Mama's body to the hearse. I whispered to that camera dude, "I want that tape," then kept going. What if Charles was setting me up? We slid Mama's coffin in the back. I asked one of the guys, "Dude, who was taping? Y'all know him?"

One of them said, "Yeah, he's cool."

"How much y'all trying to add on to our bill for that?"

"Two."

"Two what?" Beaux asked.

"Hundred. But you're not obligated," he said.

"You damn straight," Beaux answered.

We had their number. If we wanted it, we could get it later. It was time to go to the cemetery. Beaux got into my Super Duty truck. We didn't want no fancy limo driver. Closely we followed the hearse.

Looking behind his seat, Beaux asked, "What's in the suitcase?"

"A million dollars."

Beaux laughed. "Yeah, right."

While my brother was busy laughing, I'd just come up with another brilliant idea.

CHAPTER 3

Madison

"Hush little baby don't you cry. Your daddy will buy us whatever I say."

Did I need Roosevelt's money? No. Did I want his money? Of course. My resources were solid until my father jeopardized our business, sold my car, leveraged my home, and pawned my engagement rings. If I were to maintain my lifestyle and secure my family's financial future, control over all of Roosevelt's resources—bank accounts, investments, and inheritances—was what I needed.

In some cases, a man would stay married in order to live the good life. My man had generational wealth. He could replace me and replenish his accounts at the same time. In order to maintain my position as first lady in his life, I had to capitalize on his weakness, our son.

Asking my man to spend his money wasn't the most effective way to have my monetary desires met. For an established guy like Roosevelt, it was best to mention what I wanted and let him take the

initiative to do the rest. Gradually, he'd start to
trust me, then add my name to his signature cards,
and once he'd done that, I could restore all that
my dad squandered and more. When my husband
discovered my father had leveraged my home and
sold my Ferrari, he settled the lien against my property and bought me a Bentley.

How many women could get a man to pay their
car note let alone purchase them a luxury vehicle?
Thoughtful wealthy men were scarce and I was not
going through nine more engagements in hopes
of finding another man as generous as the man I
was legally married to. Papa had cashed in eight
rings. The only one he hadn't stolen was the one
on my finger.

I sat in my family room in the white leather
rocking chair my girlfriend Tisha bought me. This
was no ordinary chair. It was my favorite! The
arms, seat, and back were plump and plush. It reclined, vibrated, could do a one-eighty swivel, and
it had a climate-control thermostat. The softness
comforted me while I held my child. There were
days when both Zach and I fell asleep for hours in
the chair.

Having Roosevelt come home to us at night was
my goal. I'd grown tired of our living in separate
homes. She could visit my husband, sleep in his
bed, and there wasn't a damn thing I could do to
prevent that unless I moved back in.

I knew he wasn't happy with me but everything
was temporary. My giving birth to his first and only
son was priceless. Even if his mistress, Sindy, had a
dozen babies by Roosevelt, mine was his first.

Touching my son's toes, I whispered to Zach,

"The football game is over. He'll be here shortly." I hoped she didn't change his mind about coming to visit his child. She appeared the kind that would try to monopolize my man's time.

Rocking back and forth, I'd watched from the coin toss until the last second ticked off of the fourth quarter. I think Houston won by ten but I felt as though I was losing this round. I lost track of the score when the cameras flashed to Roosevelt's suite. Sindy Singleton was by his side. I could contact the media, start newsworthy drama, but that would be to her benefit. I'd come across as desperate. I was. But the world would never see that side of me.

She tucked her long cinnamon hair behind her ears. The diamond solitaires were more brilliant than the lights in the background. Her breasts sat high and round. For a moment I was saddened remembering how I'd had my breasts surgically removed. I'd done the right thing. I was cancer free.

Swallowing the lump in my throat, I let the tears fall onto my baby's blanket. Sindy's teeth were perfectly straight and ultrawhite. The harder I tried to find a flaw I noticed this woman appeared ideal for my husband. The operative word was "appeared." Who was I fooling? Certainly not myself. There was another thing she had that I used to have: a glow of happiness. Her being there illuminated my husband's eyes.

That bitch has got to go.

Slowly, I rocked, realizing that pain was for the person who cared.

I knew where I'd done wrong but why did it hurt so bad? I didn't know how to get back to the days when my, I mean our, relationship was perfect. The more he pulled away, the more he ignored me, the tighter my fingers curled clinging to the possibility of what had already slipped away. The slime in my hands made me envious of her. But I refused to give up holding on to my first and only husband.

Accepting Loretta's stupid bet ruined my life. "Why'd I fuck Granville's dumb ass?"

Loretta had screwed up my life and moved on with hers. I saw her from time to time, wished she wasn't my next-door neighbor but she'd forever be my ex-best friend. Her daughter's father was coming around more. Staying longer. Once a woman had a baby by a man, he'd always feel entitled to fuck her. Things probably weren't going too well with Raynard's wife, Gloria. Heard her son wasn't his. Maybe Loretta was finally getting some default dick regularly. Raynard would fuck her until he found someone else and she was stupid enough to let him. I wished there were a way I could've made her a suspect in my husband's shooting. She had a gun in her purse at my reception. No one knew but Tisha and I.

"I hate her ass!"

"Whaa! Whaa!"

Wow. I'd unintentionally said that aloud. I cuddled my baby to my chest. Soon I'd have implants. I was home with Roosevelt's child and he was on national television with another woman. Didn't any of his fans care about me?

A commercial came on advertising same-day delivery for items in-store at Target. The real holidays were starting next month. At the end of this month I'd skip Halloween. Pagans honoring witches and goons didn't make sense and I was not dressing my son in a pumpkin or superhero costume.

I kissed his little nose. "Your father is your hero."

Sometimes I only needed someone to listen. Glad Zach was too young to understand; he'd become my sounding board. Squeezing my son, I inhaled the fresh scent of new life.

Thanksgiving was five weeks away. I wished I could fast-forward and skip it all. Roosevelt and his family would want to share these joyous occasions with my baby and his mistress would sit at the table breaking my bread, drinking my wine, and toasting in the New Year. Where would I be for Christmas? Home, alone? Not at my parents'. Definitely not at Mrs. DuBois's house caroling. Tisha lived on the other side of Loretta. Maybe I'd celebrate with Tisha and her boys.

More tears fell on Zach's blanket. I had to find a way to prolong our divorce until Roosevelt changed his mind. My signing the papers didn't make our dissolution final. Did it? We still had to go to court.

"Whaa!"

"Shhh. Hush, Mama's baby," I said gently bouncing Zach in my arms.

He cried louder. "Whaa!" His face turned red.

Exhaling my frustrations, I remembered I fed him a half hour ago. I'd learned in a bad way not to stick my finger inside his diaper if I wasn't sure what was in it. Laying him on my lap, I peeled the tape from his diaper. It was wet. Again.

I kissed Zach's feet, wiggled his soft toes. Fingered his full head of dark wavy hair. I loved my baby's pecan tone. Zach's skin was a combination of Roosevelt's tan and my nearly white complexion. His ears were slightly darker. I prayed his tone would even out all over to the color of his face.

Laying him on the changing table, I cleaned his private area. For a second, I thought, "Couldn't be." His penis and balls were large. Maybe that was my imagination. Perhaps they were just swollen. He was only a week old. The darkest part of his body was his genitals and the pigment wasn't fading. The tip of his ears, his cuticles . . . I closed my eyes for a moment and prayed, "Lord, please forgive me for cheating on Roosevelt."

The only thing that reassured me Granville wasn't the father was the paternity results Roosevelt and I had gotten. That, and Zach's curly hair. Granville's head was bald but that man had pubic hairs that could be plucked and used as a scouring pad. Or a clit scratcher. I couldn't lie. Granville's dick felt amazing.

There was no need for me to let my guilt give me doubts. "Thank you, Jesus." God had granted me the one thing I'd prayed for. The right father.

My doorbell rang. Tisha was on the security monitor in the top corner of my flat-screen television. I taped a fresh Pamper to Zach's bottom, snapped his onesie, and carried him to the living room.

Opening the door, Tisha instantly took her future godson out of my arms and lovingly placed him in hers. I handed her his receiving blanket.

"My boys wanted to come but I told them they had to wait until Zach was a little older," she said. "My mom is at my house, so I took a break from my kids to come see the baby. And you, of course."

"How are the boys?"

"I'm not an attorney but my understanding is sixty days from filing the executed dissolution the divorce will be final. You signed it a week ago so in about fifty-three days, right before Christmas, you'll be a single woman. But your preliminary hearing is scheduled right before Thanksgiving. You could settle out of court but whatever happens, don't buy a place where he lives. What if he marries Sindy and you have to see her all the time?"

"I'll make her wish she hadn't. I have his first-born son. But I'm also smart enough not to sell this house. Thanks to Roosevelt," I boasted, "it's paid in full."

Tisha covered Zach's ears, then leaned toward me. "I hate to say it but you fucked up a good thing, Madison. Let him go. Make sure you don't miss your court date next month. When it's over, meet another man."

"With no breasts," I protested.

My doorbell rang again. I glanced at my monitor.

"You are the sexiest woman I know. I'm not feeling sorry for you. Not having breasts is temporary and you know it. I'll get the door," Tisha said.

When she opened the door, my dad walked in. "Madison, sweetheart. You've got to stop him. Roosevelt gave me a notice. He's stealing my company."

Eager to get the check Roosevelt had offered, my dad signed 51 percent of Tyler Construction to my husband. As Mrs. Tyler-DuBois, I held partnership in the controlling interest.

"Papa, don't be rude," I said tilting my head toward Tisha. "Here, hold Zach." I placed the blanket and his grandson in his hands. "Hold his head."

Papa sat in a chair facing the sofa, then placed Zach on his lap. "Hi, Tisha. How're the boys and your mom?"

"Everybody is fine, Mr. Tyler. I'll tell my mother you said hello." Tisha lifted Zach from Papa's lap and placed him in my dad's arms.

Papa lamented, "I know how to hold a baby."

"Madison," Tisha said, pointing at the papers on the coffee table. "Call me later so we can continue our conversation. Bye, Mr. Tyler."

"Bye, Tisha."

I was glad my girlfriend had left. I needed to speak with my dad in private. "Papa, he's not stealing our company. He's putting it under new management pending our divorce being final. He can't sell without my consent."

"But he doesn't need your permission to fire me."

Zach spit on Papa's suit jacket. My dad stared at me, then said, "Women. If Tisha hadn't moved him he would've puked on himself. You know how much this suit cost."

"He's a baby. Have your suit cleaned."

"That's not the point. Now I have to go home and change clothes."

Heaven forbid he went home and missed an appointment at the office to get his dick sucked by his personal assistant. When I found out Papa was cheating on my mama, I lost respect for him.

Papa kept the blanket, handed Zach to me, pulled a tissue from the box on the table, then dabbed the throw-up. "Damn. If I lose my job, what am I supposed to do? Sit around the house all day with your mother?" He stopped trying to clean his jacket and took it off. "If I'm forced to be with Rosalee all the time, we'll be next to get a divorce."

"Obviously you don't love Mommy anymore but I do. Are you worried about not having a *PA*? Or are you seriously concerned about the company?"

Regardless of how Papa felt about Mama, he wasn't going anywhere. After I walked in on my father at his office having sex with a young girl he'd put on payroll with our company, I was in favor of his replacement. What if one of those girls got pregnant? I was not raising my son with my father's kid.

Papa paced the full length of my oriental area rug. Back and forth he marched as though whatever he came up with would work. "You can stop him."

I could, and I would, but not for my dad. "Papa, would you agree that women are more intelligent than men?"

He stopped pacing. Frowned. Nodded. "Most, not all."

"Do you believe I can outthink you?"

I wasn't challenging my dad. He didn't come from money. He grew up in Port Arthur. His parents were poor. But I can proudly say when my papa was a young boy he had a field full of dreams and a heart filled with love.

The harder Papa tried to get one of those "good jobs" at one of the three refineries in town, the more they gave him the runaround. "Come back tomorrow" or "We're not hiring right now." They lied to his face and hired workers from Houston, Lake Charles, even New Orleans, the same day. Nonresidents were given a golden opportunity to earn a decent salary while some of the locals continued to pay twenty dollars for a loaf of bread off the back of a truck.

Papa had told me when he was little there were no restaurants or grocery stores on the black side of town in Port Arthur. Today, not much had changed. There still weren't any restaurants.

When I turned five, Papa decided to move Mama and me to Houston and start his own company. That was thirty-one years ago.

"Sweetheart, my ego says men are smarter. My head knows better."

"You think you owe me an apology for leveraging my house, selling my car, and pawning my engagement rings? You act as though those things never happened."

I only had one papa. No amount of money could make me disown him no matter how ruthless he was at times. That didn't mean I agreed with what he'd done. If it weren't for Roosevelt, our baby and I would be living at home with my parents.

Papa sat on the sofa beside me and patted Zach on the back. My dad shook his head, stared at the floor. "I'm sorry, sweetheart. But—"

"No buts."

"Let me finish—," he said.

"It's not necessary. I'm going to speak with my attorney. I've got a plan to change Roosevelt's mind about divorcing me."

My divorce hearing was next month. There was time for me to come up with something.

"But—"

Interrupting him again, I picked up the papers, then said, "I signed this under duress. He was stupid to come to the hospital and force his wife to sign over her company and grant him a divorce. I—you're really going to like this—"

My thoughts transitioned into silence. I wasn't sure how far my husband would go but I knew how many days I had to change his mind before our hearing next month.

Papa smiled. "Love what?"

I kissed my son's stomach. "It doesn't matter. Zach means the world to my husband and we're a package deal."

"Sweetheart, there's something I've been meaning to tell you."

CHAPTER 4

Chicago

"Call me later if you have time, baby," she whispered.

Sindy wrapped her arms around me and held me close. Her choice for simple words like "if" instead of "when" was alluring. She'd given me the option to contact her, at the same time I knew she wouldn't call me. In time, that would change.

Women started acquaintances adhering to their standards and principles. Gradually, one standard at a time, the pendulum would swing more in my direction. I admired a self-assured lady. If Sindy had pursued me, I wouldn't have fallen for her. Sexing an aggressive woman was easy. For a man, often the two, liking and sexing a female, had little in common. What was there not to lust for when it came to Sindy?

The way she spoke made me want to dial her number before she walked away. The way she swayed her hips as she stepped to me made me want to ease her dress over her head, and take my time trailing kisses from one set of lips to her other.

Inhaling her perfume, I fingered the edges of her long cinnamon hair that dangled right above her ass. "I'll give you a ring soon as I . . ." Not wanting to say, "Leave Madison's," I paused then continued. "Soon as I'm headed home. I miss you already."

Sindy whispered in my ear, "Take your time, Roosevelt. You're worth waiting for." She caressed the nape of my neck. Slowly she let me go.

Men were visual creatures. Women were audio lovers. I loved every sense of Sindy's sexiness. Holding her hand, I touched her ring finger, then asked, "What's your size?"

"One size smaller than my shoes, a six. Congrats again on your W," she said. Then she showed me the most captivating smile I'd seen in quite some time. That shit made my dick hard. She knew exactly what the fuck she was doing and I loved all of it and her.

Sindy opened her purse, removed then opened a case. "These are for you." She slid a pair of dark designer sunglasses over my eyes. "Not that you have anything to hide. People shouldn't always see where you're looking."

By the time my fifty-three days were up, I was putting a ring on it on fifty-four. It took all I had not to pull her back in. Her head high, shoulders straight, back arched, I watched her curvaceous hips move side to side until she exited my suite. Quietly, I exhaled. When she wasn't around, I wanted her with me.

"Somebody's got it bad," my brother Chaz said patting me on the back.

"Yes, Lord." God had definitely smiled on me. I needed to show Him some love and make it back to the tabernacle soon.

"Those frames make you stand out. I'm going to have to invest in a pair of those."

"Anyone who can distract him from that horrible Madison," my mother commented as she entered my suite from the private restroom, "is good. Don't forget to come by for dinner tomorrow. Bring that new one with you," she said.

Kissing my mother on the cheek, I said, "Her name is Sindy."

"Bring her too, but I meant that baby."

I shook my head. "Mother, my son's name is Zach."

Chaz sang in my ear. "That baby don't look like you."

My mother said, "I love you too, Chaz. Bring that sex machine woman you're dating. Your father could use a boost."

Chaz and I laughed. My brother said, "She a sexologist, Mother. And yes, she can help Dad with his stamina but let me talk to Dad first."

I never imagined our father not being able to perform. Men measured their longevity by that of their dad. Those deep-breathing techniques and PC contractions Madison taught me made my dick stronger. My concern was when would I share my improved manhood with Sindy. If I simply wanted to get my stroke count up, there were countless volunteers. I'd wait.

"I like those sunglasses on you. Guess I shouldn't

keep your father waiting in the car." Mom fanned a good-bye as she left.

"Was that a farewell or did Mom just flip us the bird?" I asked.

Chaz shook his head and smiled. "You're tripping. Does it matter? Thanks to your marrying Madison, Mom isn't a real fan of Sindy or Numbiya. She's not slick. Mom is not going to let another woman touch Dad. She wants to find out more about our women. I'm going to prep Numbiya. You should do the same with Sindy."

The older Mom got, the bolder she'd become. That was why if Madison's dad Johnny was going to have any dignity after clearing out his office at Tyler Construction, I had to handle every aspect of his termination.

I glanced up at the flat-screen television mounted on the wall inside my suite. My head coach and star quarterback were giving post-game interviews. Thankfully, I didn't have to engage in that part.

"I admit. I like Sindy a lot. And it's all your fault for introducing her to me."

I sat in a chair overlooking an empty stadium. Chaz sat beside me. "How does it feel being single?"

"Seems like time is going by slow as hell. It's not final yet. We still have five weeks before the preliminary hearing. Seven before it's all over."

"Knowing how treacherous Madison is, get ready for a curveball. She's not going to settle out of court."

Confidently, I told Chaz, "She can't stop the proceedings."

At least I'd be free to legally remarry before

Christmas. I'd dreamt about the joy that would come from not being a family with Madison and Zach. I didn't want to be one of those public pretenders putting on a show to satisfy others. "Aw, they're such a sweet family." A lot of the married people who pass judgment on others weren't happy in their own relationship. The simple thought of Sindy's fingernails traveling down my spine made me smile.

Looking up, Chaz exhaled, then said, "This is Texas, dude. The wait period is a formality. You are technically a single man, big brother. But keep Madison close so no matter what she throws, it won't stick."

The fans who loved me might boycott the games if I publically abandoned my wife right after she'd given birth and had a double mastectomy. My time shared with Sindy probably should be more private. With her in the suite, the cameras couldn't detect the depth of our feelings during a game. Our hugs came when only those in the room stood witness but viewers weren't stupid. The media hadn't exposed any allegations of an affair. They, like me, were happy I'd survived.

Had I done all that I could for Madison? Would it be selfish of me to put my desires ahead of hers? I'd been married, soon to be divorced, and I had a son by the age of thirty-two. I felt my timing was right. Clearly, the woman I'd proposed to was the wrong one.

"I don't want to be single but I guess I am. I don't want to be in love with Sindy but I know I am. And I want to stop loving my wife but no matter how hard I try, I can't."

Chaz snapped his head toward me. "Try harder.

You gon' mess around and lose a good woman holding on to a tramp."

A what? I shook my head. Madison wasn't a tramp. A loose woman is one who's never satisfied. She freely opens her legs repeatedly for men even when she has a man. Loretta influenced Madison to sex Granville. Although Madison shouldn't have shared her body with anyone except me, it was hers to do with as she pleased. Might be time I start thinking the same way about my dick. Temptation was real. Even if I were happily married to Madison, I'd still want to fuck Sindy.

"That tramp, as you call her, just had my first-born son."

"Zach is cool. He's family. She's not. I love being his uncle and all but if you love Madison so much, why'd you serve her divorce papers? I told you, you can be a great father without being her husband." Chaz was leading the conversation in a bad direction. I felt it.

I patted my brother on the shoulder. Attempting to change the flow, I told him, "You're right. What difference does getting divorced make now that the baby is mine?"

"What difference does it make that Granville tried to kill you? Don't change your mind about letting Madison go, Chicago."

My brother's comment about Granville pulling the trigger always concluded our conversation. "I promised her I was coming by to see Zach. I'll catch up to you later."

"Make sure you serve her those custody papers you got so we can see Zach too. And whatever you do, don't fuck her."

I was glad Chaz was my assistant general manager but I didn't need his advice outside of work. Leaving my brother sitting in my suite, I exited the stadium, then got into my car. My cell phone vibrated reminding me I still had it on SILENCE. I started to press IGNORE, then decided to answer, "Yes, Mom?"

"Roosevelt, you're taking too long. I'm going to lock Johnny out of the office today."

Quietly, I chuckled wondering why my mother disliked Madison's dad more than she hated Madison.

I heard my father say, "Helen, no you're not. Leave Chicago alone. He's a man. He can handle it."

"Like he's handling giving that Madison those custody papers for that baby. Looks like I'm going to have to do that too."

The next voice I heard on Mom's phone was Dad. "Son, deal with your business like a man. I'll take care of your mother."

"If you were taking care of me, Martin, we wouldn't need Chaz's sex machi—"

I ended the call, wishing I'd never answered. Wait until Chaz finds out Mom was serious about Numbiya helping Dad. Shaking my head, I smiled.

Clicking on the MESSAGE icon, I selected Madison's name, then pressed the microphone. I waited a few seconds for the beep then clearly spoke into my iPhone, "I'll see you in thirty minutes (period)."

Reading the text, I saw that Siri had gotten it right. I touched SEND.

CHAPTER 5

Madison

Thirty minutes was exactly what I needed to get presentable for my husband.

I ushered Papa to the front door. "Roosevelt is on his way. Whatever it is you have to say can wait." Papa's jacket was draped over his arm. His white button-down shirt was crisp, ash-gray pants perfectly creased. "If you're going home, tell Mama I'll see her tomorrow. Bye."

He stood on the wrong side of the threshold. "Don't bite the hand that's fed you all your life, sweetheart. I need my job and I want Tyler Construction back. Tell Roosevelt that."

Whatever amount of money Roosevelt had given my dad, I was sure my mother didn't know how much or where it was. Papa was smart. He still had that money and his private jet. His lifestyle hadn't changed but his ownership had. I didn't blame him for wanting complete control over his assets. He'd created his problems and added to mine.

"I'll think about it. Now go."

He moved one step closer to the doorway. It felt strange hearing Papa, once a proud business owner, say the word "job." He'd worked hard to build his company. Greed to expand beyond his means created his demise. The lack of commitment he had to our latest development project cost us hundreds of thousands. With my newborn and my upcoming surgery, I couldn't put his agenda ahead of my own.

Helen never cared much for Papa but the fact that I'd told Roosevelt that my father was sexing young girls instead of taking care of corporate duties put Papa on Roosevelt's termination list. If everything went my husband's way, by the time I was divorced, Papa would be unemployed. I wasn't going to let that happen but my dad should suffer the consequences for his infidelity.

Nudging my dad outside, I was not jeopardizing my chances to remain Mrs. Madison Tyler-DuBois by defending my dad's dishonor. "Go home, Papa. Call me later. And tell Mama I love her."

"Madison, wait. Zach—"

Now I had twenty minutes. I closed my front door.

He needed to go home but God only knew where my dad would end up after he left my house. Mom was probably at peace when he wasn't there with her. Awkward as my situation was, I didn't want Roosevelt and me taking one another for granted. I couldn't undo removing my husband from life support when he needed me most but if I made the proper decisions moving forward, my marriage was salvageable. My husband should never underestimate what I'd do to keep him.

Carrying Zach upstairs, I placed him in his crib, then turned on the television. *Yay!* I'd managed not to spy on my husband after my release from the hospital. "You're doing great. Don't do it, Madison." The more I resisted, something inside my head made me click a few buttons on my remote. I didn't need to see this.

The video cameras I had the contractors install at Roosevelt's condo before I'd given birth to our son were still working. The contractors did an impeccable job of hiding the lenses in the corners between the crown molding in each room. The crib, playpen, and baby toys I'd set up in Roosevelt's second bedroom were still there. Sindy might have a slim chance of replacing me as Roosevelt's wife but no other woman could trump that I was the mother of Roosevelt "Chicago" DuBois's first child.

Elated that I'd done something right, I showered, changed clothes, and refreshed my make-up for my husband. Brushing my short platinum-blond hair, I made sure not a strand was out of place. If I was going to stay ahead of this younger woman Sindy, I had to be flawless. Five, almost six years wasn't a major gap but the fact that I was almost four years older than my husband meant I had to keep myself together at all times. Having a baby and no breasts were no excuses for me to let myself go.

Zach was seven days old and my stomach wasn't flat as it used to be. In another week I was hiring a nanny and a personal trainer. I detested wearing body shapers. Those hideous garments were designed for women who didn't keep their mouth shut and their ass moving. Desiring help to temporarily restore my former hourglass figure, reluctantly I put on the one I'd bought from Victoria's Secret.

"Damn, I look better but I can hardly breathe."

I fastened my custom-made 36-double D padded bra, then dabbed my favorite perfume at the nape of my neck. Didn't want the fragrance to make contact with Zach's skin. I eased into a short blazing cerulean cotton dress that softly hugged my hips, then carried my shoes and our son downstairs.

The man in the BMW I'd waited for arrived. I slipped into my shoes. Cradling Zach in my arm, I stood in the doorway waving and smiling.

Roosevelt's blue suit, red shirt, and striped tie were impeccable. The dark designer sunglasses were different from the ones I'd seen him in. I liked these more. Hopefully Sindy hadn't given them to him. His shoes were polished to perfection as always. His thin mustache was neatly aligned with the corners of his mouth. I missed having his lips all over my body.

"I'm glad you guys won today," I said puckering for a kiss.

"Hey little fella," he said sliding his hand behind Zach's back. Roosevelt paused, pressed his lips to mine. He looked into my eyes, said, "Daddy loves you," then scooped his son out of my arms.

Men often sent mixed signals but I had my situation figured out for him. I was certain there was hope for us staying together.

I closed the door. "You want something to drink?" A part of me felt like a stranger to my husband. The other half was all too familiar.

"I'm good. I can't stay long but I'm coming by

tomorrow to get him. My family wants to see the baby. I can keep him overnight to give you a break."

Time away from my baby wasn't what I needed. "Let's give it another month or two before he's around other people." I was genuinely concerned. I didn't want strangers touching Zach's face and hands. What if he got sick? Who was going to care for our son? Not Roosevelt.

If my husband didn't change his mind about divorcing me, we'd have to let the judge determine his custodial rights. For now, I had complete control over our son's whereabouts and I refused to relinquish my power.

Roosevelt stared at me. His lips tightened as his eyebrows drew closer together. Speaking between clenched teeth, he said, "You've controlled enough, don't you think. I'm not asking. I'm coming to get my son tomorrow. I'll be by around three after I'm done at the office."

I slid my hand down his back, and he stepped away. "I only said that because Zach is only a week old. His immune system has not developed and he could catch something."

Roosevelt's lips relaxed.

"Baby, are you sure you want a divorce? Zach deserves both of his parents."

Silence filled the room until Zach cooed. Roosevelt kissed his son on the mouth, then held Zach to his chest. "Daddy got you, dude."

Tears filled my eyes. "Have me too. We both need you."

Roosevelt shook his head; he tightened his jaw. Silence.

He didn't have to say anything. I was winning

and he hated it. *Take another bite of my apple, babe.* Inside of me, I screamed, "I hate you for having a life of leisure and I'm stuck in the house with our son by myself!" then I cried uncontrollably.

"Don't perform in front of my son. We're not raising him to see us argue and no matter what we have to deal with, I don't want him to see you cry."

On the inside, I smiled then prayed for a positive outcome. Why did he always have to take the high road? The more in control he was the more I felt that I was on the verge of a nervous breakdown. Hmm. Would he divorce me if I faked one?

Kicking off my heels, I told him, "I'll give you guys time alone. I'm going upstairs. Call me when you're ready to leave."

I had to say and do that before I did something I'd regret. Screaming "You cheating bastard! Why did you have that bitch in your suite?" wasn't going to make him love me the way I loved him.

Removing my dress and body shaper, I kept on the bra and put on a short silk gown and slightly longer robe to expose my long sexy toned legs. Loosely, I tied the belt. I skipped the panties, turned off the television, then lay across my bed and cried myself asleep.

I'd do whatever I had to do to keep my husband.

CHAPTER 6

Granville

Alone time wasn't best for me so I'd taken on extra hours at my job.

Mama always said, "An idle mind is the devil's workshop."

Beep. Beep. Beep.

Sitting high in an excavator, I backed up the construction equipment. I loved operating this gentle giant machine. Powerful, big, and smooth, the SL 210 LC was kinda like me. The main difference was I didn't need anybody making me do anything.

I hit the controls to spin the cab a hundred and eighty degrees, then drove forward. Dropping the bucket onto a mound of dirt, I maneuvered switches until the bucket was full. Driving a short distance, I released the load, picked up another, then transported it a few feet. I'd shoveled, leveled, compacted, and excavated dirt for the past two hours.

My son should receive my health benefits. Madison couldn't control my adding Zach as one of the two beneficiaries on my life insurance policy. My brother Beaux would get paid after I was buried. Mama would want it that way. I was going to provide for my kid even if I couldn't see him. Now that Mama was dead, I needed someone to take care of.

"Granville," my supervisor yelled, flapping his arms.

Looking down at Manny, I turned off the engine, then answered, "Yeah, boss!"

Manny was six feet tall and he was fluent in English and Spanish. Speaking loud was the norm. It was hard to hear people talking on the site with machinery humming, banging, and drilling. Our eyes had to be our ears. Sometimes I made up country songs that went along with the motion of my machine to make my job fun.

"*I was digging her. She wasn't digging me. Until I went deep. She was feeling me.*" Well, who cared what I sang. They couldn't hear me.

"Can you work another split shift tomorrow? I need you!"

"Sure thing, boss!" I cranked up, dropped my last load, safely parked the excavator, secured all components, then hopped down. My blue jeans, denim shirt, and steel-toed boots were covered with dust.

I snapped my teeth like a starving animal. The ruggedness made me feel manly. The extra hours made a big difference in my clothes. There was no way I was changing to come back and get grimy again. The best part was the extra money in my paycheck. I was so hyped I felt like I could do ten hours seven days a week without a problem.

"You're doing an excellent job," Manny said patting me on the back.

At least someone was proud of me. "Thanks, boss."

"I'm thinking about promoting you to site supervisor. You want the job?"

The smile on my face gave him my answer but just to be sure, I yelled, "Helllll yeah!"

Driving home I wished I had a woman waiting for me. A hot meal on the stove. My bathwater waiting. I could walk through the door and say, "Honey, I'm home and guess who made supervisor?" Picking her up and spinning her around, I'd give her a big ol' juicy wet kiss. Loretta hated my kisses. I liked hers. Yum. Raspberry.

Suddenly I became sad. Where was my son? Who was holding him? Had he gained a pound? Was he happy? I imagined he was but I wanted to be happy with him and Madison. I could afford to buy Zach whatever he needed. How much could a one-week-old eat?

I laughed. Mama used to say, "Boy, you gon' eat us out of a house and a home." Wasn't that the same thing? I missed my mama.

Taking a detour off of Westheimer Road, I drove by Madison's house. Chicago's car was parked in her driveway. I stopped, stared at the front door. Turning off the engine, I opened my truck door, got out.

Looking up at the house next door, I saw Loretta standing on the balcony. She placed her hand on her hip, rolled her eyes, then went inside. The protection order she had against me was still in place

for another few years. I wasn't here to see her but
Madison's house was less than one hundred feet
from Loretta's. Just in case Loretta was calling the
police, I didn't need any trouble. My boss might
fire me if got arrested. I couldn't hold my son
while wearing these dirty clothes anyway. I got
back in my black Super Duty and headed home.

We didn't have assigned spaces but I liked when
my favorite one was available. Didn't have to worry
about my neighbor's car door hitting mine. I
parked at the end. Walked up to my penthouse on
the second floor. Opening the door to my one
bedroom, I headed straight to the fridge, grabbed
a brew, then sat on my couch.

My funk. My filth. My furniture. I stared at the
suitcase Charles Singleton gave me. If the million
dollars, the gun, and the cell phone he mentioned
were actually inside, I would need that promotion
for an incentive to stay. Actually, I loved my job. If
I'd won a million playing the lottery—guess I'd
have to play first—I'd still work.

But if I carried out Mr. Singleton's request to
kill Chicago, I might end up back behind bars.
Beating attempted murder charges was one thing
but there was no way I'd get off for first-degree
murder. I sat my beer on the floor, placed the case
on my coffee table.

What was Charles Singleton's motivation? I
mean, I loved Madison but did Charles love her
too? Why did he have his bodyguards show up at
my apartment, break in, and force me to go to his
place? Then he sat in the dark so I couldn't see his
face. That day felt like a movie scene. I didn't

know that dude. But I'd bet he knew all about me. I hadn't checked this case because . . . what was really inside? I'd waited long enough.

"Let me see." I opened it. "Shit! Fuck!" I covered my mouth. That old dude wasn't lying!

My body trembled. I'd never seen this much cash in my life! I picked up my cell, dialed my brother.

Beaux answered, "What's up, bro?"

"Get your ass over here right now," I said then ended the call.

Since I'd heard on the news recently that the government was eavesdropping on everybody's calls, I couldn't take a chance on them overhearing me. I knew they'd come get my black ass.

I downed my beer, grabbed two more from the fridge, then spread the money out on my living room floor. Waddling in it like a kid, I yelled, "I'm rich, bitch!"

Bet Loretta wished she could get some of this cash and dick. I squeezed my shit so hard I almost came, then I started laughing.

Bam. Bam. Bam. "Open the door!" my brother said.

Beaux was going to be in for the shock of his life. Grinning like a kid left alone in a candy store, I cracked the door. "Close your eyes, dude."

He pushed. I shoved him back.

"What you up to? Move out the way," he said trying to force open the door.

It didn't budge. "Seriously, do it now. Shut your damn eyes."

Beaux did as I said. I released the door, then

touched his shoulder. "Don't open them until I tell you. Now come in." Locking the door, I said, "Open them."

My brother's eyes grew the size of gumballs. "Nigga! Who the fuck you robbed?"

"I know, right?" I didn't want to tell him everything but I couldn't lie. "I told you on the way to Mom's funeral that I had a million dollars."

"Now tell me how you got it," he said picking up a handful of hundreds. One at a time, he held them up to the light.

"You think my shit is fake?"

"I don't know," he said holding up another. "Probably."

What if it was? I hadn't thought about that. I could kill Chicago, get away with that, and still end up in jail for pushing counterfeit dollar bills. Charles wouldn't do that. Tomorrow after my first shift, I was taking two of them bills to the bank to make sure dude ain't tryna play me. I couldn't ID his ass. I didn't know where he lived, but my fingerprints were on shit in his house. He had my address. I couldn't call him. But he had my number.

I told Beaux, "I haven't earned it yet. I'll get another mil after I kill Chicago." That idea that I had after Mama's funeral might work.

He slapped the back of my head. I barely felt it. He said, "What the fuck, bro? Are you stupid?"

"The worst that can happen is I'll end up behind bars and you'll be a millionaire. But, if I dump this into an offshore bank account, let it earn interest, and never attempt to kill Chicago, I can give Charles Singleton back his money and we can keep the interest."

Beaux slapped me hard, on my back this time. I stumbled. "Bro, you just made Mama proud. That's the way to go. I got your back on that." My brother fell on top of the money.

"Dude, we're gonna be frickin' millionaires!" Madison loved my dick. I bet she'd crawl on her knees and beg me to take her back when she found out that I was a rich man.

CHAPTER 7

Chicago

"Madison."

Standing at the foot of the stairs, I waited for a response. "Madison," I said a little louder. I didn't want to go up to her bedroom where she'd let Granville fuck her in the ass. I'd never lay my body in that bed again.

A flashback of her enjoying sex with another man made me want to go up those stairs and . . . my son smiled at me. Hugging him to my chest, I confessed, "If it weren't for you, dude, I would not be here."

Madison could finally stop lying about how or why she opened her legs for Granville. My wife didn't owe me an explanation but a sincere heart-felt apology would've . . . done what? Pissed me off more.

What was she doing? She'd been upstairs for an hour. "Madison."

Sleepily, she answered, "I'm coming, babe."

Seeing her slowly take one step at a time, as

though she was in pain, I felt bad. "I'm sorry. I should've known you were resting."

"You have to go?" she asked. Her eyes filled with tears that didn't fall.

"Naw, no," I lied. I had to get to Sindy before she'd be pissed off with me. "I need to change his diaper and I didn't know where they were. Didn't want to go searching through your things." There was no telling what I would've accidentally found. Pictures. Another video. Some dude's stuff he'd left.

Madison took Zach from me. "I'll do it."

"But I want to."

She kept walking up the stairs. "It won't take long. I'll bring him right back."

A text message registered on my cell. Hey, babe. You home yet?

Texting, Will be another two, I sat on the sofa in the family room, then paused. Better not put a time on it. Had to make a stop. Will call you when I'm in. I hit SEND, switched to VIBRATE, then locked my phone.

I leaned back, clamped my hands behind my head, then spread my thighs. Eight bedrooms. Ten bathrooms. An outdoor garden. An outdoor Jacuzzi. Madison's peach stucco mansion with layered red clay roof tiles resembled a Miami castle. Zach will enjoy growing up here.

Closing my eyes, I imagined Sindy straddling me. I'd run my hands through her hair, hold her face, pull her into me. My lips would caress hers. Unbuttoning my shirt, I could hear her whisper, "Roosevelt, I want to feel you inside of me."

"Roosevelt," Madison said handing Zach to me. "He's fresh and clean."

Madison turned to leave. I called her name. She continued walking. I followed her. "Madison, wait."

Pausing in between steps, she glanced over her shoulder, then answered, "Yes?"

"Is Zach *my* son?" I had to hear her say it. Hear how she'd respond.

"Of course he is. He looks just like you. Paternity tests don't lie but I understand your asking. I'm tired. Bring him to me when you're ready to go see her." Tears coated her eyes again. Looking away, she sniffled.

Why should I sympathize with her? That woman could lie like an actress. I was the one who should cry. I held Zach a few feet in front of my face. It was hard to tell who babies resembled most. Hopefully my wife wasn't lying to me again. Did she really think I couldn't change a diaper?

Handling kids was all about coordination. I knew Zach was little but I could've changed and fed him at the same time. The ball skills I'd acquired from being a running back in high school and college were amazing. I got out of the game to pursue a more lasting career. Managing a team was better than coaching or getting beat up on the field. God knew my heart had gotten enough abuse from Madison. I'd rather take a thousand hits on the field than deal with wondering if a kid was mine.

Sitting in the white leather chair, I held Zach in the palms of my hands, one behind his head, the other underneath his butt. I'd love to say seeing a sex tape of my wife with another man didn't matter since the test results proved I was Zach's father, but that was a lie.

Before I arrived at her house, my intentions

were to tell Madison, "I forgive you and I'm trying to forget the bad and focus on the good in our relationship."

When she asked, "Are you sure you want a divorce? Zach deserves both of his parents," I thought, *And what do I deserve? A whore for a wife?* My emotions were in turmoil.

I laid my son on my lap, then texted Sindy: You're perfect. I want to get to know you better. What if she were an opportunist too? Fool me once. I exhaled.

God whispered, "Trust in me. Sindy is the one."

Rattling my head, I couldn't remember the last time I'd gone to church, read my Bible, spoken with my pastor, or kneeled to pray. Madison didn't go to church. Loretta. Hmm. She was a member at Lakewood too. We used to be prayer buddies. How did Loretta consider herself a Christian? After setting Madison up, Loretta fell in love with me, a married man. And if I would've given her a ring, I know she would've accepted. I understood why Madison didn't speak to Loretta anymore.

Zach smiled at me, exposing his gums. His eyes were full of light and joy. Respect was free. I shouldn't think of his mother as a tramp. I was hurting because I cared and it seemed as though Madison didn't. Wish I were more like Chaz when it came to women.

The innocence of my lil fella made me remember when my relationship with Madison was pure. I trusted her. Once she broke that trust, I knew the day would come when I'd do the same, to her or someone else, out of spite. Was Sindy a rebound to help me deal with my pain, or did I genuinely care for her?

Hmm. Sindy. What was there not to love about her?

"Hey, little man. I wish I could say I'd teach you how to know when a woman was lying but I can't. I can't protect you against heartaches from girls but I promise you I'll do my best to make sure I never let you down. And Daddy will always be here for you no matter what."

His legs kicked as his lips curved down. Quickly, I held him to my chest, patted his back. "It's okay, son. I told you. I got you."

God whispered, "I've got you too."

I swear I wanted to cry. What was happening to me?

The vibration of my phone made me eager. Anxiously, I looked at the screen and smiled. It was Sindy. I braced Zach in one arm while reading her text: Save some love for me. I have a surprise for you.

Excitement stirred in the pit of my stomach. The last time I'd been this happy with Madison was the day I'd said, "I do."

My new woman made me want to leave here, go straight to my jeweler, buy her that size six engagement ring, and put it on her finger before I changed my mind. Perhaps what I needed was time, not another commitment. But Sindy was different from Madison. I'd respond later. This was Zach's time.

"You guys okay?" Madison asked entering the family room.

"We good."

"I couldn't sleep. You want to feed him or you want me to do it?"

"I'd love to feed him," I said sticking my finger

inside his diaper. "He needs to be changed first. I can do that while you fix his bottle."

"No!" Madison replied, swallowing as she shouted. She coughed. "Something's caught in my throat. I meant to say, not again."

She took Zach from me, then headed toward the stairs. "I'll change him while you heat up his bottle. It's in the refrigerator. How much longer are you going to be here?"

Long as I'd like, I thought. I'd paid off her mortgage. I know she wasn't rushing me. But I did want to get that surprise Sindy had waiting.

Instead of heading to the kitchen, I turned toward the living room. "I'll call and check on Zach later. I can see myself out."

I paused, expecting her to ask me to stay . . . but she didn't.

CHAPTER 8

Granville

He couldn't stay at my woman's house forever. My new cell that Charles Singleton had put in the briefcase was on the table. This time I'd give it ten minutes before checking Chicago's location again. I tapped the heel of my cowboy boot to the floor while juggling my phone from one hand to the other. Glancing at the clock on the wall in the food court, I exhaled heavily. Two minutes felt like ten had gone by. Spinning my phone, I remembered when I used to play spin the bottle. The girls gave me the same dare. "I bet you won't pull out your dick, Granville." I felt like taking it out now. Playing with my shit took my mind off of everything else.

Indecent exposure was for guys with small wood. I had a two-by-four big enough to spank a woman without my nuts touching her ass. I tapped my heel harder.

I had to tell Madison how Beaux and I were going to start the process to open a Swiss bank account tomorrow. If they questioned how we got the mil, Beaux wanted to say the cash was from us winning the lottery. I decided we'd say it was an inheritance from our recently deceased mother. *No, dude. Don't let Madison know you rich. You want her to love you not your money.* All the madness in my head didn't matter. I wanted my woman by any means.

Holding my phone, if I were a genie, that wouldn't work. I'd have to grant, not make wishes. I liked *I Dream of Jeannie.* Whatever happened to that show? I know Jeannie would've loved me. If I could've gotten her away from Major Nelson. He was cock-blocking like Chicago. I closed my eyes and made a wish: "Dude! Be gone!"

Five minutes left. I put my phone on the table. The Galleria Mall on Westheimer Road was close to Madison's mansion. It was closer to the Grand Lux Cafe where I'd taken Loretta on our last date. Bet that bitch wish she would've kept my engagement ring.

I sat in the food court by the ice-skating rink watching women dash by me on those thin blades. Most of them wore tight jeans and T-shirts. Madison would never wear blue jeans. She was too classy for that. I didn't want any of those girls. One kept smiling at me each time she zoomed by. I found myself focusing more on the dad who was teaching his kid how to skate. Tears clouded my eyes. I was going to bring Zach here when he was old enough to learn how to skate.

I checked the iPhone Charles gave me, and Chicago's location showed him on Kirby Drive. "Yeah! It's about time, dude!" The moment I'd waited for was here. Chicago had left my woman's house. He was on Kirby Drive, probably headed to his condo. Who cared?

I asked myself, *How do you know this thing is working for sure?* What if he was still there or planned on going back?

An incoming call on my personal iPhone distracted me. I pressed IGNORE. I felt like a celebrity with two phones. Immediately he called back.

"What's up, bro? I'm busy."

"Why you lying? I see your ass sitting in the food court."

I looked up. My brother Beaux was leaning over the rail. I asked him, "What you doing up there by the Michael Kors store? Buying a purse?" I laughed, then sang, "You ain't got no girlfriend."

Beaux wasn't gay or anything but he hadn't gone steady in a long time. Maybe I should hook him up.

"Meet me up here. I'm starving. Let's go grab something to eat at 51Fifteen," he said. "My treat."

"We ate there two days ago, dude. I'm good," I lied. I was so hungry I could eat a cow and her calves too. Food could wait. My mind was made up to make Madison let me see my son tonight. "Stop stalking me, dude."

Beaux's taste buds had gone from Pappas Bar-B-Q to fine dining almost every day since our mama died. He refused to take anything for granted. I felt the same. That was why I had to see my kid. With this windfall, ain't no telling what Beaux would upgrade to. Me, I was forever a Texas cowboy who loved pussy, pretty women, and the simple life.

"I'm not asking," he said. "We can go wherever you like. Stay there. I'm coming down."

Soon as he was out of my sight, I ran toward

Rainforest Cafe, dashed out the exit, and got in my truck.

In a matter of minutes, I was at Madison's. Chicago's car was actually gone. What did I have to do to start tracking Madison again? My online satellite was blocked. How'd she do that? She would never let me close enough to her phone again so I could download a GPS app like I'd done the night she passed out while riding my dick.

The one time Madison sexed me was the best of my life until our baby was born. Tears clouded my eyes. I parked my Super Duty a block from Madison's house. If she saw my truck, she'd probably get scared. I didn't get out right away.

Had to talk with my mama first. I touched my forehead, chest, right then left shoulder. "I'm getting ready to see your grandson." I missed my mama. I'd make sure Zach knew who Sarah Lee Washington was. I should've brought a picture of Mama for him. Next time.

Hawking up the mucus in my throat, I opened the door and chucked it in the grass. "Fertilizer." I sat in the driver's seat. I used the phone dude gave me and typed in MADISON TYLER on Facebook hoping she'd posted pics of our son. A few matches came up for her name but none of the profiles were her. I entered MADISON TYLER-DUBOIS. She came up but only friends could see her page.

What the hell? Why was I friends with Chicago and not her?

I started to send a request then remembered that Charles Singleton had warned me not to change the Facebook settings on the cell he'd given me. Adding or deleting friends was prohibited too. My sole purpose was to keep track of Chicago until I killed him. If I sent a request from my phone, Madison would know it was me. My friend page had photos of mountains and sunsets. Too many of them to count.

My personal profile name was Kilamandingo. I had lots of friend requests but didn't have a pic of myself anywhere on my page. Didn't want those football fans attacking me for shooting Chicago. I didn't accept any friends. Having no friends was true in my everyday life too. Watching other people was my main reason for signing up.

Getting out of my truck, I strolled past Madison's girlfriend Tisha's home. The next house was Loretta's. I stared at her place. Loretta's lights were on downstairs. I paused for a moment then continued my stride. I didn't care for her anymore. If she called the cops, she'd be doing me a favor. Breaking the protective order Loretta had against me wouldn't count when I explained to the police I was going to visit my son. I had the right to do that.

Sensor lights came on as I approached Madison's front door. I rang the doorbell then waited. Playfully I put my finger over the peephole. Laughing, I moved my hand. Hoping she'd be happy I'd come, I didn't hide my face. "Hello, dear." I was prepared for Madison not to let me in soon as she saw me but she couldn't leave me standing out here forever.

"You need to get your ass away from here right now nigga and never come back."

I balled my fists tight, held them high in the air as I turned around and swung.

"You heard me, nigga. I ain't scared of you," Johnny Tyler said, stepping back. "Get!"

"I ain't no dog, dude." This old man wasn't my boss anymore. I was glad Madison had fired me. Otherwise, we couldn't be together. "You want some, old man? I ain't come here for no trouble. I came to see my kid."

"I called the cops! They're on the way!"

My head snapped in the opposite direction. My fists were still raised. Dropping my arms to my side, I stared at Loretta standing in her front doorway. "You need to call 1-800-JENNY."

What did I ever see in her? She still hadn't ditched that dreadful ponytail. I wasn't close enough to see if that raspberry lip gloss was smeared across her chocolate lips. Can't believe I'd sucked it off twenty-three times. Yuck!

She yelled, "Don't leave. I want you to go to jail!"

"Oh, so now you neighborhood watch, bitch! I came to see my son, not you! Did you lick any pussies while you were in prison?" That should shut her up.

She threw up her middle finger. I saw that white T-shirt tucked into those skin-tight blue jeans just before she slammed the door. "You gettin' fat!"

"Granville, you need to leave and never come back."

My head jerked in another direction. This time it was Madison standing in the doorway of her house. These bitches lived too close together. I looked toward Tisha's place expecting her to be in the driveway, then I heard sirens in the distance.

"Nigga, you deaf?" Johnny said.

"I got your nigga," I told him then quickly thumped my cowboy boots along the driveway. When I made it to the sidewalk, I saw a cop car heading in my direction. I took off running toward my truck.

A big house with an alleyway leading to a backyard was to my right. Too big and too black to hide in this upscale neighborhood where owners like Madison had motion lights surrounding their property, I kept it moving.

I made it to the corner, dashed across the street while shoving my hand into my front pocket. My keys were on my fingertips and my truck was less than fifty feet away. "You can make it," I told myself. I looked over my shoulder before crossing the street.

The cop's car bumper was literally on my ass when he pulled into the driveway next to my truck. His door flung open.

The police yelled, "Freeze! Take your hand out of your pocket or I'll shoot!"

I put both hands up in the air. The phone Charles gave me fell out of my pocket. I motioned to bend over to pick it up.

Pow!

"Ow!" My left knee hit the grass, then my right. My chest was flat against the cement sidewalk. The left side of my body ached. I braced my head inches from cement. I might not be the most handsome man in Houston but my face was not scarred. Had to keep it that way. It felt like blood rolled underneath my armpit to my chest.

The officer said, "Don't move!" then I heard him say, "Suspect in custody. Cancel backup."

He was the one that needed to back his ass up. "Man, I was surrendering! I don't have a gun," I said. "You didn't have to shoot me. This is racial profiling."

"Put your hands behind your back," he said.

My body was numb. "I can't. I'm shot."

He grabbed my arms, held my hands behind my back. Tightening the handcuffs around my wrists, he said, "You have the right to remain silent . . ."

I became quiet, praying he didn't realize the Super Duty was mine. Everything Charles had given me was at my penthouse except the cell underneath my shin. I should've gone to dinner with Beaux. Now, I was going to have to call him to get my truck and bail me out of jail.

I'd shot Chicago three times. This cop hit me once somewhere in the back and I thought I was on my way to heaven where my mama was. Mama was not going to be happy to see me. God wouldn't have to whup me. Mama probably had a strap waiting for my behind.

"Get up!" the cop demanded. He placed his hand under my armpit.

"Man, let me go and call an ambulance. Can't you see I'm bleeding?"

"It was a stun gun. You're sweating," he said. "Now get up before I shoot you for resisting arrest."

I felt the iPhone beneath my knee. Getting up I placed the heel of my cowboy boot on top of the cell then crushed the screen, praying I'd destroyed the device and the SIM card. Mama had probably put it there. I felt my personal phone in my opposite pocket. The cop never noticed the phone in the grass. He put me in the back of his car and drove off.

Had this Charles dude set me up?

All I wanted to do was spend a little time with my son.

CHAPTER 9

Sindy

What appropriate gift does a single woman give to a married man?

Something tangible? Intangible? A tie was too basic, yet safe. A hand-painted partially nude tasteful image was thoughtful of her, inconsiderate of his wife. A lap dance was sexy, would make him very happy, and last an eternity in his mind, especially if his wife had never given him one. The latter was what I'd planned.

Being in Roosevelt's presence made my pussy pulsate with pleasure. His sexual energy was dynamite and kryptonite rolled together.

"I know it's been a long day, for both of us," he said. "Thanks for meeting me here." He refilled our glasses with champagne.

The red belly-dancing outfit I'd bought was in a bag in my car. At Roosevelt's request to the owner, we sat alone in the Lexington Room at Corner Table restaurant. A ten-foot-tall mirror was closest to our table. The curtains were drawn. No one could see in. We didn't want to see out.

The waiters were informed not to disturb us. An extra bottle of Cristal was on ice. A small feast of strawberries, chocolate, whipped cream, an assortment of cheeses, and red grapes decorated a silver platter that sat in the middle of our round table.

I wasn't hungry for food. Neither was he. We focused on one another. My being a virgin didn't mean I was inhibited. Creativity and exploration over the years made me more aware of my erogenous zones.

"I understand. You have a lot of responsibilities. Your team. Your son. Your family. Your—"

He kissed me, then said, "You. I want you, Sindy."

The sentiments were mutual. My pussy, although it'd never been wrapped around a dick, craved his. Holding his hand, one at a time I pressed his fingertips to my lips. "Which one is your favorite?"

"The longest. It's the perfect length to stimulate your G-spot."

I liked that he knew where it was but he wouldn't be sticking anything in my vagina. My ass, maybe. I eased his hand under the table, between my legs, then let him touch my precious pearl. I put his middle finger in my mouth, then let him feel me again.

"Pleasant surprise," he said, this time dipping his finger into the whipped cream.

Perhaps he was referring to the fact that I didn't have on panties. Or that I'd initiated contact. Roosevelt smeared the thickness onto my wetness. I was wet before he'd touched me. Impromptu foreplay was not what I'd planned but it felt so good.

I squeezed my thighs together. "Ah, yes, babe."

Gripping his wrist, I moved his hand. He dipped his finger again, resumed playing with me. This time I curled my hips into his rotation, then closed my eyes. Roosevelt positioned himself under the tablecloth. The white cotton draped his head.

Opening my eyes, ours met. When his tongue brushed against my clit, slowly my eyelids covered my pupils. I scooted my chair backward. He pulled my hips to the edge of the seat. I had a stellar reputation, not the kind that would make my colleagues snicker behind my back or mumble under their breath at the annual bar conference, "Did you hear Sindy Singleton was caught having sex in public? If she's giving it up for a bottle of bubbly, she's so hot I'll buy her a vineyard."

Irrespective of how successful women were, men viewed us as objects. I wasn't sure how much longer I was going to remain a virgin but tonight wasn't the appropriate time for us to consummate our relationship.

The more I struggled to resist, the better his mouth felt. I conceded, grabbed the back of his head, and drew him into my juiciness. Roosevelt fluttered his tongue on my clit. My body tensed. I was glad I'd removed my panties earlier and put them in my purse. Teasing him wasn't supposed to go beyond fondling.

Waves of orgasmic spasms made me slide off the seat and under the table. Suddenly my back was flat and my knees were bent. I felt like a freak and a sexually deprived woman at the same time.

Roosevelt bit my nipple through my dress. He slid my strap off my shoulder and suctioned my areola into his mouth.

I bit my upper lip to keep from cumming. I exhaled, "Ah, damn."

His lips trailed down my stomach, belly button, and back to my clit. He suctioned me in.

I started screaming, "Babe! I'm creaming!"

Silencing my climax, I'd forgotten where we were. I prayed no one came in while I was still cumming. The tail end of my orgasms turned into laughter.

"You are so crazy," I told him. "I can't believe we're under a tablecloth doing this."

"Doing what?" he asked gazing into my eyes. "Say it."

I was not going to tell Roosevelt "making love" or "I love you."

Peeping out, I crawled from under the table, stood, and straightened my dress and hair. "Let's get out of here." At least I didn't have to worry about being videotaped like Madison.

The valet retrieved our cars. After that amazing climax, I had to lay my head on Roosevelt's chest and shoulder tonight. I followed him to his place.

Being a virgin didn't mean I'd never experienced an orgasm but this one was head to toe. There were more alternatives to intercourse that would take the edge off for both of us. I was confident I could please Roosevelt sexually but I wanted to be reassured he was the one. I'd hate to have waited until I was thirty to let a man cross my hymen threshold then have regrets.

Roosevelt pressed his brother's buzzer. Shortly afterward, Chaz opened the door.

"Good to see two beautiful people together. Numbiya is here. Come in."

"I just wanted to say thanks and you were right."

Roosevelt nodded, then added, "I'll see you at the office tomorrow." He interlocked his fingers with mine, then kissed the back of my hand.

Raising my brows, I smiled. "Hi, Chaz. Bye, Chaz." Based on his actions, I was certain Roosevelt's statement was in my favor.

Although I lived in a River Oaks mansion designed by John F. Staub in the 1930s, I was tired of living in ten thousand square feet of space alone. A real man didn't ask a woman's ring size to get her a token of his appreciation.

I saw myself moving in with Roosevelt after he'd proposed. From the theater on the entry level to the ballroom on the top floor, his condominium building at The Royalton had all the amenities I desired and more.

Walking a few doors down, we were at Roosevelt's place. Taking a good look at his firm buttocks, I entered behind him. This man was heavenly to hold and behold.

Yet, how could I be 100 percent certain this was the right man for me? I couldn't. I'd do what I believed would work. One, continue getting to know him. Two, be patient. Three, trust my gut instincts. I placed my purse and bag on the bar countertop.

"Hey, baby. You hungry?" I asked him opening his refrigerator.

He looked down at my hips.

"For food," I said smiling.

"My chef prepared a chili bean casserole and a spinach quiche. It's in the oven. If you don't mind heating it up, that would make your man happy," he said kissing me.

Wow, if I weren't a woman of reason, I'd truly

believe he was my man. Underestimating what Madison would do to keep him wasn't in my plan.

"Anything for you, handsome." I meant that believing he'd do anything for me.

"I'm going to take a quick shower." He bit his bottom lip, slowly eased it from between his teeth, winked, then entered his bedroom.

Quietly, I exhaled and removed my Jimmy Choo red, sparkling, open-toed, slingback stilettos. The football team's colors, red and blue, had become my new favorite since dating Roosevelt.

I placed my heels next to his sofa, then washed my hands. A real woman never did more for a man than he did for her. Everything wasn't monetary. I possibly had more money than Roosevelt could give me. For that, I thanked God. I probably should thank my father too, but the way he'd earned his millions wasn't honest. Siara. I needed to Skype soon with my sister. I had missed a few sessions since being with Roosevelt.

What I wanted from this man was simple—love, respect, and consideration. Those were my non-negotiables. As basic as that was, most men didn't give those things to a woman because he didn't want to, she didn't require him to, or he didn't care about her feelings.

The test I used to gauge how badly a man wanted me was to walk away shortly after meeting him. The one guarantee in every relationship was men displayed their characteristics and character flaws early. When a man showed me he was no good, I didn't try to change him. I released him to the women who liked wolves.

Programming the oven to 350 degrees, I set the

dinner table for two. I poured a glass of scotch for him, champagne for me.

The day Roosevelt took me to Brennan's for dinner he'd patronized my profession, mildly devalued womanhood, and stepped away from the table to make a call. Since he'd done all of that on our first date before we'd ordered entrees, I left.

If he'd called me later that night, which he did, he showed he cared. If he would've phoned the next day, that meant he was prideful and needed time to restore his ego. If Roosevelt hadn't called for two days, I would've been done. A forty-eight-hour delay was the sign of an insecure man and I'd never invest in that type of person.

Glancing up at the beautiful white crown molding around his ceiling, I frowned. There was an unusual gap in the corner. A closer look revealed the spacing in the other corners was consistent. I imagined it was a construction defect.

"Hey, the table looks nice," Roosevelt said as he stood behind me. He hugged my waist, gently swept my hair over my shoulder, then kissed the nape of my neck.

"Is there something wrong with your molding?" I asked pointing toward the ceiling.

"Let's focus on what's right. You and me."

I faced him. Eyes didn't lie. This man loved me so much I felt it. "In fifteen minutes, you can take the dishes out of the oven and placed them on the table. It's my turn to shower."

Pressing my lips to his I opened my mouth, sucked his tongue, then swallowed our saliva. "Sweet. Let's save some of that for dessert toppings."

Seductively walking away I entered his bedroom. There were no visible signs of Madison ever living here. I'd asked him to get rid of her belongings. A man who'd justify holding on to his woman's or his wife's property after they'd separated wasn't over her. Since Roosevelt's mother and brother weren't fond of Madison, I didn't imagine he'd store her things at their place. Most condos had a storage space for each unit. I'd be happy if he'd put them there. I was not treading on insecurity. I was thinking ahead. And I wasn't sharing room in his space with another woman, especially his estranged wife. My toiletries had replaced hers.

I preferred a bath but opted for a shower. I cleansed my body head to toe and every space in between in ten minutes. Another five to brush my teeth and dry off and I was ready to enjoy what was left of our night.

"You ready for me to fix the plates," Roosevelt called from the dining area.

"Yes, sweetheart."

"Your cell phone is ringing. It's your dad."

I hurried to the living room before it went to voice mail. There was no telling what Charles Singleton was up to. "Thanks," I said then answered, "Hi Daddy."

"Have you heard?"

"Heard what?" That Granville had changed his mind about the hit my father put on Roosevelt? If that were true, it'd be the right thing for Granville to do. I wasn't supposed to know any of this so I didn't mention it. Even if I wanted to tell my father off, I couldn't do it in front of Roosevelt.

"Granville?" my father said.

"What about him?"

"He was arrested for violating his protective order."

"And?"

Roosevelt mouthed, "Everything okay?"

I nodded.

"I heard from my sources that Nyle Carter is going to tell the police that Granville told him he's plotting to kill Chicago again."

"And?"

"Okay, baby girl. What I heard sounds a lot like I was listening to you. Are you behind Granville being arrested? Are you still trying to protect Chicago?"

"I think you know the answer to that question. Bye Daddy." I didn't tell my father I was about to have dinner with the man who had done no wrong to my dad, Madison, or anyone. And yes, I'd do everything I could to protect Roosevelt, but I wouldn't take a bullet for him or any man.

"Sindy."

Lost in thought, I realized I hadn't ended the call. Whenever he called me by name, he was serious. "What, Daddy?"

"I'm going to bail Granville out." That meant I was getting Nyle out.

While my dad was saying, "You are going to marry this billionaire who has already paid for you or he's going to kill me. Don't cross me. I'm not asking," I was texting my inside contact: Release Nyle Carter immediately.

I wasn't backing down. The inside guy couldn't do what I'd requested on his own. I had a few more texts to send. I never gave my father permission to accept money from a wealthy stranger in a foreign country in exchange for my virginity the way he'd done with my sister, Siara. My gut told me our mother wasn't dead. My sister believed she was.

Siara had said, "If she's alive, why hasn't she contacted either of us?" My sister loved her family.

I was with the man I wanted to marry and there wasn't anything my father could do to make me change my mind.

"Good-bye, Charles."

CHAPTER 10

Madison

The five minutes I'd planned on spying on Roosevelt turned into my barely blinking for a half hour. This was not supposed to be the life of Madison Tyler-DuBois. All the foul things Loretta had done to me didn't compare to Sindy seducing my husband.

I checked on Zach, who was asleep in his crib. Babies blessed with good parents didn't have to worry about their needs being met. My need for Roosevelt to love me was not coming to an end over her!

Tears streamed down my cheeks. I swiped them aside before they stained my dress. Didn't want any outward signs of sadness. Papa was on his way over. Said he had something to tell me. Refused to say whatever it was over the phone.

Pacing in front of my television, I kept watching them. I knew there were some who would say, "She deserves this," and there were others who'd sympathize with my agony because they too had been a fools for love. A split decision was what my husband had made. He couldn't have both of us. When he was here, he'd shown me that he cared for me.

Think, Madison, think.

I recalled the look on Sindy's face when she was on the phone. Seemed as though she'd been told something important. I watched my husband sit at the dinner table staring at Sindy. She tucked her hair behind her ear. I wondered if her strength was in those long beautiful strands and if I could get close enough to cut them and her off. I couldn't hear her clearly and had no idea to whom she was speaking or what they were saying but the distorted expression on her face indicated there was a problem.

When Sindy had pointed up at the ceiling earlier, I sat on the edge of my bed praying she hadn't spotted the hidden cameras. I had to find a way to enter Roosevelt's condo during his next game to close the gaps where I'd had the devices installed behind the crown molding.

What if the person on the phone with Sindy told her Granville had come to my house claiming Zach was his child? Damn, Madison. Stop waddling in your guilty conscience.

Standing over my son's crib, I placed my hand on his back, then under his nose. He was fine. I wasn't. The truth was undisputable. Paternity tests didn't lie. What if Sindy was the envious one who'd sent Granville here? I bet that's exactly what happened.

I turned off the television, picked up my baby, went downstairs, and sat in my favorite chair. My doorbell rang. Turning on the TV in my family room to check my security monitor, I prayed he wasn't back. It was Tisha.

Exhaling, I opened the door. "Come in, girl. I'm happy to see you."

"I'm just checking on you. Loretta told me she saved you from Granville by filing a report against him for violating his PO. She said you don't have to thank her. She was doing what any friend would've done. Call her, Madison."

"Not my problem," I told her.

"I can't believe this boy is sleeping through our conversation," Tisha said taking Zach from me.

"What am I going to do?" I asked, sitting beside them on the sofa.

"Get your own protective order." She cuddled Zach in her arms.

"I wasn't talking about Granville." I picked up the remote, changed the channel to Roosevelt's condo.

"Madison, no. You can't be serious. That's invasion. You could end up in jail if he finds out."

Roosevelt wouldn't do that to me. He loved Zach too much.

"Oh, oh. You might want to turn that off," Tisha said staring.

That slut was on her knees and had her mouth all over my husband's dick.

The words I wished I hadn't heard were loud and clear. "Oh, shit, motherfucker, damn! I'm cumming," Roosevelt shouted.

"Nasty bitch."

"Madison, excuse you. Zach heard that," Tisha said covering up his ears. "Why don't I take him to my house for a few hours until . . ." She paused, then said as if she were reading my mind, "You're not going to go over there, are you?"

I stared into her eyes.

"I'll just stay—"

The doorbell interrupted her sentence. Papa's face was in the upper right corner of the screen. Tisha stood, placed Zach in my arms, picked up the remote, then powered off the TV.

"You don't have to leave," I told her.

"Actually, I do. I have a date," she said opening the door. "Hi, Mr. Tyler."

How was she going to take Zach if she had plans? I could've used a break but she was right. If I didn't have my baby, I would've definitely gone to Roosevelt's place.

Papa said, "Thanks for keeping an eye on Madison, Tisha. Bye."

I handed Papa his grandchild, headed to the kitchen, filled a goblet to the rim with champagne, then drank half.

Papa was sitting in the oversize chair facing the sofa. This time he had the blanket over his suit like a bib.

Opening my mouth to laugh, I burped loud. "Excuse me," I said drinking half of the half that was left in my glass.

"Slow down. The baby can't be causing you to drink that much. At least not yet."

"What took you so long to get here?" After I'd asked, I said, "Don't answer that."

"It's okay, sweetheart. I was home all day with your mother. We're talking more these days."

I wished I could say that were true for Roosevelt. Did Sindy swallow my husband's semen? What were they doing now? Papa's timing was not good.

Taking my baby from Papa, I decided not to question him for details of his conversation with Mom. I had to get back to watching my husband.

"What is that you've been meaning to tell me, Papa?"

He cleared his throat, glanced at his wristwatch. "About what, sweetheart?" he said reaching for Zach. "We were still bonding."

Moving my child away from Papa, I cradled my son and rocked him. Silently, I stared at my dad. My lips pressed tighter together. He was the one who'd said he needed to tell me something; now he was acting like he hadn't come here for that.

"You'd better not give me any bad news," I told him. "You've hurt me way too much, Papa." I wanted to cry. Not for what my dad might say. I couldn't erase the image from my mind of Sindy down on her knees.

"Okay, I'll tell you but you have to keep this between us."

I shook my head and remained quiet. My heart pounded hard against my chest, reminding me I had no breasts. There were times when I didn't focus on having had a double mastectomy. The one regret I had was not trying the newer procedure and having everything done at once—removal, implants, and nipple preservation.

"The test," he said.

I stood preparing to hear the rest. "What about it?"

He sighed, looked up at me. "Okay."

I yelled, "Don't play games with me!" then cried. "Say it."

Zach screamed. I started crying. *God, please.*

Papa hung his head and talked at the floor. Covering his mouth, he mumbled.

"What was that? I didn't hear you, Papa."

He looked at me, then said, "I paid the lab technician to make sure the test results were in favor of Ro—"

Shaking my head, I said, "Get out."

"Sweetheart, it could be his baby. We don't know for sure. I did what I felt was best—"

"For you, Papa. You always do what's best for you!" Bouncing Zach in my arms, I rubbed his back. "Leave, Papa! And don't ever come back to my house!"

"I deserve that," he said walking toward the door. "But Roosevelt can still be the father. I don't understand why you jump to conclusions before you have all the facts. You want me to—"

"You know damn well Granville came here because . . ." The words "It's his baby" were caught in my throat. I could not imagine having to co-parent with that fool. Gasping for air, I could barely breathe.

"You've done enough. Go!"

Zach was screeching and jerking. His arms and legs were flapping. I wanted to do the same.

"Sweetheart, you make sure I keep my job. I'll make sure I keep our secret. One hand washes the—"

Slam!

I didn't care if the door hit him in his face. I took my baby upstairs.

Glancing at the video monitor, I saw that Roosevelt and Sindy were naked in his bed. I should've turned off the camera but I couldn't. I didn't know which hurt more. Watching them engage in foreplay or wondering who Zach's real father was.

The one thing I was sure of was Zach was my child. Or was he?

CHAPTER 11

Granville

"You know the routine," he said citing my inmate number.

They'd left me in a holding cell for hours. How did he remember that? Maybe he looked it up while I was waiting. Wasn't like I could leave but I wanted to go home and get in my bed.

"Step into the cage and put this on," he said handing me shower shoes, a tan uniform, brown underwear, and the same color socks. "I knew you'd be back, black. You're almost done processing in."

I felt like an animal. Not the kind that would pounce on a pretty girl and give her my hard wood. I felt like a dog locked in a kennel. I was loyal and that was my fault. No matter how long Madison disowned me, I would always love her.

The small fenced-in area didn't have any privacy. They'd already taken my cell phone, keys, wallet, and my cowboy boots. I removed my jeans, shirt, and underwear. Let my big dick hang low. I made it swing side to side before putting on the boxers they gave me.

He opened the gate. I gave him the clothes I'd taken off. "I ain't donating nothing. I want everything mailed to my brother."

Guess I was familiar with the process. My stomach growled. This was a fine time to get hungry. I couldn't buy any snacks. Had no book for Beaux to put money on yet. Wasn't asking my cellmate for shit. Wasn't getting my shit packed while I was in here either.

"Walk this way," he said leading me to a small intake room.

I sat in the small plastic blue chair. He sat at the rectangular steel desk.

"Here's your blanket, black. Kept it warm for you." He slid it across the desk.

Hardy har har. How dare dude call me "black" twice like he was my friend. If we were outside and he didn't have on that uniform, his mouth would be shut or I'd shut it for him.

"What made you so sure? My being back behind bars isn't my fault," I said dropping the brown rolled-up blanket to my feet. Before he answered, I told him, "I should've left town after I won my case, huh?"

The only persons keeping me from moving to Louisiana or California were Zach and Madison. What was California like? Did LA really have that many beautiful women? All the ones I'd seen on them reality shows seemed more high class than Madison.

Maybe I'd find me a Southern Barbie doll, marry her, then move to LA. Like my chicken, I only ate dark meat. I frowned; Madison would get jealous and take my son away from me if I did that. I loved my brother but I could live in a different state and not miss him the way I would my woman and my kid.

Interrupting my thoughts, he said, "Most of the guys come back because they're stupid. They violate parole, commit the same crimes, or they're selectively institutionalized. You can't reform stupidity. You. You're ignorant. That can be changed through proper education. There's hope for you if this is your last time in here. But you're also back due to that thing called karma." He shook his head. "Just because you weren't found guilty doesn't mean you're innocent, black. You deserve life at state. You know that. Plus, you shouldn't have smirked at that female the judge sentenced to thirty days for perjuring herself during your trial. Judges hate when you disrespect them."

I frowned at him, then shook my head. He wasn't at my hearing. These workers in the courthouse needed to sign agreements to keep their mouths shut about my personal business. What else did he know? I squinted and tightened my lips real hard.

He laughed. "Ain't nobody scared of you." This time he called me by my number. "You don't get it. Women never forget. Loretta will probably hate you the rest of your life. Why did you violate the protective order?"

He knew her name. "I wasn't trying to see her. I'd broken up with her almost a year ago. I was going to see my kid."

Loretta must've gained at least twenty pounds since I let her go. All that sitting in the window keeping watch over Madison made her lazy. She was probably waiting to get a glimpse of Chicago. Nursed him back to health and he still didn't want her. Hell, Loretta probably didn't want herself.

"That's not the way the police saw it and it sure isn't the way to comply with an order." He stared at me. "You serious. You really believe this kid is yours and not Chicago's?"

Was that a trick question? I didn't think so. He didn't have to ask that but I was glad he did. He had my respect now.

"I know he's mine."

"How?"

Hunching my shoulders, I hung my head, then told him, "Just do."

"If you want to stay on the other side of these cement walls, keep away from that woman and *her* kid." He cited my number again.

I'd talk to him as long as he wanted. I was in no hurry to return to Unit Six on the sixth floor. That was where I was the last time. It was the only male unit that was directly across the hall from the only female unit. But I could end up in one of the other five units where they housed the men.

"How long I'ma be in here? I can't afford to lose my job." Shit! I'd forgotten about my promo. "Can I get out on good behavior? I gotta go to work tomorrow."

"You should've thought about that before you ended up back in here, black."

I looked up and saw Nyle Carter on the other side of the door. I stood.

"Sit, dude."

I pressed my face against the glass to be sure it

was him. "He can't leave. He still has more than two years. Plus, that's my inside attorney. I'm going to need him for advice."

"Sit down, I said!" he shouted standing up to me.

I frowned at him again, then sat in the chair. "Am I going back to Unit Six?"

I asked but it didn't matter. My former cellmate, No Chainz, had been released. We kept in touch while he was on the inside. I put money on his books. After his release, I hadn't heard from dude. He probably had enough sense to leave town. I couldn't care less about making new friends in here. I wasn't staying long. How was Nyle being released at night? Something wasn't right. I had no way to get in touch with that Charles dude. If I did, that'd be my one call.

"Stay to yourself if you don't want to end up in state. I know you haven't heard the latest but it's rumored that you're planning on trying to kill Chicago."

My jaw dropped. "Where the fuck you hear that?" That Charles dude had set me up. Or was it Nyle? Or were football fans guessing? Maybe someone had started a social media lie on purpose.

"Why the fuck didn't you deny it?" he asked reciting my number.

I swung hard. Left. Right. Left right. One punch after another I threw blows to my face. "How could I be this stupid!"

The intake guard opened the door, shoved me to the floor, then clamped my wrists together before locking on handcuffs. "Fifty-one-fifty!"

Several guards rushed me. I was already down. What's wrong with them? I should've decided to shut up an hour ago.

"Take him to twenty-four-hour suicide observation and keep him there until he goes before the judge."

Just like that. Dude had turned on me. I hadn't touched him. My head was hard as a rock. Beaux and I exchanged blows all the time. I barely felt the punches I'd landed to my face.

I yelled, "I'm not trying to kill myself. I'm upset." I cried like a baby, "All I wanted to do was see my son."

If the police believed that rumor about my trying to kill Chicago, I might not get out of this hell-hole.

CHAPTER 12

Chicago

Waking up with Sindy in my arms was comforting.

A man needed a woman to lay her head on his shoulder. Literally and figuratively. I wanted to protect Sindy from the bad people in the world, from anything that might break her heart, or upset her.

As I stroked her hair, the ache inside me was a good pain. A welcome discomfort. I was definitely getting her the ring. I'd call my jeweler later today. There was no way she'd say no when I knelt before her, held her hand in mine.

Wow. I recalled her looking up at me last night with her beautiful lips wrapped around my engorged head. This woman was incredible. Why hadn't some man snatched her up?

Her naked flesh next to mine felt better than pure silk. It was like she was coated with that liquid body glide Madison had introduced me to. Tilting her head, she gazed into my eyes.

I whispered, "I want you soooo bad I'm about to erupt like a volcano." I swept my finger over her nipple in a featherlike motion. God knew my needs.

The way her stare lingered made my dick harder. I squeezed my head to reverse my blood flow. The more pressure I applied, the longer my shaft grew. Sindy was a woman filled with unspoken challenges. I liked that. Her silently letting me take the lead was a test I was not going to fail.

I exhaled imagining turning her on her back, spreading her thighs, and giving her all of my erect manhood. Eating her pussy for the first time under that table was sweet but I was trying hard to be a gentleman and not allow my urge to have sex control my actions. If I just wanted pussy, that wasn't a problem. Sindy was different. She'd earned my respect by withholding sex. Whatever move she made was what she wanted. I'd wait a moment and follow her lead.

On our first date, she compared playing chess to the mentality of men. I was not a man chasing pawns. I wasn't a rookie or a disillusioned knight. I was a king with character, discipline, and patience.

Slowly she peeled back the cover exposing my excitement. "Nice," she said straddling me.

Finally. I'd waited long enough to experience what she felt like on the inside. Was she tight? Could she make her vaginal walls pump my shaft like Madison? My heartbeat raced. My dick pressed against her vagina.

"Keep him right there," she whispered. "Don't penetrate me."

Gently grinding her opening against my head, I had to exercise restraint not to thrust my throbbing erection deeper. Focusing on her, I saw that

Sindy was flushed. I frowned. Concentrated on her surface movements.

No way. There was no way my head was hitting a barrier to the opening of her vagina. I wanted to ask but didn't.

Touching herself, then me, she said, "I'm going to take care of this." Lightly she scratched her nail along my shaft.

When she raised her butt, I wanted to grab her hips, and pull her pussy back onto me. Her hand caressed my dick. "Lay back and relax. I want to take things slowly."

We'd done that last night. Oral was amazing but I wanted in.

The heat of her mouth, moisture of her tongue, cupped my nipple. Precum oozed from the tip of my penis. She sucked my erect nipple, gradually increasing the intensity. I wanted to stroke my shaft with the rhythm I knew would make me ejaculate. I wasn't in the mood for foreplay.

Her fingernails teased my other nipple. Twirling and squeezing one side, she licked and sucked the other. Gradually, the combined stimulation created a lump in my throat.

"Baby, I want you," I moaned eager to release a load.

Condoms. I didn't have any. The risk of impregnating Sindy wasn't worth a few seconds of climactic bliss. I hadn't had intercourse since before Madison gave birth. I inhaled through my nose, then opened my mouth. As I exhaled, she covered my lips with hers. Her pussy was sweet, soft, hot, and juicy.

She lowered her clit closer to my tongue, then moaned, "Roosevelt, don't stop baby. I'm cumming and it feels cool like a waterfall." She glided her pussy back and forth occasionally thrusting, pulled back then glided again, as she stuffed my mouth.

I started stroking my erection. More precum seeped onto my head. I wanted to fuck Sindy. Getting her pregnant while I was married to another woman . . . I massaged the slipperiness of my semen onto my frenulum then slid my hand down my shaft to my balls and squeezed real tight. *Oh, my, God.*

Fornication was one thing. Adultery.

As she eased her hands between her legs and peeled back her labia, I suppressed my guilt when Sindy moaned, "Keep your tongue right there."

She was engorged, almost the size of her pinky finger. Raising up a little, she rolled her hips forward, lowered her clit on my palate, then slid back. A trail of her juices coated my taste buds. Repeating the motion, she increased her pace as she grabbed the headboard.

"You, are, the, best, I've ever had . . . Oh, my, God . . ." She'd spoken what I'd thought as her head leaned so far back her long cinnamon hair covered my dick.

Her back was arched. Her protruding shaft had turned from pink to a blushing red. Grabbing her hips, I sucked her pussy into my mouth and started bobbing my head until . . . she exhaled "Roosevelt" long and slow.

Sindy lay on her back, propped a pillow behind her head. "Get up here. Straddle my face. Bring me my dick now. I've got something special for you, baby."

God knew I loved this woman for not quitting after she'd gotten hers.

She trailed kisses from my head to my balls and back up. Circling the tip of her tongue underneath the circumference of my head, she stopped. Devoured my erection in one gulp.

I came instantly.

Sindy eased out of bed and disappeared into the bathroom.

My cell phone vibrated reminding me I'd put it on SILENCE. I started to press IGNORE, then decided to answer, "Hello."

"Hey, Chicago."

Wishing I hadn't answered the blocked call, immediately I regretted hearing her voice. "What's up, Loretta?" She hid her info because she knew I wouldn't have talked to her.

"You got a minute?"

I hesitated. I could hear the water running in my shower. I said, "Not really."

"Congratulations on your win," she said sounding cheerful.

It was too early for this shit. Was she ignoring me? "What's up, Loretta?"

This chick was predominantly responsible for Madison fucking Granville. If she'd never made that bet with Madison and introduced Madison to that deranged dude Granville, I'd be a happily married man.

"It's about Zach," she said then became quiet.

I grunted with anger. "What about *my* son?"

"Calm down. Madison won't let me see him."

And that was whose fault? "If that's why you're calling me, I can't help you."

Quickly, she said, "That's not why I'm calling," as though she anticipated my ending the call.

The water in the bathroom stopped running. "Then, what's up, Loretta? I gotta go."

"I just thought you might want to know Zach isn't your son. That's all," she said, ending the call.

That woman was bad news. The only one who could help her was God and I was beginning to doubt He was willing to save Loretta from herself.

I wasn't falling for Loretta's jealous shenanigans. Test results didn't lie.

Loretta was not squashing my orgasmic high. Sindy was the one.

I texted my jeweler: Need to see you soon. Real soon.

CHAPTER 13

Madison

I'll teach her to suck my husband's dick.
Roosevelt's sperm was not her delicacy. It was mine!

I recorded the footage from my television onto my Blu-ray. I made popcorn then sat in my bed all night fast-forwarding and rewinding each scene. Occasionally, I pressed pause to attend to Zach's needs.

Getting out of bed, I hadn't slept all night. I placed Zach in his crib, showered, then stood naked in front of the mirror. Seeing another woman lay flesh-to-flesh with my husband, I knew she was prettier. Her body was flawless. I wasn't jealous. I was pissed off at her.

He was going to see this. I powered on the television, pressed record from my cell phone, and videotaped part of the footage of the two of them having sex.

Grateful I hadn't gotten stretch marks from having my baby, I lathered my body with lotion. Couldn't remember the last time I'd massaged my pussy with my special irresistible white chocolate extract concoction. There was no man to lick me until I came. That was going to change.

I bathed my son, dressed him, then myself. For the first time since we'd been home, I packed his diaper bag and left my house.

"You wanna be a tramp?" I said unlocking my car. "I'll give you that opportunity!"

Buckling my son into his car seat, I glanced over at Loretta's home. That bitch was standing in her doorway. Did she get fired from her pharmacist position at the hospital? Was her ex-husband, the gynecologist, paying all her bills? She waved. No way in hell would I ever trust her again.

I ignored her, got behind the wheel of my Bentley, and sped off.

Driving faster than the law allowed, I was making record time to my destination until I encountered a traffic jam. Seemed as though suddenly every driver was on the road to block my intentions. Quickly, I glanced over my shoulder at Zach, then focused on the cars ahead. He was staring out the rear window.

Honk! Honk! "Move out my way," I shouted motioning for the woman in front of me to stop switching lanes just so she could stay ahead of me.

She sat at the green light. Curved her tires to the right, moved a few inches. Then she cut to the left when I attempted to go around. When the light showed yellow she crept across the intersection.

Ooh I wished we were in bumper cars, I'd knock her ass on the curb.

I wanted to hit this woman and run Sindy over.

Once I saw the green light, I made sure I stayed ahead of every car behind me on Westheimer Road. Turning left onto Kirby Drive, I parked in the lot, got my baby out of his car seat, left the diaper bag, and stormed into his office.

"I need to speak with my lawyer now!"

Standing in front of the receptionist, I rocked my son in my arms.

"He's with a client, Ms. Tyler. Do you have an appointment?"

"Are you hard of hearing or just dumb? What part of 'my lawyer' don't you understand? And it's Mrs. DuBois, not Ms. Tyler."

Zach started crying.

"See what you've done!" I told her.

My divorce attorney's office door opened. A woman walked out smiling. I bypassed both of them and stormed in. Standing in front of his desk, I said, "Close the door, Vermont."

He stood with his hand on the knob. "Madison, we do not have an appointment."

"We do now," I said inviting myself to a seat. "We have to do something about my husband sexing another woman. I want to sue Sindy Singleton for alienation of affection."

He closed the door, sat in his chair, then shook his head.

"Don't tell me no. I pay you. Look at this video." I placed my cell on the glass covering his desk.

He exhaled. "The first thing you need to do is calm down. And yes you are on the clock."

I didn't care about the money I'd have to pay him. I was getting it back from Sindy. She'd screwed the wrong woman's husband.

Vermont firmly said, "You can't sue for alienation of affection."

"Are you watching?!" I pointed at my cell. "She's a home wrecker."

If the baby in my lap wasn't Roosevelt's, as Zach got older he might start to look like Granville. Sindy would probably be the first to notice since her ass wanted my man.

"This videotape doesn't matter. You can't sue because alienation of affection is not against the law in the state of Texas."

"What! Says who? Why not? Goddamn Republicans. That's why they send their wives to the crazy house and get away with it. Well, nobody is sending Madison Ty—I mean DuBois—up the river. I'll drown that bitch first."

Zach started crying. I rocked him in my arms.

Vermont shrugged his shoulders. His crisp white shirt and designer gold tie were immaculate, just like him. If he weren't twenty years my senior, I'd let him put an engagement ring on my finger.

The ring was mandatory. I didn't believe in dating a man exclusively unless he proved he was serious.

"Texas is a testosterone state, so to speak." A smile crept across his face. He placed my phone in front of me, then leaned back in his chair.

Guess that was why he never married, had no kids. The more I thought about it, most of the divorce attorneys I knew were single.

"I'm serious about getting rid of this woman. Preferably the legal way. What can I do?"

"You can say three Hail Marys and hope Chicago changes his mind." He laughed.

I didn't. I wasn't joking with him. Vermont was always good for comic relief but if that were meant to be a joke, his timing was off.

"You're entitled to half of whatever he's earned since the marriage."

I thought about the ten million Roosevelt's grandfather had given him but that was before we walked down the aisle. His buying Papa's company was after we were married.

"I need to sue Sindy! Not my husband."

My lawyer stared at me, then exhaled. "You can subpoena her to court to testify about her relationship with your husband but that wouldn't work in your favor. Regardless of what Sindy says, the judge will still grant Chicago a divorce. And let's not forget, the man you had sex with shot your husband. Chicago could subpoena him to court. And, if that happens, depending on how the jury deliberates, you may end up with nothing. Court is tricky, Madison."

Yeah, and you're no damn magician. I know. "Walk away with nothing. Over his dead body," I said. Even if Roosevelt took it that far he wouldn't deny his son because he didn't know what my father had done. For a second, I hated Johnny Tyler.

"Watch your words. That crazy guy is already back behind bars. And it's alleged that he's going to kill Roosevelt. You go threatening Chicago and the community will think you're the one who wants Chicago dead."

"What are you talking about? Granville is back behind bars for violating his protective order."

"You need to get back into the world soon as possible. It's all over social media. I think some guy started the rumor. Probably a football fan.

Whether it's true doesn't matter. Watch what you say to others. Maybe you shouldn't follow this stuff. All the online drama can be a waste of your time. Get out of the house more. That's healthier."

"Zach is one week old. I can't take him out for another five weeks."

Quietly, Vermont raised a brow.

"I'm not leaving my baby with my mother before then." I scooted to the edge of my seat, picked up my phone. "Watch the video again. There's got to be something here we can use," I said pressing PLAY.

This time Vermont watched until it stopped. Looking at the expression on his face, I wasn't sure if he was trying to decipher what to do, or if he was being entertained.

Placing my cell in front of me, he said, "I refuse to present this as evidence. I don't even want to know how you got this but I can tell your method is illegal. I suggest you delete it immediately."

He was saying delete while his eyes were fixed on me and barely blinking. "I'll decide what to do with it but I'm not getting rid of it."

Vermont walked to the door and opened it.

"Madison, it's time for you to leave. My best legal advice is for you to let the Sindy situation go. If you truly want your husband, focus on Chicago and how to win him back."

CHAPTER 14

Granville

I couldn't believe I was back here.
Blah, blah, blah, blah, blah. I wanted to wobble my head and smirk at her. Whoever gave her a robe should give me one too. She wasn't the boss of me. I already had one supervisor. Hope Manny hadn't fired me.

"Mr. Washington. You're charged with violating the protective order Loretta Lovelace has against you. You were within five hundred feet of her residence. How do you plead?"

Was there a right answer? I thought it was supposed to be one hundred. Could I get off on a mistake? If I said I was guilty, I couldn't go back to see my son. If I plead innocent, I'd be found guilty because Madison's house was next door to Loretta's.

I hated this orange jumper they'd given me. I didn't need a court-appointed lawyer. I'd represented myself on an attempted murder case and won. Hopefully, I could beat this charge too.

Standing tall, I squared my shoulders. Confidently, I said, "Your Honor. My girlfriend lives next door to Ms. Lovelace. I was within five hundred yards by default. I'd like to request a court order granting me visitation to see my son. I mean, can the protective order be modified so I can legally visit my kid? Besides, Ms. Lovelace failed to appear so technically my case should be dismissed."

That judge stared at me through narrow eyelids the width of a sheet of paper. How'd she do that? She looked scary. I leaned back a little. Did the same. Where were all the male judges? Why did I always have a woman deciding whether I was right or wrong?

"Mr. Washington, how do you plead?" she said.

"Oh, wait. Strike my last comment from the record. I meant to say feet. Not yards."

I swore she didn't blink those big brown eyes once she opened them wide. I did the same but I couldn't hold out as long as her. She won. I blinked. If she let me do her, I bet she'd shut her eyes and open her mouth and scream my name.

I could tell when a woman was fed up with me. I said, "No contest." Before she got mad, I said, "I mean, not guilty." I shook my head. "No contest. That's it. I don't wanna say either way."

What difference did it make? She'd probably already made up her mind. That's how women were. Decision already in their head and they messing with me.

"Who's your girlfriend, Mr. Washington?"

I stood taller. "Loret—I mean Madison."

"Mr. Washington, you think my courtroom is a platform for your humor. Thirty days mandatory in the Federal Detention Center."

I'd seen on television how that football player

slapped his attorney on the ass after the judge let him off. That female judge gave him thirty days. Somebody on a talk show said if the player would've apologized, he might have gotten that judge to change her mind.

"I'm sorry, Your Honor. But I made a mistake. Please forgive me. Please, please, please." Get out of my head, donkey! "I wasn't joking. I wouldn't do that." Of all times for me to think about *Shrek*. I hung my head. Mama would be embarrassed for me if she were alive.

She banged her gavel. Handing my file to the clerk, the judge picked up another file. "Lyons versus Perkins."

"Your Honor, I don't understand. What you decide?"

Ignoring me, she spoke to the bailiff. "Get him out of here."

At least I didn't have to go back on suicide watch. That glass-enclosed room was freezing cold. The cover they gave me was a sheet, no blanket. Guess all of that air conditioning was to keep my mind off hurting myself, which was never my intention.

I'd lain in that bed staring at the ceiling. No cellmate. The only way I could communicate with the watch guard was to speak through that beige telephone receiver. Mama used a telephone something like that. She never had a cell phone. But hers had a long spiral cord.

Checking back in, I was happy to get that brown blanket. I got another pair of tan pants and a matching colored top, socks, and shower shoes. Last time I served, I got a green shirt and pants. That was for inmates with jobs. The only job I wanted was my construction one. Hopefully, Manny would hold it for me for twenty-eight more days.

"Fuck!" I yelled.

The guard put his hand on his gun. "If you're going to go upside your head again, man, I'm sending you to isolation on the seventh floor."

I shook my head. "I'm good." *Chill out, dude!* I wished I could trade places with him for one day.

Solitary confinement would've kept me from getting into trouble. The seventh floor was where the worst prisoners were housed. A few that should've been transferred to state pen had been there for more than the three-year limit at FDC. One kid should've been sent to state but the warden didn't send him because he was eighteen, small framed, blond haired with blue eyes. She knew what was going to happen to him if he transferred. It had probably happened here. Just not as often.

Where was Charles Singleton? I needed his number so I could call him. Now that I thought about him, he should've bailed me out. Maybe he wasn't in a hurry for me to get dude. If Charles was trying to break me, that was not happening.

The door to the cell closed. I had a new cell-mate.

Being raped wasn't my concern. I was worried about my being promoted to supervisor and by the time I got out I'd probably get fired. Manny was a good father to his kids. If he gave me the chance to explain my side, I was sure at a minimum I could keep operating heavy machinery. Before all this mess, I hadn't missed a day of work. Finally got the recognition I deserved. Now it might all be gone because I wanted to see my son.

My son! I'm not crazy. That boy looks just like me!

CHAPTER 15

Sindy

"Is Madison going to let us get Zach today?"
Babies were adorable, cute, and innocent. If Zach were Roosevelt's, I had to accept him into my heart, help rear him as though he were mine. He'd have two moms. Lucky kid didn't know how amazing his life was going to be.

I recalled the day Madison was in labor with him. The moment I stepped into her birthing room, Roosevelt was magnetically drawn to me. That was not the case right now.

I wrapped my arms around him. Roosevelt shook his head. He slouched on his sofa. Clamped his hands behind his neck.

"You look like you could use a hug," I told him.

He sat motionless beside me. I held him. There was no reaction.

I knew Madison didn't want me in her delivery room a week ago. But with her being in bed with her legs up, what could she do? Her mother was passive. Rosalee hadn't told me to leave, nor had she attempted to escort me out.

"Baby, what's wrong? Talk to me. Are you upset from last night? Was it my not wanting to have intercourse?"

"Sindy, please."

Please, what? Go away? Shut up? That wasn't going to happen.

If my mother had spoken up, she might still be alive. It was foolish of me to hold on to the possibility of her not being dead. My father had done ruthless things but I'd never proved him a liar. My mother hadn't seen any of my sister's three children. Someday I wanted two, maybe three kids by Roosevelt. I'd never give up on them or him.

If that were me in that birthing bed, and my husband's mistress walked in, and my mother was there, I was sure the other woman wouldn't have made it past step two. But what would Roosevelt have done?

He moved his hand, then moved my arms. "Please, Sindy. Not now."

Had the things I'd done with him, to him, made him reject me? I went to the kitchen, poured a tall glass of orange juice. The doorbell was a welcome interruption. "You want me to see who that is?"

Roosevelt didn't move. "Sure."

I opened the door.

"Hey, Sindy," Chaz said kissing me on the cheek. "Hey, man. Why you not answering your phone? We're late. Let's—" Chaz paused then looked at Roosevelt. "Not this again. Let's go. We can discuss it on our way to the office."

Slowly, Roosevelt got himself together. He picked

up his cell, wallet, and keys. "I'll call you later," he said somberly.

Why was he acting and sounding like someone had died?

"Long as we have our health, honey, everything else is secondary," I said trying to lift his spirit. "I'll lock your door on my way out."

He knew that but I didn't know what else to say. Normally, he'd respond, "I love having you here. Stay long as you'd like." This time he didn't say anything. Men internalized too much. I was not wasting time speculating. When he was ready, he'd bring it up.

When the door closed, I called my contact, the prison guard at FDC.

"Hey, I haven't heard from you since we took care of Nyle last night. That GM must have you on lockdown." He laughed, then asked, "Do I hear wedding bells?"

"We're getting there. Listen, I called to find out if you know anything. I know why Granville was arrested but what is he saying?" It was best to start the conversation discussing business first.

"He's pretty much kept to himself. The judge is making him do the full thirty. It's only been two days but he's staying out of trouble."

Narrowing my quest for information, I asked, "Does he talk about family?"

"Aw, man. I see where you're headed. When I processed him in . . . that dude is bent on seeing his kid. Claims Chicago's baby is his. I don't know if he's crazy but he's definitely bananas over that lil boy. Hopefully he won't do anything stupid like kidnap the kid. Have you seen the online posts about that dude?"

I thought about Roosevelt's sudden mood change. Had Nyle started spreading the allegation of Granville attempting to kill Chicago? "Thanks. I've got to go."

"Anything for you."

We ended our call at the same time. Swallowing a sip of juice, I placed the glass on the counter, then retrieved my iPad from my purse.

A reminder popped up. My Skype session with Siara was in fifteen minutes.

I googled "Granville Washington." OMG. This was not what I expected. We had a major problem. Nyle was ahead of me. I texted him: Don't do anything else until we speak.

Instantly, he replied: What about Port Arthur?

Nothing.

He responded: OK

The threats had to be the reason Roosevelt was despondent. Calling my dad wouldn't help my position. I googled "Sindy Singleton+Granville Washington." Various listings popped up. Nothing connected Granville and me. Did the same with Nyle Carter. Thank God there were no pics of us together.

Exhaling, a search for "Granville Washington+ Madison DuBois" didn't reveal a connection. I sensed that baby was his. At least I prayed it was. Now I had to prove it.

Inside contacts at FDC were invaluable. One call to my friend at the Federal Detention Center and I'd concluded Granville had no intentions of violating his protective order to harass Loretta. Madison's home was his destination. Still, I needed Granville behind bars until I reevaluated my strategy. If my father hadn't hired Granville to kill my man, I'd talk to the judge, request Granville's release, and help him present a case for paternity.

Granville had a heart. A huge one. His emotions made him dangerous enough to kill. He needed an incentive to do right, not wrong. That man believed Zach was his son and I did too. Now it was time for Sindy to form a stronger alliance against Madison and my father. I had the perfect personal assistants in mind.

First, I had to face-chat with my sister. Opening Skype, I clicked on her screen name. Her eyes sparkled. "Hey, you look more amazing than usual. What's the good news?" I asked.

"The kids are excited. We're leaving for Toronto tomorrow. My husband has business there so we're all going."

I waited for an invitation. There wasn't one. "This is a good opportunity for me to meet your husband and kids."

The shine in her eyes faded. "You know that's not going to happen," she said.

Was I indirectly responsible for making the people I love unhappy today? There was no point in mentioning Mom. That would make Siara sad. "Look, I have to run off. Got some important matters to tend to," I said.

Siara smiled, then asked, "How's Roosevelt?"

"He's fine."

"Sindy, I do want you to meet my family. When the time is right. I feel like I've waited so long, I don't know how to introduce you to them."

"It's okay," I lied. "I know you still blame me for what Dad did to you. But you don't hold him accountable."

Was it easier for her to suppress what had happened? If I didn't address the situation, she wouldn't. I had my own problems.

"Sindy."

Watching Siara was like staring in a mirror. Seemed as though my mom had twins two years apart. "Yes?"

"I respect your decision not to marry the man in Dubai but you could at least meet him. Dad was wrong for marrying me off but I love my husband. I love you too. Dubai is a beautiful country. Don't say no until you're sure."

"Bye, sis. I love you too."

Ending our session, I left Roosevelt's condo. Twenty minutes later I parked my Bentley in the driveway in River Oaks and rang the doorbell.

Greeting the woman of the house, I extended my hand. "Sorry to come without notice but I'm here to discuss your son."

"Next time call first. Come in," Helen DuBois said opening the door wider. "I know Chicago is a little upset. I just got off the phone with him. Have a seat here in the guest room. Give me a moment to make us tea."

My mother and Helen exhibited similar hospitality. Whenever company came by, Mom always prepared tea. Depending on how long guests visited, she'd prepare hors d'oeuvres.

Helen didn't wait for a response. Roosevelt's mom headed toward her kitchen. Her silk pewter dress loosely hugged her flattering figure. Pearls circled her neck. Rubies clung to each earlobe.

I wasn't sure how old she was but her flawless mocha skin, high cheekbones, and pepper-and-salt, shoulder-length hair indicated she'd taken excellent care of herself over the years. Fifty was my guess. Not a day over would've meant she had Roosevelt when she was eighteen. Somehow I doubted that.

Standing in front of the mantel, I stared up at the DuBoises' family portrait. Roosevelt's mom and dad stood behind a woman seated in a large Victorian chair. I presumed she was the matriarch. But was she Helen's mother or Roosevelt's father Martin's mom? Between Helen and Martin a tall handsome man had his left hand on the shoulder of the woman seated in the chair. Presumably that was the woman's husband.

"Yes, dear. That is the DuBois family," Helen said entering the room carrying a silver platter. On the tray were an old-fashioned white ceramic teapot decorated with blue flowers and streaks of gold, two tiny cups, a small dish with lumps of brown sugar cubes, honey, and lemon.

"Please, let me help you with this," I said taking the platter.

I placed it on the coffee table, then sat on the sofa.

"Come, dear," she said, walking to the mantel. "That's Martin's mother." She pointed at the woman in the chair. "You met Martin's father, Wallace, in Chicago's suite at the game."

Ah, of course, I thought not wanting to interrupt.

"And you know the rest of us. This portrait was hand-painted by a famous artist twenty years ago. I was forty then."

I stared at her. "You look stunning," I complimented.

"Compared to what, my dear? If a woman takes care of herself, age never comes before beauty. Come. Sit next to me on the sofa and tell me what's so significant that it's brought you to my front door unannounced."

"I apologize. It won't happen again."

"Indeed. Out with it dear. I have commitments and I won't be late."

I wouldn't dare tell her my father had arranged a hit on Roosevelt by the same man who had shot her son three times. If I had, I think Helen would've gotten her gun and killed Granville and my dad. She definitely appeared to be the kind of woman who could handle a firearm and a man with no problem.

"It's about Zach."

She raised a brow. "Continue."

"I don't believe he's your grandson."

"Well, hell, Sindy. Neither do I. If all you have are suspicions you're wasting our time."

Continuing, I said, "That's why I believe Madison won't let Roosevelt keep the baby. She knows something she's not revealing."

Helen held up her wrist, glanced at her diamond Rolex. I had one on too. Women with money had an unspoken respect for one another. I'd work for someone else if I merely had Madison's money.

Obviously Madison was financially dependent upon Roosevelt after her father, Johnny, signed over Tyler Construction. Every day they remained legally married she'd get a little more in the divorce settlement. If I thought Madison would go away, I'd write her a check today.

"Darling, the tea is cold and I must go. *Call* me when you have facts and not speculations."

"I respect that. But I need your help. When Madison has her breast implants done, you will offer to keep the baby—"

"That won't work."

Why was this woman apprehensive? I had to keep trying.

"Or you can request Zach over the Thanksgiving holiday."

Helen shook her head.

"Hear me out. If you don't want to keep the baby, I will. But we have to get Zach long enough to have Granville take a test."

"Are you trying to divide my family, young lady?" she asked standing.

"No, ma'am," I responded shaking my head. I stood not knowing what to say next.

"Haven't you heard that Granville is back behind bars?"

"Yes, and that's perfect. I'm a lawyer and I have friends at FDC. I can have Granville's blood drawn and sent to the lab for a DNA test. I love your son, Mrs. DuBois. I want to marry him."

"No need to buy the cow," she said. "Don't get ahead of yourself, dear."

"No ma'am. I'm nothing like Madison. I'm still a virgin."

She raised that one brow again. Scanned from my face to my feet then met me eye to eye. Shaking her head, she said, "I've got to go and so do you."

CHAPTER 16

Madison

She was with him again.

When Roosevelt had left, she'd walked out shortly afterward. When he returned to his condo, she was with him. My heart ached knowing I'd pushed him into her arms. The one thing I was not doing again tonight was watching those two engage in sex of any type.

Sindy was a tease. She dangled her pussy in front of his face. Not once had I seen him penetrate her. For that I was grateful. At least if she'd claimed she was having his child, I could prove her a liar.

The way she was monopolizing his time pissed me off. He had a baby. Just because I'd said he couldn't keep Zach overnight didn't mean I wanted Roosevelt to abandon us.

Tired of waiting for him to call, I dialed my husband. Soon as he answered, frantically I said, "Roosevelt, I need you to come over right away. I don't know what's wrong. I don't know what to do. I need you."

"Whoa, slow down. Is Zach okay?" he asked. The compassion in his voice made me lie.

I was prepared for him not to have concern for me. She was by his side. If that bitch wasn't there, he would've picked up keys, been out the door, in his car, and on his way here.

"I'm not sure what's the problem. He feels really hot."

I bucked my eyes, then narrowed them. Clenching my teeth, I stretched my mouth wide. Zach cried, "Whaa!"

Teasing him one day, I discovered scary faces made my baby wail as though I'd taken a bottle out of his mouth while he was starving. I didn't want Zach to continue crying.

"Hurry, Roosevelt," I said ending the call.

He called right back. Zach was still crying. "Daddy is on the way. I'll be there in twenty minutes. Call me back if you need to."

Rocking Zach in our favorite chair, I kissed him knowing he'd be asleep by the time Roosevelt got here. "Shh, sweetheart. Mommy loves you."

Staring at the monitor, Roosevelt kissed Sindy. "That was Madison. I'll be back. I have to go check on Zach. He's sick."

"You want me to leave?" she asked tucking her hair behind her ear.

That cutesy move wasn't going to work forever. In fact, it started to irritate me. "Tell her yes."

"No, baby. Please, stay. I'll text you the details."

Huh? About our son? She didn't need to know anything.

I raced upstairs, put Zach in his crib. I showered, brushed my teeth, then slipped into a long semi-sheer white gown. I styled my hair, but it was too perfect. I scratched my scalp all over with my fingernails until it looked like I hadn't combed my hair all day. I brushed a light coat of red blush on my cheeks and smeared a hint of smoky gray shadow under my eyes. I was tired but wanted to make sure I looked exhausted.

I had to hurry. I got a fresh onesie, sprayed water on the front and back, then balled it tight in my hands. I turned his bottle upside down and let a few drops of milk stain the chest area, then rubbed it in. Removing his clean dry T-shirt, I replaced it with the damp one, then tucked his body in a cotton blanket. Tugging at the center, I made sure the stains on the front of his shirt were visible.

When my doorbell rang, I lay Zach in his crib and raced downstairs. Leaving my baby in my bedroom was the only way I'd get Roosevelt upstairs. Opening the door, I gasped. Roosevelt was more attractive every time I saw him. Maybe that was because I seldom saw him in person.

"Is he okay?"

"I'm good," I said. Closing the door, suddenly I felt foolish for making myself look sickly. He hadn't asked how I was. What if he found me undesirable?

"Where's Zach?" he asked. He didn't give me any indication that he noticed my see-through nightwear.

If I took it off . . . I paused my thoughts. I'd forgotten to put on my padded bra. At this point should I put it on or leave it off for sympathy?

"Upstairs. He's dozing a little but I can't figure out what's wrong with him. Thank you for coming."

"Of course. That's my boy."

Roosevelt led the way to my bedroom, went straight to Zach. He placed his phone on the dresser, then gently picked up our baby. This was the first time he'd been in my bedroom since he'd seen the sex tape of me riding Granville in my bed.

Hopefully, Roosevelt would notice that bed was history and so was Granville. I'd bought new furniture, rearranged the room, and replaced my bedding—sheets, sham, bed skirt, comforter, and pillows. The room was repainted and I had the carpet replaced.

I'd prayed every night that Granville would grow old behind bars. Someone should beat his ass while he was in prison and extend his stay. I prayed for the kind of aging that made one's hair turn completely gray. He should have the life sentence that would make his spine curve and feet drag against the floor. I never wanted to see him anywhere. Maybe I should have Vermont file a protective order for me against Granville in case he was thinking about coming back to my house. I didn't care if Granville had a personal revolving door at the Federal Detention Center, county, or state.

"Thanks for coming, Roosevelt. He spit up on his shirt. He was running a high temperature earlier but I think it's down." I got the thermometer. "You check him."

"How?"

I placed the tip in his ear. "Hold it there for a few seconds. You know the old-fashioned way is to insert the tip into the rectum."

Sindy probably hadn't given Roosevelt's ass an oral massage. I missed licking my husband's asshole. He loved that. Maybe I could convince him to let me do it tonight.

"Not my son. The ear is fine. Did you call his doctor?"

"Yes," I lied. "He said every hour give Zach water and check his temperature." I started to say, "And give him a cold bath," but stopped. Roosevelt would want to bathe Zach and I wasn't ready for him to see our son's big, dark genitals. I continued, "If he's not feeling better in the morning I should bring him in."

This was his last night in town before his road game tomorrow. Desperately, I wanted this man. Legally, I had the right to have him to myself. I had to make sure he stayed with us tonight. That would give him three days away from Sindy and time for me to figure out how to get rid of her.

"I'm going downstairs to get a bottle of Pedialyte water for Zach."

"I'll get it. You lay down and rest. You look tired."

Maybe my make-up and no bra made him notice. "You sure? I'm used to doing it all by myself."

"Positive, babe."

Soon as he left, I picked up his phone. A security code was set. Quickly, I entered 4263 for g-a-m-e. That didn't work. I tried 8463 for t-i-m-e. *Damn!* I couldn't set his phone to DO NOT DISTURB so I switched the side button to VIBRATE, powered it off, placed it back on the dresser, then lay across the bed on my stomach. Using my ass to tempt my husband wasn't going to work. I had to get close enough to lick his. I slid under the cover, turned my back to the door, then pulled the sheet up to my neck.

"The divorce hearing is coming up soon," he said entering the room. "I don't want to fight you on this. Whatever you need, long as it's reasonable, I'll agree."

I heard him open and close a few drawers in Zach's dresser. "Why didn't you change his clothes? He's wet."

Sleepily, I said, "I'm exhausted. Can you stay for a while? I need a break."

"I'll clean him up. When was the last time you changed his diaper?"

Shit! I hadn't thought about that. I lied again. "Right before you got here. His diaper is fine." I'd change Zach soon as I could.

"There you go, Daddy's big boy. I love you, dude."

I felt my husband lay in my king-size bed. He placed Zach between us, then said, "He seems to be doing better. He's not hot anymore."

"Maybe he just needed his daddy." I really meant we, not he.

"Yeah, he does. He has two parents, Madison. We don't have to wait for the judge to grant me custody. Let me keep him when I get back."

"Okay," I lied.

I remember my mother saying, "If you'll lie, you'll cheat. If you'll cheat, you'll steal. If you'll steal, you'll kill."

I'd done two out of four. Or was it three? I closed my eyes and pretended to be asleep. Since I couldn't sue little Miss Sindy for alienation of affection, I'd have to use Zach to get my husband back.

Roosevelt quietly said, "If you fight me on this, I'm filing for sole custody."

I wasn't sure what his intentions were, but giving up my parental rights was not happening.

CHAPTER 17

Chicago

"**O**h, shit! What time is it?"

"Don't worry. It's only five," Madison said, laying my son on my chest. "You still go in for eight, right?"

She had those blackout curtains in her bedroom. It seemed later. "Yeah but I need to get home. You sure that's the correct time?" Zach's head bobbed.

"Hold him, Roosevelt."

"Hey, little fella. Your mom worries too much. I got you," I said to my son, then told Madison, "Top of the morning to you."

He stared at me and my heart softened. I hated that Loretta had called me. She'd put me in a fucked up mood. The way I'd treated Sindy after she'd been wonderful to me was messed up. Now I'd left her at my condo all night. Fuck!

I hadn't completely dismissed Loretta's comment about Granville being the father but it was best I did. That female was nothing but bad news.

Asking Madison for sole custody last night was a test to see how she'd react but she'd fallen asleep before responding. My doubt was stupid on my part, especially since I had the results.

Madison took Zach from me. "Good morning. I see I wasn't the only one that was tired."

"How the fuck I end up sleeping in your bed?"

She didn't answer.

Sitting on the edge of her mattress, I looked at the nightstand, then asked, "Where's my phone?"

"Right where you left it," she said picking it up from the dresser. Handing me my cell, she said, "Everything happens for a reason. I have no regrets. Roosevelt, I love you with all my heart. I wish every night could be like last night."

"What do you mean by that? You sounding like we had sex."

She shrugged her shoulder. "Guess I'm still hopeful. Roosevelt, I want us to be a family. I don't want to be a single mom raising Zach in two different households." Madison sat beside me with our son in her arms. "Isn't he beautiful? Doesn't he deserve to be raised the way we were?"

I stared at my wife. What she'd done was wrong but having my son was right. "What would be different?" I asked taking Zach. "I'm not sure I could love you the way I used to."

"You'll never be sure, baby, if you don't try."

"Try what?" I asked her. She made it seem like falling in or out of love only required the press of a button. I rocked my son. His eyes closed.

"For starters, I haven't broken my wedding vows, and I won't."

Aw, here she goes. At this point fidelity didn't matter to me. Madison could sex whomever she wanted. That wasn't completely true. Long as she had my last name, I wanted her to keep her legs closed.

Madison continued, "What happened was before we said, 'I do.' I made the biggest mistake of my life. I need you. We," she said pausing for a moment before continuing, "need you."

She probably thought her timing was impeccable. I didn't want to be cruel or hurt her feelings. I sat quietly. Was I that unforgiving? I wanted our son to have what we had too. A two-parent household.

"You know I'm seeing Sindy and I don't want to disrespect her or hurt her the way you did me. She has feelings too."

Sharing another hour with Zach didn't matter at this point. Sindy would be pissed, gone, or both by the time I got home. I made a mental note to get Sindy's engagement ring.

"Sindy can find herself another man. She probably already has one you don't know about. But nothing can change the fact that I just had your baby. I love you, Roosevelt. Let's get counseling or something but don't go through with the divorce."

Madison placed her hand on my thigh. This time I didn't jump. It didn't make sense for me to be confused. Sindy was the right choice. God had reassured me.

"I've got to go. I love you too. I promise you I'll pray on it again."

I placed Zach in Madison's hands. She put him in his crib.

"I'll walk you to the door," she said then pressed her lips to mine.

Instantly, I became weak for her. Was this the

way Adam felt when he opened his mouth and took a bite of the forbidden fruit? Opening my mouth I welcomed in my Eve. Our tongues danced the way they used to. My chest swelled with the kind of energy that was undeniable.

Madison whispered, "Make love to me, Roosevelt."

Blood rushed to my dick. She thrust her pussy against my hardness. My fingers undressed her gown, then unsnapped the bra she wasn't wearing last night. I kissed where her breasts used to be. Kneeling before my wife, I tugged her panties to the side and licked her sweetness.

"You still taste the same," I moaned then sucked her clit.

Her hands caressed the back of my head as she released her juices into my mouth. I waited until she'd finished enjoying her orgasm. Instead of removing my pants, I let go of her lace panties, pulled her straps over her shoulders, then picked up my phone.

"I've got to go."

"But—"

"But what if you get pregnant again? Plus, we're not the only two involved, Madison. *If* we're going to parent together, we have to do this right," I said then left.

CHAPTER 18

Sindy

My cell rang. I pressed IGNORE.
It rang again. I did the same. The third time I answered, "What, Roosevelt?"

"Stop ignoring my calls. Where are you?"

I refused to ask, "Where were you all night?"

Sitting poolside at my house, I gazed up at the sun through my designer sunglasses. I sipped my mimosa, then replied, "I do have a business to operate."

Being in love could be all good or an unnecessary headache. If he wanted to play games, he had the wrong woman. I'd called him three times last night. That was once more than my maximum to phone any man without a call or text back *and* he hadn't accepted any of my calls. Did he honestly believe I'd still be at his condo when he got there?

"I know what you must be thinking and I know you've cursed me out but—"

I interrupted, "Why would I do that without having all the facts associated with your disappearing act? Feel free to volunteer any pertinent information you so desire."

Men loved for women to get emotional when they screwed up. That way they could tug on her strings as if she were a puppet and make her dance to his commands. Roosevelt couldn't even kiss my suntan oil–coated ass right now.

"I owe you an apolo—"

In a very low tone, I told him, "No you don't. Have a safe trip to wherever you're headed. I've got to—"

His voice quivering, he said, "Sindy, please. Hear me out."

His actions had spoken louder than any explanation he'd give. He wasn't man enough to tell me the truth. I'd passed the bar! I was not going to let Roosevelt test me. He'd taken his ass to her house, probably fucked her, and now he was like most men, confused. I didn't care how horny I'd made him. He should've kept his dick in his pants.

"I've already heard you. You want her back. I wish the two of you the best."

The tone of his voice said, "I'm guilty, babe," without his confessing. He had to drive from her place to his. He didn't call while he was in the car because he was preoccupied with rehearsing his lies for me. Guilty as charged!

"Okay. Fine. I'll talk to you later. Bye," he said then ended the call.

Defensive. That was another sign of guilt. I pressed END then sat my cell on the table. I felt like throwing it in the pool but what good would that do? I wasn't working from home or headed to my office. My heart was broken. My head was flooded with anger.

Biting my thumbnail, I hated that I'd secretly admired that man since he played college football. I had a chance to make him mine and he'd jeopardized our future to backtrack to trash. The trees surrounding my house stood tall. The branches were motionless. It was nine in the morning, no breeze, and we'd already reached eighty degrees.

Sipping my drink, I questioned if Roosevelt was worthy of having me. The one thing I was not going to do was pursue him or any man. His spending the night at Madison's was his choice. What he'd done sexually with her was his business. What if she had a sexually transmitted disease? If there were to be a next time for us, his wearing a condom would be mandatory. I was not touching his dick until he got tested.

His not responding to any of my calls was the worst. All of what he'd done let me know I needed to rethink my interest in him.

The world was filled with men who would love to have me as their woman, their wife. There was no pride or joy in my having a man who would worship me knowing he didn't deserve me. The billionaire who thought money could buy me should get his investment back from my father and marry a woman he knew. Maybe Siara was right. What harm would it do if I met the man in Dubai?

My truth was, I was in love with Roosevelt. And what he'd done, hurt.

I texted Nyle: Dig her up. Take photos. Show me what you have when you get back.

Roosevelt made me feel excitement in my heart and twitching in my vagina at the same time. His aura drew me closer to him. Admiration and exhilaration drew me closer to Roosevelt but I was not competing for a man if she already had the trophy. Nor was I going to allow sensitivity to make me have doubt.

Finishing my drink, I stepped into my pool. A few laps would've decreased my frustration if I hadn't imbibed alcohol. Leaning back, I floated. Staring at the sky through dark-colored lenses was my life in this moment.

I did not want a package deal. I was willing to take on Madison, not Roosevelt and Madison. I'd decided to give Roosevelt the space he needed to choose which woman he wanted.

I was cutting off all communication with him, starting now.

CHAPTER 19

Madison

"Vermont, I took your advice. I did it!" I screeched.

I'd won! I pranced in the center of my bedroom. Focusing on the task, I resumed packing. There was no hope for little Miss Sindy. I had to move quickly. Soon as Roosevelt left, I fed then burped our son. Zach was asleep. By the time he was hungry again we'd be home sweet home.

I shoved onesies, booties, and outfits in the middle section, then zipped the bag. Pacifier, bottles, diapers, and formula went in the side compartments. Whatever I didn't have I'd buy online and have it delivered to The Royalton. Or I could come back for more.

"And?" he asked.

Priority number one was establishing position. "You were right. Roosevelt wants us to come home. I'm packing as we talk." We had to get out of here.

"Isn't he in Kansas?"

The questions were starting to slow me down. "Yes, he is. What's your point? I thought you'd be happy for me."

"He asked you?"

As I exhaled heavily, the joy in my voice dissipated. "Yes he did. In so many words." It was clear to me. Roosevelt wanted us back. I was saving him from having to ask.

"Madison, divorce is a serious matter. Don't play—"

"That's Roosevelt calling." I ended my conversation with Vermont and answered, "Hi, honey."

"Madison, don't act as though everything is good. I'm heading to the airport later. Got a lot to do before I take off. I'm calling to tell you we need to talk when I get back," he said.

Ignoring the fact my husband sounded sad, I asked, "About?" Forget doing things right. His call had something to do with Sindy and I didn't want to hear it.

"Us."

I led him in my direction. "Are you saying what I think?"

"Yes. I'll come see you when I return. Gotta go."

"Okay," I said. Not wanting to tell him bye, I waited until he ended the call before I did the same.

Checking my underwear drawer, I pushed my lace panties aside. That reminded me of Roosevelt making me cum with his mouth this morning. I needed that.

Good. It was there. I held it up. Hugging the key to my chest, I waltzed around the room to the music in my head until my legs were tired.

I checked on Zach. He looked peaceful sleeping in his crib. I showered, slipped into the first dress my hands touched. I woke up Zach, gave him a quick bath, dressed him in a T-shirt, shorts, and socks, then put him back in his crib.

Racing to my car, I put our bags on the front seat, went back to get Zach. He was asleep. I scooped him up, carefully trotted down the stairs.

Opening the door, I was too late to escape. "Hi, Mom and Tisha."

Mom, I was expecting. Tisha, not. Why did my girlfriend always pop up without calling? At first it was okay. If I didn't get rid of them before my favorite doorperson was off duty at Roosevelt's place, I might end up back here.

"Come to Godmommy," Tisha said taking Zach.

"Come to Grandma," my mother said taking my baby from Tisha.

Before I said, "Come in," they were seated in my living room side by side on the sofa. I went to the kitchen, poured a mimosa. Downed it. Refilled my flute, prepared two more, then joined my mom and friend.

"I don't have long. We might as well have a quick toast before I'm off to my appointment," I said handing them a mimosa. "To my mother's new hot and sexy look. Don't think I missed it." I sat in the oversize chair Papa would normally sit in.

My mother's hair was silky straight and cropped into the sexiest bob I'd seen her with since I was a little girl. The edges lined her jaw.

"When did you do this, Mrs. Tyler?" Tisha asked easing the baby into her arms.

I had to get up, then lift and finger my mother's hair. Silk strands flowed into place. "You look hot. I love it."

My mouth was still open. I admired the peachy cropped-sleeved dress that lightly hugged my mother's hips. Her legs crossed as she seductively swung her three-inch slingback.

"It's the new and old me. Seeing how nothing stops you from being a woman and watching Helen in your delivery all dressed up helped me realized I'd become detached from my womanhood."

Tisha chimed in, "I like that, Mrs. Tyler. A toast to reclaiming womanhood." A small sip crossed her lips as she placed the glass on the coffee table and began playing with Zach's thighs.

"Besides your obviously taking excellent care of yourself," Mom asked, "What's happening with you, Tisha?"

"I'm not home-schooling my boys this year. I enrolled them. My ex-husband Lance is engaged. I'm legally divorced, dating, and happy."

Tisha left out the part about the seven-figure settlement Lance gave her. I bet he wouldn't have given her that much if she hadn't filed for a divorce from Darryl. Couldn't blame him. A loser like Darryl would've sued Tisha for half. My reuniting with Roosevelt meant I didn't have to worry about money. I'd stay at home a year with our son then it was back to running Tyler Construction.

My mother smiled at Zach. Her eyes shined. That red lipstick made her appear years younger.

"Has Papa seen you?"

Shaking her head, she said, "He will. Whenever I get in."

Papa was sure to adore Mama. "I'd love to continue this moment but I have to leave. If the two of you aren't busy later, we can do lunch." The key to Roosevelt's condo was in my purse. It wouldn't matter in a half hour. If I were still here, I might as well stay.

Legs still crossed, Mother said, "I decided it was time to stop sitting home while your father runs around sleeping with wayward women."

I took my son from Tisha. I believed Mom's makeover was to get Papa's attention.

Forcing a smile, I stood. "I'm happy if you are, Mom." This conversation could be continued over the phone. She needed to get up. I had to go.

"I want you to know, I'm going to divorce your father."

My smile vanished. I shook my head, sat in the chair. Zach had dozed off. "No, Ma. Don't do that."

"I'm not asking for your blessings or permission, Madison. I've already consulted with Vermont. He's preparing the dissolution."

Then what was her point in holding me captive?

Tisha picked up her mimosa, then commented, "I applaud you for making the decision, Mrs. Tyler."

"If that's really what you want, Mom, I salute you. How long have you known about Papa's affairs?"

"Honey, those are not affairs. An affair is when two people care about one another but one or both of them are married. Your father has become a male whore."

Jesus! I screamed in my head. She made me think about Sindy. I'd never heard Mother speak a negative word about my dad. She was obviously just warming up and I was about to boil.

"Don't act like you're shocked. You know he's having his way with young girls in the office. Now that he thinks Chicago is going to fire him, he's been hanging around the house like a stray puppy dog. That's why I'm moving in with you."

Oh no she was not. Avoiding eye contact, I asked, "Where is Papa? You should go home and show him your new look. Or, what you should do is have him meet you somewhere."

Tisha sat listening attentively.

"My intentions were to be gone by the time he got up and not see him until tonight," she said standing.

Finally. I exhaled, then stood. My mother took the baby and sat down beside Tisha.

Mom fingered Zach's cheek, then continued, "I've started volunteering my time to assist breast cancer survivors."

Tisha said, "Mrs. Tyler, that's great."

Tears clung to my eyelids. Not wanting to sound insensitive, I said, "Mom, that is great."

"Madison, I can't begin to tell you how good I feel. I was wrong for not telling you about our family history of breast cancer. I've finally forgiven myself for that."

How did we get here? Not this again. By the time I'd realized I'd rolled my eyes, my mom saw it. I redirected the conversation. "Speaking of forgiveness, I've got good news too. Roosevelt and I are getting back together."

I expected my mother to be happy for me, like I was understanding of her situation. She returned my gesture as her eyelids closed then opened.

"You are your father's daughter. Why is everything always about you?" Mom asked.

Tisha hunched her shoulders, nodded, and remained quiet. They'd invaded my space, now I was the one under attack.

I wasn't self-centered. Reassured, yes. "Why would you say that, Mother?"

She stared into my eyes, then asked, "When are you going to tell your husband this baby isn't his?"

CHAPTER 20

Granville

Two weeks in. Two more before I get out.
I ate breakfast, lunch, and dinner alone. Didn't attend any of the group classes. Let the barber shave my head once a week. Didn't want to let myself go, especially if I had a chance to get with my wife and raise my kid.

I didn't talk to my cellmate at all. He tried but once dude realized I was never going to respond, he chilled out. He didn't mind my picking up and reading his books. I'd finished *When It All Falls Down* by Dijorn Moss and had started on *Politics. Escorts. Blackmail.* by Pynk. If things didn't work out with Madison, maybe I could marry Pynk. Was it legal? The things she'd written? How did dude get this book in here? I was trying some of this with a woman soon as I got out. I wasn't religious but God had become my friend in my head.

Outside of my brother, I had no relationships with men. Didn't go to any of our football games lately. I used to be a big fan but after I'd done what

I did to Chicago, I didn't feel right sitting in the stadium. If I followed through with the hit, how was I going to get close enough not to get caught? We had a good basketball team too but I didn't go to those games either. The round ball wasn't my favorite. Had never seen a polo match or horses race around the track. There was a lot to do in Houston and thanks to Charles Singleton, I had enough money to afford the best seats.

Today, I sat on the floor in a corner by myself eating lunch while reading. When I first got here a few guys would come by and try to make conversation. I didn't respond. The only person I spoke to was the guard on duty.

One of them was headed my way. He stood in front of me. "You good?" he asked.

I nodded, then turned the page. If I didn't have to use words, I didn't.

This was the first time in my forty-five years of living that I realized I needed to shut up. The words "politics" and "blackmail" gave me lots to think about. Staring at the pages, I couldn't focus on the words. Dude standing over me felt weird.

When I got out, I was not going to contact Madison or try to see my son. If she wanted me back, she had to make the first move. The feeling of knowing Zach was mine and I may never see that boy . . . I braced my forehead on my knees to hide the tears. He was three weeks old. I bet he'd feel like a loaf of bread in my big ol' hands. Besides eating and sleeping, what was he doing all day?

I smiled. I'll be all right. I frowned. Maybe this was my punishment for what I'd done to Chicago. Day three in here I almost confessed. Then I felt like what good would that do? Freedom was more important than telling the truth. That's why people hired lawyers to get them off the hook.

Not doing anything dumb to come back here was my final decision. If that meant I'd never see Zach until he was eighteen, I'd live with that. Once my kid was grown, wasn't nothing Madison could do to stop me. I'd set aside money to pay him back child support.

Beaux hadn't come to visit me. I told him not to. Hopefully, the funds in our offshore account were growing. Regardless, I was giving Charles Singleton back his million dollars, his gun, the briefcase it came in. I was no killer. I was a man trying to keep my broken heart from crumbling. Charles could do his own dirty work.

I felt a tap on my shoulder. I looked up. Lost in my thoughts, I'd forgotten dude was there.

The guard said, "You need to come with me."

Didn't sound like I was getting out early like Nyle. Hoped the thoughts I had from reading this escort's book wasn't going to add time to my sentence.

Standing, I wondered, "What now?"

CHAPTER 21

Chicago

"Baby, make love to me."

Had I heard my wife right? It was six o'clock in the morning. The usual time I'd wake up since I'd let her move in. My dick wasn't hard. I think he was depressed. Missing Sindy as much as I was. Madison was the last person I'd had intercourse with and that was almost ten months ago before our wedding.

We were pregnant before the ceremony. I wanted to penetrate her after the wedding and before the reception but we were late so she'd opted to give me head. There were times when I'd become aroused just thinking about how my dick felt inside of Madison. Now I fell asleep wondering what it would feel like to penetrate Sindy. I pictured Sindy on her knees sucking my dick. Instantly, my head started rising.

The second I'd landed at Bush International returning from Kansas City, Madison had texted We're in the lobby. The doorperson won't let us up.

Damn, she hadn't given me time to take off my shoes, enjoy a glass of scotch while propping my feet on my coffee table. I hadn't confirmed I wanted them to move in with me. Hadn't fully had that conversation about our future. Obviously I sent mixed signals.

I'd given the doorperson permission to let them go up. Figured we'd have an adult discussion. I didn't want her back like this. I was hoping to let her know Sindy was going to be in our lives. Truth was, Sindy wasn't even in my life. She had not called since I'd left for Kansas. No "Congratulations on your W."

Madison and Zach had spent one night. Then another. I didn't want to be alone. I didn't want Madison. But I didn't know how to ask her to leave.

Zach had his own bedroom, which was separated by the living area. Madison had ordered a small crib online, then had it assembled in my room. I pointed to the baby.

"He's asleep," she said. "Please make love to me, Roosevelt."

Love? I could fuck her. I could fake it. But I couldn't make love to Madison.

She pulled back the cover. Instantly, my shit stood tall. It was hard. Not because my wife had turned me on. The memories of Sindy sexing me were . . . damn my shit felt good. Massaging my dick, I started masturbating. Getting myself off was smarter. "Don't you have to wait two more weeks?"

"I'm ready now." She raised her gown over her hips, then straddled me.

I covered my dick with my hand. Shook my head. "We can't. I don't have protection." That was a lie.

After Sindy started sucking my dick like it was her favorite flavor, I had bought a three-pack of Magnums in anticipation and preparation to make love to her. The one thing I knew was women liked when they could see the pack of condoms hadn't been opened. If I used one with Madison, I hoped I'd have to buy another pack for Sindy. I missed her.

"I can't get pregnant and I haven't been with anyone since the last time I was with you."

Wanting to believe her, my dick grew larger. Not sure who needed to release more, I moved my hand. "You sure you can't get pregnant?"

"Positive," she said putting the head in.

Her pussy was warm and incredibly tight. She squinted, froze, then said, "Ow."

I held on to her waist. "I told you it was too soon. Get up."

Opening her mouth, softly she exhaled. "I'm good." Slowly she lowered her pussy and I remembered why I fell in love with her. She eased down to my balls and sat there.

"Get up. Let me get a condom." I rolled sideways. She leaned in the opposite direction. Slowly rocked her hips. She eased her pussy toward my balls. I could deny her but not the sensation.

Sex wasn't why I'd put a ring on her finger. Madison was a woman. Curvaceous. Daring.

Oh . . . oh. "Oh, no. Damn. I'm cumming. I'm cumming." Wave after wave of semen involuntarily left my body and entered hers. I should've pressed my fingers at the base of my shaft to keep the ejaculation from occurring.

Leaning her head back, Madison touched her clit, then moaned, "Don't move. I'm right with you."

I didn't want to seem selfish but immediately after I'd finished, I regretted not saving my bodily fluids. Masturbating would've been better. It was too late. I felt guilty, as though I'd cheated on Sindy.

Madison whispered, "Thanks, honey. I needed that." Her lips traveled toward mine and I turned away. This was the same woman who had left me for dead. *Fuck!*

All of a sudden, I hated Madison.

She got out of bed, went into the bathroom. "Keep an eye on Zach," she said, then I heard the shower.

I slapped my forehead four times. *Idiot!*

Lying in bed, I had to be honest. The second Madison and the baby crossed the threshold of my condo, I knew I'd made a huge mistake letting her in. Now I'd made a bigger one.

I'd overreacted to Sindy's not communicating with me but she was right. I was confused but I wasn't anymore. Sexing Madison made my stomach upset. I had the sensation of regurgitating.

I should've given Sindy three things: time, space, and the truth. My emotional indecisiveness gave my manipulative wife another advantage.

Madison and Zach had been in my place for three weeks. Zach was a month old. Halloween had come and gone. No treats. Thanksgiving was next week. Had to figure out how I was going to balance spending time with Madison, my son, and my mom. Numbiya would be at my parents' with Chaz. Everyone would be happy, except me.

Every night I'd gone to bed with Madison, I'd thought about Sindy. She hadn't called. My mother hadn't come to a home game since I'd reunited with Madison. My brother didn't socialize with me outside of business. Whosoever believed a person didn't marry the other person's family was wrong. My entire family had divorced me because I hadn't divorced Madison. Things had to change.

Except what we'd done moments ago, each day was the same. Madison awakened early with the baby, bathed and dressed him, showered then put on her clothes, and sat in the living room.

What was taking her so long in the bathroom?

I used the bathroom connected to Zach's nursery room. Scrubbing my privates repeatedly, I felt dirty. After the fourth time, I rinsed my body, brushed my teeth, toweled dry, layered on lotion, then dressed. My wife was sitting on the sofa.

"Madison, we need to talk." I turned off the television and sat beside them.

She smiled. "Zach has his one-month checkup tomorrow. I scheduled the first morning appointment so you could go with us," she said bouncing him on her knee.

"Madison," I said staring into her eyes. "I thought I could do this but—"

"But you haven't given us enough time. We're doing fine. We have to work through things, baby. It'll be okay. Let's get counseling," she said trying to give Zach to me.

Refusing to let her use our baby against me again, I scooted away. "Madison, I'm miserable."

"With me or without Sindy?"

I refused to lie. "Both. After his checkup tomorrow, I'm taking you guys to your house. We'll work this parenting situation out. I'm not going to take him from you. I want joint custody and I'm going through with the divorce proceedings next week."

Silence surrounded us as she stared at the black screen.

My head tried to give my wife another chance but my heart couldn't do it. For me it was, "If you can't be with the one you love, leave the one you're with." What was I trying to prove by mimicking what my parents had?

"I'm not leaving," she said kissing Zach.

Firmly, I answered, "Yes, you are."

CHAPTER 22

Sindy

Life without Roosevelt was terribly lonely.
He'd brought a unique high-class element to my social experience that was exhilarating, not stuffy. Being in his suite on game day, having cameras capture me by his side, mingling with my best girlfriend who was dating his brother classified as a standing double date. I felt ostracized. Numbiya was at the game.

Tired of being home alone, I entered the bar area in pursuit of an adult beverage to drown my sorrow. The charming ambience where I'd first met him surrounded me. Patrons cheered. Not for me. For Roosevelt and his football team. The game was like our relationship—almost over. In two minutes, the players would have what I desired.

Closure.

"Nice shoes," a woman said staring at my feet.

How long had I stood here? "Thanks," I said, walking toward the small stage. The band was setting up for their usual gig except this performance wouldn't be celebratory for me. Madison Tyler-DuBois hadn't won. Roosevelt couldn't be that foolish.

The saxophonist was tall, white, and handsome. He winked at me. A contrived smile parted my red lips. Was it true? Musicians were the best lovers. They knew how to tune a woman the same way they did their instrument.

Why was I preserving my virginity? What did I have to prove? Perhaps I should flirt with the sax—. I held my breath as he licked his lips then pressed them to the tip of his horn. Whatever name he'd given her, lucky girl. He blew. My pussy clenched. Not for him. As I internalized the sensation of Roosevelt's dick against my clit, a sexual sensation penetrated me. I twitched.

The booth where Chaz, Numbiya, Roosevelt, and I had our first date was empty. Slowly, I eased into the same spot where I'd sat. That night, Madison was still with child while I'd shared pleasantries with her husband.

What did it feel like to be pregnant for a man who was out enjoying himself with another woman? I never wanted to know but I was glad I wasn't in Madison's position. When a woman messed up a good relationship, she needed to not be a sore loser.

Looking at my lap, I brushed away a speck of lint. Today I'd dressed to show my support for Roosevelt's team. I meant our team. My red skinny pants, off-the-shoulder red top, thin blue belt, and my sparkling sapphire platform stilettos made me look superhot. On the inside I didn't feel very sexy like the red Victoria's Secret thong I had on.

The score for the end of the fourth quarter flashed on my phone. A roaring cheer resounded throughout the bar. Houston had won the home game by seven.

Typically there wouldn't be enough hours in the day to run my business and enjoy the company of my man. Now my days and nights alone seemed endless. I hoped he'd called. Apologize. Ask me out. We could talk about what went wrong. Standing firm on my solid principles for four consecutive weeks was beginning to make me feel small. Was I trying to prove my love was stronger or that I was stronger?

Sindy. Sindy, I said to myself. *How did you get here?*

"What can I get you, beautiful lady?" the waiter asked placing a glass of ice water and a menu on the table.

A text from Numbiya appeared. Hey, where are you?

I replied: Eddie V's, then told the waiter, "I'll have a glass of Moët & Chandon." I had no reason to celebrate. I wanted to numb the ache in my heart.

"I'll be right back with that."

"Wait. Bring the bottle." While I was certain I wouldn't consume that much champagne, I didn't want to wait for a refill.

"You got it," he said whisking away.

Speaking into my cell, I voice-texted Numbiya, "So he's undefeated (period)," then pressed SEND.

Since I hadn't seen Roosevelt, outside of work I'd seen Numbiya less. She and Chaz had become inseparable. I wasn't jealous. I was happy to see Numbiya in love.

"We're leaving the suite. On our way."

I said, Where (question mark) And who is we (question mark), then sent the message.

Chaz and I are coming to meet you she replied. You want me to invite Roosevelt?

"No (period) See you guys when you get here (period)"

Okay, girl. But you sure can't tell he won by the look on his face. He's missing you.

She texted me a photo.

Inhaling slowly, I held my breath. The shine I normally saw in his eyes whenever we were together was absent. His lips flatlined. Not the slightest indication of victory was exhibited. Blinking away my tears to hide my feelings, I became sad.

The waiter sat the ice bucket at the end of the table, then filled my flute. Politely he asked, "Would you like to order or should I give you a moment?"

I didn't have an appetite for food. "I'll wait until my friends arrive."

He nodded, then walked away.

Staring at the picture Numbiya had sent, a part of me prayed Roosevelt would come with them. A part of me didn't want to see him. I should've asked Numbiya where he was going. Did I really want to know? As I scrolled through the contacts in my phone, the hurt in me wanted to delete his number. My love for him would regret not being able to call him or know if it were him calling me. I removed his number from my favorites then checked my calendar.

Wow. After I'd stopped talking with Roosevelt, I'd hoped that my father had abandoned his mission with Granville. I phoned my dad.

"Hello there," he answered. "Change your mind yet?"

"The appropriate question is, 'Have you?' "

"About what?"

He had to ask what I wasn't supposed to know. Maybe I should meet the billionaire in Dubai. I could vacation there. Go skiing indoors at the mall then shop until all my bag carriers' hands were filled with jewels, clothes, purses, and shoes. A woman could never own too many pairs. Maybe I could rationalize with my father. If giving up my virginity would save Roosevelt's life, why shouldn't I do it?

Siara was happy with her family. That reminded me I needed to Skype with my sister this week.

My dad said, "You called because Granville is being released tomorrow."

I whispered, "Listen. You can't go through with your plans." I didn't realize his thirty days were up. Any display of desperation would lead Dad to believe he had an edge.

"And what plans would those be?" he asked.

I shook my head. He had to have known that I knew about his contract hit on Roosevelt. "I don't want to talk about this on the phone. I'm coming over to your house later."

"Call first, Sindy," he said ending our conversation.

The debt had to be paid. I was considering giving in, going overseas, and marrying the billionaire who had paid my father millions in exchange for my hand in marriage. Perhaps I should arrange to meet the man here in Houston. He might be nice. After the ceremony I could divorce him.

For a moment, I wondered how a man with that much money earned it. What was his house like? What did he wear? Eat? How large was his bed?

How many housekeepers and groundskeepers did he have? How old was he? Was he at least six feet tall? Did he have kids? Siblings? Why did he live in Dubai? Was he born there? Was he nice? How had he met my father? I wasn't the only thirty-year-old virgin in the world. How much had he paid and why me?

I wasn't for sale. But what harm would be done if I met this man? I tried convincing myself the outcome might be positive.

An incoming call interrupted my thoughts. "Hello."

"Hi, dear. You have a moment to talk?" she properly inquired.

I should've said, "No," but replied, "Yes."

"Can you come to my house?"

"Now?" I asked.

"Do you have a better time?" Helen DuBois questioned.

"I'm meeting friends for drinks."

"Chaz and Numbiya. I know, dear. What time will you arrive at my house?"

"Eight."

"Fine, don't be late," she said then ended the call.

Hopefully Roosevelt was at his mom's and Helen had spoken with him. Soon as she hung up, I remembered I'd told my father I'd stop by to see him. I had to meet with my dad before Granville's release. If I waited until the morning—

"Hey, queen," Numbiya said approaching the booth.

Easing to the edge of the seat, I stood and gave my girlfriend a big hug. Chaz opened his arms, then wrapped them around me.

"We missed you today," he said.

Glancing over his shoulder, I looked toward the door.

"He's not coming," Numbiya said sitting next to me.

My girlfriend knew me well but my heart remained optimistic.

Chaz sat on the opposite side. "Give him time, he'll come around. At least he's moving Madison out of his condo."

What? When had he moved her in? So that was why I hadn't heard from him. Frowning, I looked at Numbiya. I hated being right about Roosevelt wanting his wife back. I didn't want to be wrong about how well my girlfriend knew me. I stared at her.

She fingered the edge of her big red afro. "It wasn't worth my mentioning. Plus, Chicago was the one who needed to tell you. Not me."

She was right. What would I have done if I'd known? Be more upset than I am now. Mentally preparing to exercise whatever options I perceived I had, I told them, "I've decided I'm going to Dubai."

"Excuse me," Numbiya said.

"For what? Vacation?" Chaz asked.

"More like, for whom," I said.

Numbiya stared into my eyes. "You can't be serious."

"You want to go with me?"

"Absolutely. You can't visit that billionaire by yourself."

If she'd told Chaz about my dilemma, that was okay. Maybe he'd mention this conversation to Roosevelt.

Chaz chimed in, "That what?" He looked at Numbiya. "You left that part out. But I don't care how much money he has. You're not going. If that's what Sindy wants to do, she's a grown woman." He glanced toward me. "Go. But whoever he is, he's not Chicago."

Why was Chaz upset?

Numbiya boldly said, "I'm not Loretta. I'm a fully grown woman. If Sindy is going to Dubai, I am accompanying her."

"Chaz, I know how much you love Roosevelt. I love him as well. Your brother made his decision. And I've made mine. Excuse me. I have someplace to go."

"Are you going home?" Numbiya asked.

"I'll text."

Numbiya stood. "Call me. Tonight," she said hugging me.

"Bye Chaz."

"I'll tell my brother you asked about him."

Men. I didn't bother responding. I got in my car and drove to Helen's.

CHAPTER 23

Sindy

As I parked in front of Helen's house, the digital on my dash displayed 7:50.

Roosevelt's car wasn't in the circular driveway as I'd hoped. Maybe he was in transit. Perhaps not. What difference would it make if he came?

Chaz just told me, "He's moving Madison out of his house." That meant my suspicions were accurate. He hadn't come to Eddie V's and he wasn't coming to his mom's because he was with them.

I can't fucking believe he's back with that trifling bitch and he wasn't man enough to tell me! That was his prerogative but I had the right to know he'd moved on. Selfish, inconsiderate adulterer. Regardless of what I'd done, I wasn't a fornicator. What I was, was glad I hadn't given my virginity to him. I didn't wait this long to have regrets.

The main thing I required was respect. He'd opened his mouth to perform cunnilingus but he couldn't tell me the truth. Wow. Maybe he thought not saying anything was respectful. Or was he still waiting for an opportune time to explain his decision? Or did he believe he'd move her out before I'd find out?

I'd bet if I never mentioned I knew, he'd never tell me. *Sindy you know his intentions were to keep you as option number two in case things didn't work out with Madison.* As long as that baby had Roosevelt's last name, I couldn't compete with a kid.

Exhaling, I had to regroup before getting out of my car. I didn't like using profanity but some men could make me outswear a sailor. My lawyer colleagues believed obscenity was for those with a limited vocabulary. I felt communication was primary. Long as I understood, word choice was just that. Sometimes a woman had to curse in order to be heard. I could use a shot of scotch instead of that tea Helen probably had brewing. Liquor would intensify my mood. Although I wanted one, I didn't need a cocktail.

I doubted Roosevelt was on his way anywhere by himself. Madison probably didn't let him go too far without activating a tracking device on his phone or dragging that baby along with them.

I stared into the rearview mirror. I had to admit, out loud, "I love that man." If I didn't, I wouldn't be sitting outside his mother's house.

The sadness in my eyes resembled Roosevelt's in the photo my girlfriend had sent. He missed me. I felt it. I touched up my lipstick, swept my hair behind my back. Not wanting Mrs. DuBois judging my partially provocative attire, I raised my blouse to cover my shoulders. Seasoned Southern women were slow to teach young girls how to be ladies but quick to judge how females presented themselves.

Holding my cell, I wanted to call him. *Forget*

about him. My pride decided not to dial his number. I dropped my phone in my purse.

The door opened exactly at eight. Helen motioned for me to come in.

Slowly, I got out of my car and closed the door. Forcing a smile, I walked toward her.

She glanced from my face, to my feet, and back to my face. "Lovely shoes, dear."

"Thanks," I said, not sure if Helen's compliment was genuine.

"How are you?" she asked closing her front door behind us.

How the fuck you think I'm doing? "I'm doing well and you?" I replied scanning her head to toe.

She glanced at me. "Hm. You don't look well to me but if you say so. Come, dear." She led the way

Then why in the hell did you ask? The blue tapered short-sleeved dress stopped above her knees. A thin strand of pearls circled her neck. Diamonds decorated her ears. Her wedding ring sparkled with clarity. Her red two-inch slingbacks were soft leather. Her thick pepper and salt strands were permed to perfection. The silky edges framed her face. Her hair, tucked behind one ear, curved at the nape of her neck.

Entering the family room, I admired the photo above the mantel. The innocence in Roosevelt's eyes beamed full of happiness. He was probably one of those boys who craved approval for doing what was honorable. Why else would he have taken Madison back?

Redirecting my focus to Helen, I answered, "Outside of missing your son, I am doing well." Did she honestly care about my feelings?

"Good. That's what I was hoping to hear. That

means you haven't lost interest in him. Sit next to me." Balancing her rear end on the edge of the sofa she fluffed a decorative pillow. She filled two small porcelain cups with hot tea, then handed me one.

Repositioning the pillow behind my back, I inched away from her. There was space for a third person to comfortably sit between us. Already emotional, I didn't want to be close enough to cry in her arms.

Her pinky finger straightened, then curled. "That's fine," she said sipping her tea. "I'll get right to it, dear. I want to know what you had in mind about getting rid of Madison."

Was she interested in helping me or herself? Staring into my cup, I shook my head. "I've let that go. I'm moving on. Roosevelt wants Madison and he has the right to be with her."

It was best I hadn't had sex with Roosevelt. Maybe his good dick was what Madison was holding on to.

"Moving denotes movement, dear. My son does not want her. He's told me he asked her to leave but she won't get out of his house."

I thought for a moment, then softly said, "Why did he move her in?" I paused wondering what she expected me to do about that situation.

"He didn't. He told her they needed to talk and next thing he knew she showed up at his place with that baby. He couldn't leave her and that baby sitting in the lobby of his building while he was at the airport. That would've been all over social media. Besides, I reared him to be respectful. He had no idea she had their belongings with her."

Respectful? Or had she handicapped her son

like a lot of mothers? The number of African-American youth being incarcerated was alarming but the moms who defended them were in denial.

I held in my laughter. Madison was willing to look pathetic to keep her husband. No man honored pity. Okay, now his erratic behavior appeared logical. Maybe I'd view this differently, if I hadn't kept cutting him off when he tried to explain.

"I love your son but I'm sure you didn't chase Mr. DuBois for his hand in marriage."

Elongating her spine, Helen raised her shoulders a few inches. "And you are correct. However, relationships were different when I was younger. Women didn't treat men as though they were children and men didn't act like little boys. I knew Martin was the one for me and he knew it too," she confidently said.

Not wanting to cut her off, I'd waited until she completed her sentence, then asked, "Why should Roosevelt be my concern?"

"Dear, I didn't ask you here for a debate. She's got to go. Answer my question."

"I don't want to get involved."

"Too late for your wants, dear."

Damn, she should've been an attorney. Exhaling, she was right. There was an element in love that didn't consider wants, needs, or desires. Love was rational, irrational, exhilarating, terrifying, and unpredictable at the same time.

My heart and head were out of sync. Eventually I'd get over Roosevelt. But I couldn't live my life wondering if the next woman would take my next man. Even if I didn't win back Roosevelt I was going to take the trophy away from Madison and beat her over her head with it. She wasn't that smart.

Plotting against Madison would give me satisfaction and entertainment. I remained silent.

"Fine. Then tell me the details and I'll handle it," Helen said.

If I were right, everyone except Madison would be happy. If I were wrong, I could lose Roosevelt forever.

"Out with it, dear," Helen said. "Why did you want me to get that baby?"

"I suspect that Granville Washington is the biological father."

"Suspect? When there's documented proof he's a DuBois? Nonsense."

"Documentation can be altered. I wanted you to get the baby so we can have Granville take a paternity test."

Helen crossed her arms and legs. "This is absurd. I love that baby."

I placed my cup on the silver tray, then stood. "Then let's just let things remain."

Firmly, she held my wrist. "Please, sit. That Loretta girl told me it was Granville's baby but you can't believe a word that comes out of her mouth. She'd say anything to get my son. She's nothing but trouble. Loretta is in love with Chicago too you know."

Instantly, my eyes scrolled upward. "Is any woman good enough for your son?"

"You tell me, dear," she answered, then stared at me.

I refused to respond. Woman to woman I did not have anything to prove to her. If she believed she'd done an exemplary job of parenting her boys, why did Roosevelt marry Madison? I was beginning to observe the manipulative similarities between Madison and Mrs. DuBois.

"Well, I'm sure I can get my grandchild from my son but what good will your plan do when the results come back the same?"

"Trust me. They won't."

Helen raised a brow. "How will you get Granville to agree to taking a test?"

"My father knows him."

"Really?" she said dragging the word out.

"No, he was not involved in the shooting."

Her eyes darted to the side then back toward me. She folded her arms under her breasts. "Did I ask you that?"

I stood, then picked up my purse. "I have nothing to prove to you. If you want my help, you have my number."

Following me to the door, Helen said, "I certainly do, dear."

When the door opened, I almost bumped into Madison and the baby. I stepped back into the foyer. I stared at Helen. She didn't look in my direction. She had to have known they were coming.

She reached for Zach. "Come to grandma." Briefly our eyes met. She smiled, winked at me, then held the baby in her arms.

The baby's eyes, nose, and lips resembled the DuBoises'. Zach's head looked a little like Granville but most babies had big heads.

Sarcastically, Madison said, "Hello, Sindy," then asked, "What are you doing here?"

Helen replied, "Madison, this is my house. Your house, where you should be living, is on the outskirts of River Oaks, dear. Remember?"

Helen's comment should have provided me relief as she referred to the location of Madison's place, not Roosevelt's. It didn't. River Oaks folks like us did have an added touch of arrogance. I gasped when I saw him. I felt trapped. Madison stood next to Roosevelt blocking the doorway.

I glanced at Roosevelt then quickly stared at my shoes.

"Hello, Sindy," he said in the saddest, yet sexiest, tone.

My heart tightened as I struggled to force back my tears. I looked at his pants. Slowly my eyes moved up to his knees, his thighs, his hips, his stomach, his chest, his shoulders, his neck, his chin, his lips, his nose. Reluctantly, I gazed into his eyes.

Slap!

Anger dictated my reflexes. Before I'd do the same to Madison, I parted the two of them then marched toward my car.

"Oh, no you didn't hit my husband," Madison said following me.

My husband? The husband who was feasting on this good pussy?

I stopped. Turned to face her. I'd never had a fight but I had mastered self-defense. "Don't let the dazzling stilettos mislead your steps." I was so full of anger, if I had hit her, I would've zoned out. Neither Roosevelt nor his mother could've pried me off of her.

Why did I hate Madison when Roosevelt was the one who'd hurt me?

Helen said, "Madison, bring your narrow ass in here."

I kept walking, then I heard the front door close.

Soon as I slammed my car door, a flood of tears gushed into my palms. I couldn't stop crying.

Tap. Tap. Tap.

"Sindy, can we talk?" Roosevelt asked standing by my window.

Why did I have to meet him? My life was drama-free before Roosevelt. I couldn't stop the flow. I didn't want to see his face or have him see mine.

I yelled into my palms, "Leave me alone!"

Calmly, he said, "Sindy. Please."

Lowering my window half of an inch, I said, "Please what? Let you explain why you didn't have the decency to give me closure?"

"Yes."

Would his version match Helen's?

"What good is talking going to do? If you really wanted to talk, you would've called me. If I hadn't run into you tonight . . ." Uncontrollably, more tears poured. I raised my window. Regardless of what he would've said, when he was done he was going into his mother's house and he was going to be in there with Madison and Zach, not me.

"Sindy. I'm begging you. Let me explain."

Drying my tears, I started my engine and drove off. I wasn't in the mood or right mind to hear what Roosevelt wanted to say. I'd probably shoot my father, if I went to his house. What had he done to our mother? "I hate men!"

That wasn't true. But in the moment, that was exactly how I felt.

Instead of going home, I pulled over and dialed his number.

"Hey, Sindy."

If one more person said my name without enthusiasm, I'd scream. "Hey, Dad. I'm not coming over. After Granville is released tomorrow, the three of us need to meet."

"About—"

"Stop it! Stop it! Make sure Granville is at your house. I'll see the both of you tomorrow, Dad. Good-bye!"

I'd do all I could to keep my father from having Granville kill Roosevelt but I was not leaving my country for two men who didn't give a damn about me.

Make that three.

CHAPTER 24

Granville

Last time I was locked up I walked out of the courtroom a free man. I never thought I'd be back in the slammer. Thirty days was a long time to have kept my big mouth shut. Processing out, I was happy to be on the other side.

Loretta got back at me for making her do thirty days but I did not want this to be no game of you're it. I would call and apologize to her, but I wasn't sorry for trying to see my son. I should've broken up with Loretta instead of breaking her heart. It was too late to do the right thing. I wasn't going to call, text, e-mail, or go near her or else I'd end up back here again. Loretta's life was fucked up. No need in both of us feeling the same. My mama didn't raise no fool.

When dude rolled up on me talking about, "Come with me," I just knew some stinky shit was going down and my DNA was attached to it like maggots. Turned out he wanted my recipe for chili. Had heard from some of the inmates in Unit

Six (where I was housed the last time) that I made the best. I was flattered.

I was no real chef. I learned how to stir up a few things hoping to impress Madison with my Ginsu skills but my aunt Wilma took Mama's kitchen knives after the funeral. Since cutting up a chicken wasn't going to happen at my apartment, it was back to eating fast foods.

After I'd gotten out the last time I couldn't remember what I'd put in any of those dishes. I'd made up something so I wouldn't piss off the guard. Give a man a gun, he was dangerous. Give him a license to use it, he could easily become an asshole.

Halfway through my sentence, got word through my brother that No Chainz, the guy who was my cellmate the first go round, wanted to visit me. That was cool he hadn't forgotten about me but I told Beaux, "Naw, man. Tell him if he wants to hang, I'll see him on the other side of these brick walls."

That Nyle "G-double-A" Carter attorney that I'd paid for legal advice during my trial hadn't reached out since he'd gotten out. That nigga was too quiet. Now that I was back on the street, he was the one I was going to find.

I paused the madness between the folds on the back of my neck that were rubbing together. Stood still for a sec. Listened to what Mama called my inner voice. Yep. I'd heard right. Everyone was out to get me in some kind of way. Loretta. Madison. Chicago. Nyle. Mama used to say, "The only thing people owe you is respect and you don't deserve that when you ain't been decent to folk."

Listening again, had I been decent? I couldn't tell. I hoped so.

I strolled away from the Federal Detention Center for the last time—for real—then stood on the corner and stretched my hands toward the sky. "Mama, this is it. No mo' foolishness. I promise I'ma think with the right head."

Couldn't mention the big one while talking to my Mama, that would've been disrespectful. But I was glad both were huge. The scent of a woman floated under my nose. I sniffed the perfume like a dog, looked down, then barked. Her long naked legs in them short shorts reminded me of the cows our next-door neighbors back in Port Arthur had when I was growing up. I'd stuck my thing in one of them one time and came so hard it scared me. Sliding the tip of my tongue out of my mouth I wanted that red lipstick that was smeared over juicy lips all over mine. The shiny hair flowing down her back . . . I shoved my hand in my pocket and squeezed my dick.

She rolled her eyes at me.

So what. Looking wasn't a crime. I hadn't touched her. Couldn't lie though. I wanted what was between them legs. I wanted to run up on her like a beast in heat and do her doggie-style while howling at the sun, moon, the time of day didn't matter.

Gripping my dick tighter, I kept it moving. The last time I'd had a woman let me spill my seeds inside of her was a month ago. Actually it was longer. My wood ached to feel the softness of a tight pussy. Her flesh pressing against mine made me want to take my shit out now and ask for volunteers.

Indecent exposure would get me arrested. I'd rather kill somebody. A murderer had more rights than a sex offender. They weren't free even after they got out. Couldn't live near schools. Couldn't be around minors. Couldn't be in the house with they own kids.

I was not getting used to being caged like a gorilla with a bunch of dudes, beating my meat in the dark. Good thing the people walking by couldn't read my mind or they might've thought I'd meant I'd let some dude hold my dick. Never that. I handled mine.

Now that I was out I was gonna stay straight. No mo' brawling or boiling over like a teakettle using my fists to blow off steam. Maybe I'd find me a good woman at a church to give me head. Some of those Christian girls were easier to snatch up and lay with than the chicks strolling the streets. Loretta taught me that. Didn't take much for me to get her out of her ugly drawers. I hated that conniving broad. Wonder what she was up to?

I spotted my black Super Duty parked at a meter on Texas Avenue. Beaux had dropped off the blue jeans, cowboy boots, and button-down shirt I was wearing, then said, "I'll wait outside." An explanation wasn't necessary. A black man didn't want to be inside a prison even if he was a visitor.

Beaux was reclined with his eyes closed. I bammed on the window.

"Bro, wake yo' yellow ass up!"

"Damn, dude!" He sat up, opened the door, got out, then hugged me tight. "Keep your ass out this time," he said.

My brother had on black slacks and nice blue shirt. The first few buttons were undone. He smelled good. His hair was neatly cut down to a shadow. He stood six feet.

Towering six inches above him, I leaned on him

for emotional support. "For sho that. I should've went to dinner with you that night bro but I just wanted to see my son, man. Sorry for putting you through this shit again."

"No need to apologize. What's done is done," he said sitting behind the wheel. "Now that Mama is gone we're all we've got and your ass has got to leave that woman and her child alone."

Being older it was time I started acting like his big brother. He motioned to close the door. Pulling it toward me, I realized I had nothing to prove to Beaux. My gut told me baby Zach was mine.

"Don't let me off the hook. Hang my ass on the wall next time I even think about making a dumb move and leave me there until I come to my senses." I grabbed my head. "I am fucking sorry. Sorry I did that stupid shit. Ain't gon' be no next time. Get out dude, I'm driving."

He didn't move. "We've got to take care of business first. You can drive after we're done."

"Now?"

"Now," he said.

"That's why you all dressed up?" Beaux didn't answer. I stood there and explained. "I'm hungry. Take me to Pappadeaux's," I growled. "I want some cat, and some fried catfish, a woman with her ass on the table with her legs spread wide so I can eat her and my jambalaya." I bounced like Future, held my dick, while singing, "I want pussy and food at the same damn time."

"Shut up and get in the damn truck, dude! At the same damn time." Beaux slammed my door.

Frowning, I sat in the passenger seat where he belonged. "Where to?"

"Not to get you some pussy." Handing me my cell, he said, "Call your boss." A couple of right turns and we were headed toward the freeway.

My eyes got real wide. I still had my job? I slapped the dashboard. "You taking me to work! Where my clothes and steel-toe boots?" I looked behind the driver's seat. Saw a suitcase bigger than the one Charles had given me. Work was one place I could do double time. Triple if Manny asked. I dialed the number from my favorites.

Manny answered, "Hey, Granville. You back?"

Squinting from the sun almost blinding me, I lowered the visor then stared at Beaux. I'd just notice his face was shaved clean too. "What happened to your mustache, dude? Yo' forty-two-year-old butt lookin' like a kid's ass and shit."

"I don't have a mustache," Manny answered then asked, "Your brother told you?"

"Yeah, he told me to call you. When you want me to start my new position? I can come in right now, boss."

"Sorry, Granville. We had to terminate you. I've already hired your replacement."

"But I love my job. I thought you wanted me to come in. It was a technicality. I'll explain when I get there but don't give away my promotion," I pleaded.

What would I do without a job? More than the money, I enjoy laboring under the Houston blazing heat with sweat rolling down my head and face. This was my first time in almost thirty years being somebody's boss.

"Don't cut my balls off, dude."

Manny laughed. I didn't find shit funny.

"I understand you needed a break but I can't

put operations on hold when you decide to take a month-long vacation."

"A what?"

"Your brother told me you went to the DR. Hell, I'd loved to have gone with you but it was irresponsible of you to celebrate your promotion when you should've been here. Personally, I think he's lying but either way, it doesn't matter. You're still the best I've hired and the best I've fired. If you need a reference, I'll give you a good one," he said ending the call.

I stared at Beaux. "Thanks, bro."

"Don't mention it."

"No, I mean thanks for fucking up my bread and butter, dude!" I punched the dash.

Beaux laughed. "You'll get another job."

I wanted to beat his ass! "Don't need no 'nother job. I'ma lay low and roll with my dough."

"Better to have him think you were partying with a bunch of females than to tell him you were arrested for violating your restraining order by trying to see a kid that's not yours. Now we can really go to the DR and when we get back you can apply for a job someplace else."

That's it! Reaching for the steering wheel, I turned it toward me. "He is my son!"

My truck swerved into the next lane. Beaux spun the wheel to the left and merged back into the fast lane.

"Nigga! Kill yourself! Not me or the people in the other cars. I swear you do some ignorant shit. Put your hand over here again I'ma stab your ass. What if someone else did this shit and your son was in the car and they killed him and Madison? How would you feel?"

All the shanks they had in the pen, I wasn't afraid of no knife. Tears clouded my view but I didn't want to hurt nobody but if someone killed my son out of foolishness, I'd personally bury them alive.

I took a deep breath. "You taking me to the airport? We leaving now?"

He shook his head.

"Where the fuck we going then?"

He shook his head again.

"Well, tell me how's our money doing offshore?"

Beaux entered the driveway leading to this huge mansion in River Oaks. "I closed the account."

"What! Closed? Or never opened?"

"What difference does it make?"

I swear I wanted to punch him upside his head. "What'd you do that for? How much we made before you did that? Where you put the money? Why didn't you ask me what I wanted to do with *my* money?"

One question after another he never answered. Finally, he said, "We have to live right."

With no fucking job and no income? "How?" I didn't want to live right if it meant being broke. Parking my truck, Beaux reached behind the driver's seat and removed a suitcase and a briefcase.

"Let's go."

CHAPTER 25

Madison

My husband seeing his mistress made him colder toward me.

Roosevelt treated me as though it were my fault she wasn't sleeping in his bed. The only love I received since he'd seen Sindy was from Zach. As precious as our son was he couldn't fill my emotional void.

I sat on the edge of the bed feeding Zach. I didn't feel complete competing with a woman with sexy boobs. Roosevelt wasn't shallow. If he were, he wouldn't have made love to me.

The fact that he'd shown compassion after my surgery made me love him more. A man couldn't fake kissing a woman's stitches with tenderness. "I'm sorry," was on the verge of escaping my mouth. A picture of Granville flashed on the television, silencing me. Tossing Zach's bottle on the bed, I snatched the remote, then changed the channel as Roosevelt entered the bedroom.

Granville was not a celebrity. His release was not

newsworthy. Papa. He'd been quiet since his confession. He suggested the results might not be accurate. There was a chance this sweet precious baby in my arms was a DuBois.

Roosevelt loved Zach. There was no reason to give him doubt.

My husband's body glistened. Beads of water covered his chest. A drop clung to his nipple. I imagined opening my mouth, licking it off, then sucking him gently the way he'd let me do the other day when he came deep inside me. My eyes traveled from his face to his dick. His shaft and balls both sagged between his thighs. I prayed when I went in for my six-week checkup, I'd be pregnant with his second child. There'd be no questioning the paternity if I were.

Roosevelt closed his eyes, then slowly opened them as he secured the towel around his waist. "Don't look at me like that," he said with disgust.

"Like what? Like I desire my husband? I do." Once upon a time his dick stayed hard for me. Not anymore. He stooped slightly, then slid the towel over his dick. He gripped his privates, squeezed, then released.

I was no fool. I wouldn't tell him, "She can have your ass." That would encourage him to sleep at her place, or get a hotel room and leave the baby and me here alone.

A visual of my husband's mouth on her clit disgusted me. "Adultery is a sin. I know you've had sex with her."

"I'll save you the argument. I have," he said scooping our son from my arms. Flatly, my husband said, "I'm not playing this game with you, Madison."

There was so much to say and at the same time I was speechless. He'd drained my fuel to fight by admitting he'd done her, which meant he either knew I couldn't sue for alienation or he didn't care. I preferred he knew.

I stood and began packing my suitcase—toiletries, two outfits, and two pairs of shoes. It was time for me to go.

"Good morning, dude." He held Zach above his head. Zach smiled. "Daddy loves you." Zach's slobber rolled down Roosevelt's cheek. They both smiled.

Never had I imagined this man would look at me without seeing me. I grazed Roosevelt's lower back with my fingernails. His body tensed. Firmly, he said, "Please don't touch me like that."

I bet if Sindy were here at his condo rubbing her hand up and down his spine the way I'd seen her do while watching them on television in his suite, he'd enjoy that. She didn't deserve Roosevelt more than I. No woman did.

"Roosevelt, we have to move past your discomfort. Am I really that bad?"

Why did Texas Republicans deny women our rights? We couldn't sue for alienation; now they'd enacted laws that may close almost all of the forty-two abortion clinics in the state. Most of our politicians were men who wanted to fuck women in and out of bed. No matter what my husband said, I wasn't letting him fuck me over.

"I love you. I'm not in love with you. And my love is turning into a strong like and that's because you're the mother of our son. I've tried forgiving you but . . . Madison, I don't know how many times I have to tell you, I want you gone."

His words slit my wrist. I was emotionally bleeding to death. Would he dial 911 if I tried to kill my-self? Or would he step over me?

"I want you out of my house. The only reason I wanted to talk with you, not move you in, was be-cause of this dude. He deserves both of his par-ents." A tear fell on Zach's cheek. "I love you with all my heart, son. Daddy would die for you."

That was not necessary for him to say. Never thought I'd be jealous of my child but this very sec-ond I was. Roosevelt stared at the wall. His face be-came expressionless. My eyes trailed his to the TV. *Shit!* There he was again. This time Roosevelt saw him too. Picking up the remote, I powered off the damn television.

I had to get my husband to focus on me. "The doctor said if my breast augmentation goes well, I should be released in two days. You have games over this Thanksgiving holiday. My mom can keep Zach."

The darkness of our son's genitals had light-ened over the past few weeks. I was thankful. Be-fore then I'd begun thinking Granville was Zach's biological father.

"What's the recovery time?" my husband asked staring at the blank screen.

"A few months. Maybe." I had to lie.

In five days the doctor had said I could drive. Ten days I could lift Zach (or up to twenty pounds) but not over my head. Three weeks the doctor pro-jected I'd be completely functional the way I am now. I wish when they cut me open they'd replace my broken heart.

"Do not use my son against me. I told you my mother is keeping Zach and that's final." He hugged our baby tighter.

Exhaling, I lamented, "What about the divorce? If you don't tell your lawyer to withdraw your petition, it'll be final while I'm in the hospital."

"Why prolong the inevitable?" he said, standing in front of me. I wanted to snatch the towel off his waist.

"I'm giving you five million dollars. I've paid off your house, bought you a car, plus, against my mother's will, I'm giving you back your family business free and clear."

Roosevelt's generosity was an incentive to hold on, not let go. I'd decided not to tell Papa about Tyler Construction.

"Finish packing your bags. I'll send the rest of your belongings to your mother's. I love you, but for the last time, Madison. You've. Got. To. Go. I'll get Zach ready to take to my mom's." Walking away he added, "We'll be in the living room waiting."

The tightness in my chest knotted up as I watched the two most important men in my life leave the bedroom. I never thought I'd end my time on earth over a breakup with a man but I swear my husband's rejection was killing me.

CHAPTER 26

Granville

Soon as the front door opened, I knew exactly where I was.

"Hi, I'm Charles Singleton. The last time we met, you didn't see my face." He extended his hand.

That was because dude had kidnapped me and had his bodyguards bring me here.

His weak voice was all I'd remembered of him that day as he'd sat in a chair with his back facing me. His dining room was dark. Not pitch black though. Security had sat me at a long table. As I listened to Charles telling me how he wanted Chicago dead, he sounded old with that same choppiness in his throat.

"You want my arm to fall off?" he asked standing in front of me.

Why should I care? That wasn't funny. He wasn't Billy Dee but he had them kind of rich guy clothes on. "You going to bed or just waking up, dude?" I snickered.

What was up with the bedroom fit? Black shiny

pants and gold designs pasted to a smooth jacket that had a sash tied around his waist. Where was the cigar? He didn't seem the type that would have one of those vapor-smoking gadgets.

Looking at him in all those clothes, my head started sweating. It was too hot for all that. I stared at his feet. Who wore leather slip-ons?

"I don't want to shake your hand or kiss your ass, dude." I wiped my head, then slung my sweat on him. "Beaux, you shouldn't have brought me here. Let's go," I demanded.

My fists were aching to curl and lay this old wealthy guy out with one punch. I was starting to hate all people with lots of money. My mama didn't put no price tag on me and he wasn't going to either. The only thing that kept me from letting him have it was I'd probably have to fight off the bodyguards standing at the top of the stairs with their arms folded. Plus, I didn't want a jail cell waiting for me to step inside that hellhole tonight for doing something stupid. If my brother ended up in the slammer with me, who'd bail us out?

Beaux sat the two cases in the foyer. "Here's your million dollars plus interest. Granville ain't doing your dirty work, Charles Singleton."

I snatched the briefcase, clung it to my chest. "That interest is ours, not his!"

"It's not as much as you think. Put it down, Granville!" Beaux struggled to peel away my arm. I laughed. He must've forgotten where he'd picked me up from. My abs were ripped, biceps bulged like Popeye the Sailor Man. I hated spinach. Over the past thirty days I'd worked extra hard on beefing up my back muscles. Heard some women like a man with a nice strong back.

When old dude said, "That one has the gun," I let go of the case before questioning, "How you know?"

It was the one I'd gotten the cell phone from and the gun was in there at that time. The piece Charles had given me was no snub-nosed like the one I'd used to shoot Chicago. Charles had given me a silencer too. I figured Beaux had put our interest in the briefcase and the gun in the big bag with the mil.

"Damn, bro!" My fingerprints were all over the leather. Should I take it or leave it? Beaux's prints were on it too.

The latch popped open when the case hit the tile floor. A gun fell out. "Bro, you supposed to secure that shit. It could've gone off and killed one of us."

I didn't care about Charles. If he would've been accidentally shot and killed, oh well.

Charles laughed, then said, "You're right, Granville. Leave it all there. The gun is yours. The money too. You can get it on your way out. I don't want it back."

"Yes, you do, Daddy."

I turned to see the woman with the long cinnamon hair that was in the courtroom during my trial. She closed the door. My jaw dropped. Drool rolled down my chin. I swiped my hand across my lips. I wanted me one of her.

"Not even in your dreams," she said as if she'd read my mind. "Glad you made it. We might as well get straight to it then, Sindy," Charles said. "Everyone follow me."

Sindy stepped behind Charles and in front of me. The way that red dress hugged her booty, I wanted to be the spandex kissing her ass. I got closer. She stopped and my dick was on her back. I got instant wood. Sindy turned around and landed a slap to my jaw. That felt good. I hoped she'd do it again.

"Get in front of me," she demanded.

"You were the one that stopped. Not me." I stood still to let her keep her place in line. The two bodyguards that were at the top of those stairs were now behind my brother.

"Move it, Granville," one of them said with bass in his voice.

Charles didn't look over his shoulder. "Touch my daughter again and I'll personally kill you." He barely raised his crackly voice.

If he was as weak as his voice, all I had to do was step out of the way of old dude's punch and watch him fall, then cry, "I've fallen and I can't get up."

I started laughing, then stopped. The word "cry" made me think about my son. I became sad.

Charles said, "Have a seat on the sofa."

Which one? The size of the room was ridiculous. Who needed three couches? One. Two. Three. Four. Five. Six oversize fancy high-backed cushioned chairs were gathered in pairs at separate glass-top tables. Now the pool table, that bitch was sweet. Drooling, I picked up a stick. Pretended I was a professional. "Rack 'em, boys." I could earn that two million honestly and live this way the rest of my life.

Charles nodded to one of his security guys. He walked toward me, picked up a stick, then handed it to the old dude. Sindy got one.

"Let's do this." I tossed Beaux one.

Charles gestured toward the flat screen attached to the wall. One of his guards turned it on. The picture was incredible. I stared at the news reporter. "That shit looks 3D."

"It's 4K," Charles said.

Four who? What's that? I hadn't been locked up that long. When did those come out?

"Let's team up to make this interesting. I got Granville," Charles said. "Put your stick down for a minute and sit next to me. We'll shoot around in a minute." Dude coughed then told my brother, "You can sit wherever you'd like. You got Sindy."

My eyes widened. Pouting like a kid, I thought, *I want her!* Beaux could have old dude. "Bro, sit by my side," I said.

"Not so close to Granville," Charles said. "Right there is fine, Beaux. This won't take long."

"Daddy, don't do this," Sindy said then sat between Beaux and me. "I'll do it."

"Do what?" I asked.

Beaux moved to a nearby chair. Good. I didn't want to share Sindy.

"Don't act like you don't know," she said.

"Know what?" I asked.

Her eyes filled with tears. She didn't look sad. She squinted, then rolled her eyes. I wanted to move and at the same time not. I hadn't done anything to her for her to hate me. She leaned forward and stared at her father.

"Sindy, until you marry the billionaire in Dubai who has bought you, I'm proceeding with my plan." He spoke to me. "Granville, I want you to do as I've told you. Take care of Chicago."

Frowning, I focused on the television.

"My brother is no killer," Beaux said.

"Fine, then you do it and I'll give you the two

million. I don't care which one of you pulls the trigger but my life depends on getting this done."

"Ain't nobody gon' kill you over no pussy," I said.

Slap! Ol' girl hit me again. I told her, "You sho' is ugly," hoping she'd hit me harder.

"Granville," the old man said.

"What?" I asked turning to him. Couldn't he see I was busy?

Charles coughed in my face.

"Dude, I don't care how much money you got. Cough on me again and see what happens," I told him.

Beaux stood. Soon as he took one step toward that old arrogant dude, those two bodyguards blocked him. Standing shoulder to shoulder they put their hands inside their jackets.

"What the fuck? Turn that up," I said pointing at the TV. "Why my picture on there?"

Charles smiled, then nodded upward. One of his bodyguards increased the volume.

I listened to that news broad say, "Granville Washington was released from the Federal Detention Center earlier this morning."

"And?" I said. "I did my time."

"Was he innocent of shooting Roosevelt 'Chicago' DuBois? Now that Roosevelt is back with his wife and child, is there any truth to social media rumor? Is Granville out to attempt to kill Chicago again? Will Granville violate his restraining order to see the infant he claims is his?"

"It's not a claim, lady. Get your facts straight. I'll do it, if I have to," I said. Soon as I'd said that, I realized I didn't mean it.

Smack! Sindy slapped my face. "You're dumber than you look."

"You'd better stop turning me on. If you get a feel of this hard wood, you mine."

She exhaled in my face, and I inhaled. Damn, I was hoping to give her another reason to hit me but she didn't. I said, "If I kill Chicago, will you marry me?"

Smack!

Yes! This time her titties shook.

I looked at Charles. Dude didn't say a word. This moment reminded me when my mother used to tell my brother and me, "Whichever one is lying, tell the other one to shut up."

"You're the stupid one," I told her. "What woman wouldn't marry a billionaire?"

Sindy touched my thigh. Suddenly she got nice. "You're right. I apologize. I know you're hurting because that is your son. Let me help you prove it."

I tried to kiss her. She scooted back. Whatever. Her loss.

I hoped she wasn't trying to use me like Loretta and Madison had done. "I'll do whatever you say."

This time she'd kissed my cheek then glanced at her father. "Daddy we can be civil about this and no one has to get hurt." Sindy started crying.

Women sure were emotional.

"I'm still not calling off the hit until you're married. You are not marrying Chicago, and"—he paused, then continued—"Granville is going to do what I tell him to do no matter what you—"

"I hate you!" She stood, picked up a vase, then hurled it toward her father.

I swatted the vase to the floor. Charles should put me on payroll to protect him from his daughter. "I can't do this," I said watching Sindy cry. "Mr.

Singleton, may I have your permission to marry your daughter?"

That way Chicago wouldn't have to die, we could pay that billionaire dude back his money, and everyone could be happy.

Dude coughed again. This time in my face.

"What the fuck!"

Blood spilled from his mouth onto my lips. I wiped it off. The bodyguard handed me a cloth napkin. "What you got, man?"

Sindy stared at me, then at her dad and said, "He's got HIV."

Before she took one step toward the door, I pushed old dude to the floor. "If I'ma die you gon' die first." I raised my fist and aimed for his head. His bodyguards tackled me, pulled out their guns.

"Beaux, get out of here. Go!" I yelled. If the police came, I'd do the time. I was about to make them guards use those bullets or take one hell of an ass whipping.

CHAPTER 27

Sindy

"Don't shoot him," my father faintly lamented. "Give me a gun."
I shouted to the bodyguards, "Kill him! Kill! Him!" The first time I pointed at Granville. The second, my father.

Granville frowned at me; Charles stared in disbelief.

"Don't shoot me, dude!" Granville yelled.

I enjoyed watching Granville stare into the barrel of a gun. Did I want Granville dead? No. My father? Not really. He was the only living parent I had. Had he killed our mother? Was it an accident? I never asked because I never wanted to know the truth.

Everybody had a deep secret.

Granville pulled back his fist to hit my father again. "If I'm going to die, I'm going to kill him first."

Beaux shouted, "He's not worth it."

Granville's fist stopped inches from my father's

face. Not because he'd changed his mind. One of the bodyguards hit Granville's hand using the handle of his gun.

"Ow! Dude, what the fuck! I've got a beat down with your name on it," Granville said holding one hand with his other.

Charles pathetically sprawled on the plush carpet. His elbow trembled as he braced himself. "Don't just stand there. Help me up." His guards put their guns in their pockets.

If there were a category for best actor with no formal training, my dad would win the Academy Award. When his name is called, he will have to answer to God for the sins he'd committed. I prayed he didn't do like the lying, cheating, abusive murderers who'd sinned all their lives, then repented on their dying bed. If everyone could get into heaven that way, what was the point of trying to do the right thing all my life? It was time I benefited from the pass God has granted.

After our mother's death, my sister was sold or bought—depended on how one viewed the situation. She'd gone from being my best friend to more of a stranger.

I'd never forget the day Daddy said, "Siara isn't coming back. If anyone asks, tell them Siara changed her mind at the last minute and decided to go to NYU instead of TSU." His lie made me more skeptical about Mama.

I never mentioned my sister to anyone, not even to Roosevelt. When I talked with Siara via Skype during Christmas, it was the hardest time of the year not to shed tears in front of her. She'd show off pictures of her three kids but she refused to let them speak with me. She'd never mention Mom.

The day Siara told me, "I have to be a better protector of my children than you were of me," I cried profusely.

My sister could family vacation in Toronto but I couldn't join them. She could Skype but I couldn't visit her in Paris. Maybe my guilt made me passive. Perhaps she knew something I didn't. Next time we face-chat, I wouldn't ask. I'd insist. Hopefully, she wouldn't resist.

I still cry at night sometimes. I was only twenty when she was eighteen. How was I supposed to know when Daddy took her to Paris, she'd never come back? How many mentally ill men had done the same to their daughters?

Charles had lied, "Paris is my high school graduation present to Siara. Sindy, I'll take you anywhere in the world you want to go when you get your college degree."

While I watched his bodyguards help him to his feet, I should've kicked him while he was on the floor. The only reason I hadn't was once I'd start, I might not stop until I stomped the last breath out of him.

Trusting men was hard for me. I'd date. But when a guy wanted to have sex, I'd find a reason to break up with him. Roosevelt was different. I felt him in my heart. I knew I could trust him to take care of me and I'd do the same for him. We deserved each other. People don't get what they deserve. They get what they earn, or they get what they take.

Charles almost had me brainwashed. The thought of getting on a plane to Dubai, I'd considered it more than once. What was there not to love about Dubai? Never again was I entertaining my father's desire. Thank God for Numbiya. She was a true friend willing to go with me.

Agreeing with Charles not to shoot Granville was not to my advantage. Men like Granville were easily manipulated. He was the type of brute who would fight for any cause especially when he thought he was right. Loretta didn't want him but he'd claimed she was his until she filed a protective order. Then he felt upgraded when she handed him off to her girlfriend. In his mind, Madison was his woman and the baby was his. I wasn't 100 percent positive the kid was his but I had a plan to take Roosevelt's name off of Zach's birth certificate permanently.

Unbeknownst to Granville, a few words out of his mouth made him indebted to me. I could've left my father's house but I had to make myself a witness. I could have dialed 911. Instead, I stood by videotaping the incident. My part would be edited out.

I'd rather reserve my power to send Granville back to jail. If he didn't do what I'd tell him, I'd orchestrate my next moves and have him arrested for attempted murder of my father. Charles would have to hire another hit man. That was if he didn't die from an accidental overdose the way Mama had. I still believed my mother was dead before he pushed her down the stairs. My father was sick. Mentally.

Daddy didn't have HIV. My dad's esophagus was eroding from acid reflux. The lining of his throat was deteriorating. Doctors had prescribed medication that made my father's condition worse. His coughing up blood wasn't life-threatening, although there were times that I wished it were.

Turning off the video, I had enough footage to put Granville away for a few years. I watched Beaux help Granville up. My cell phone interrupted the most entertaining moment I'd had in a while, as Beaux said, "Let's get out of here, bro."

"Wait until the media hears about this. I'm sending your black ass back to jail," Daddy said with his finger shaking. The movement in his hand wasn't intentional.

Distracted by the madness, I let Helen's call go to voice mail. "Granville, Beaux, come with me."

Granville didn't deserve to go back to jail for this nonsense but he could. I was disappointed he hadn't hit my father that last time. A man with disregard for another man's life needed to feel pain. That was true for both Granville and Charles.

"Wait," I said handing the suitcase to Granville. "You've earned this. Keep it. But don't spend anything until you hear from me."

Granville didn't hesitate. "Thanks." He stared at Beaux. "I'm keeping this." Interestingly, his hand felt well enough to grip the handle.

I escorted them to their truck. "I'll be in touch tomorrow."

I sat in my car until they drove off, then I listened to my voice mail.

"I got the baby," Helen had said. "Let's get that test done while Madison is in the hospital getting her breast implants."

Whether or not I reunited with Roosevelt, I wanted to make Madison suffer for the evil things she'd done to a good man. The old Sindy Singleton was getting ready to set everyone straight.

I saved the message then dialed his number. "Please accept my call."

"Haven't heard from you in a while," he answered. "It's good to hear your voice."

"Where are you?"

"Home."

"Alone?"

"Yes. Why?"

"Stay there. I'm on my way. We need to talk."

CHAPTER 28

Chicago

When God tells you what to do and you don't listen, what happens next?

I prayed He'd give me another chance to do as He'd said. I hoped I wasn't waiting for an answer that would never come.

Standing outside the courtroom with my brother Chaz, I questioned if this was the appropriate time to abandon Madison. Taking care of her for a few months would be honorable. Then I could get back to Sindy and give her my undivided affection.

"My biggest regret is messing up my chance to get to know Sindy."

"If you ask me, stop staring a gift horse in the mouth. Sindy is the one. Leave Madison's trifling ass at the hospital. Move all of her shit out before she gets out. Let her parents pick her up. You've given Madison too much of yourself, dude."

He was right. But what harm would a few more months do at this point? "I'll think about it." Shifting my weight to the opposite leg, I glanced to the side, then exhaled heavily.

"Aw, hell no. Please tell me you didn't."

I nodded.

"You used protection, right?" Chaz asked.

I shook my head. "Soon as I ejaculated, I had regrets. She told me she couldn't get pregnant that soon."

My brother was quiet for a moment, then said, "Fuck that lying bitch Madison. She'll probably say she's pregnant even if she's not. I can't believe you let her set you up again. Never mind her. Don't call Sindy. Go to Sindy's house and apologize face to face. Take flowers. Long-stemmed red roses. All she can say is 'It's over.' But most women don't mean that shit. If she rejects you three times, move on. Don't beg her ass."

Chaz always made relationship decisions appear easy. If I were more like him, Sindy would be here with me right now.

My attorney opened the courtroom door. "We're up."

Never had I imagined getting a divorce. This was not a joyous occasion. Maybe that's why I was avoiding going through with it. The best part was, within the hour, I'd legally be a single man. Mom, Dad, and Grandpa decided not to come. I was glad Chaz was here.

The judge announced, "Case of DuBois versus DuBois."

I sat on the right, facing the judge. My lawyer was seated next to me on my left.

"Please stand and raise your right hand."

Glancing over my left shoulder, I could see Chaz

seated in the first row. He nodded. I exhaled then faced the judge. When the bailiff was done reciting the oath, I answered, "I do."

The judge flipped through the file before her.

Madison's attorney stated, "Your Honor, I'd like to request a continuance. Mrs. DuBois is in the hospital having surgery."

"Objection," my lawyer stated. "Mrs. DuBois has not contested the divorce."

"She meant to. It's just that she's been overwhelmed with taking care of the baby while Mr. DuBois is"—he nodded in my direction—"managing his football team. And my client was dealing with pre-op appointments and today she's having her breast augmentation procedure. She had breast cancer, Your Honor. We haven't had time to meet and I can't call her because she is under anesthesia the same as she was the day she was served the divorce papers."

The judge looked to my attorney. I knew we were in a losing situation at the moment. He whispered in my ear, "What would you like to do? I can stand firm on the objection but it would make us appear insensitive to women and the community."

"How much longer is reasonable?" I asked him.

"Uncomplicated recovery from breast augmentations is typically five days but I say give her thirty."

Was he serious? Five days?

"No more than thirty days."

"I withdraw the objection and request a thirty-day continuance."

"Your Honor, on behalf of my client, I request ninety days. We have a few people to subpoena," Madison's attorney said.

"Thirty days continuance is granted," the judge said then told the clerk, "Check the calendar."

After going back and forth on an available date for everyone's schedule, we were well after Thanksgiving, which was this week, and closer to Christmas. Somehow I knew Madison would use the holiday to get a continuance to the continuance.

Shaking my head, I strolled out of the courtroom. "Can you believe she told me just this morning that the recovery period was a few months?"

Chaz was right behind me. "You don't need me to answer that. I keep telling you man, let her ass go." Getting in the car, my brother said, "Fuck that bitch! Put her out of your condo and take care of your son."

I dialed my mother. Connected the call to my car's Bluetooth.

"Hey, honey. Are you officially a single man?"

"No," Chaz answered. "The judge denied his release. Now he's on a thirty-day probation."

Narrowing my eyes at my brother, I listened to our mother. "Is he serious?"

"Something like that. We have a continuance. I don't want to discuss it. How's Zach?"

"He's fine. Sleeping."

"I'll be by tonight to get him. We have to get to the office for a few meetings."

"I love you," my mother said.

Hearing those words always made me feel better. "I love you too, Ma."

"Me too!" Chaz shouted right before I ended the call.

The drive to the office was quiet. I parked in my reserved space. Walking into my office, I told Chaz,

"I have to let go and let God take the wheel on this one, man."

Chaz patted me on the back. "Faith without work is dead. You're going to need more than roses. Me too. How about we get to work? Let's go visit our jeweler."

CHAPTER 29

Sindy

I was about to go all in for a man who didn't know how much I loved him.

Roosevelt was a good guy. I couldn't blame his parents and say, "They gave that man no home training." The DuBoises had educated and emotionally supported their boys. Roosevelt was not one of the many men who had grown up without a father in the house.

Martin was an excellent father. He'd shown by example how a man should treat his wife. He was wealthy but I'd never heard him speak ill of poor people or those with less. The DuBoises were a proud family. Perhaps that pride they'd instilled in their sons was what was keeping Roosevelt tied to Madison.

Being around Roosevelt's family in the suite on game day, I loved to watch their interactions. I knew Madison was kicking herself for having slept with Granville but I was not going to ease her blows. If Roosevelt had listened to Chaz, he would've never married Madison. But if Roosevelt hadn't married Madison, there wouldn't have been a reason for Chaz to introduce us.

I appreciated that Chaz was straightforward. Numbiya and others did not have to assume what was on his mind. Chaz did what made him happy. Roosevelt did what made others happy.

As I drove through the older neighborhood of Houston, I noticed that the single-family homes were closer in proximity than where I resided in River Oaks. I had ten thousand square feet; the houses I passed averaged two thousand. This area had generational ownership. We had that in our community too. What we lacked, one could not place a price on—company.

My mother believed in inviting family and friends over but in this neighborhood, family and friends did not need an invite. They just showed up at the front door and if it was open, they'd walk in. I noticed a few trailers on lawns adjacent to houses. The grass was partially brown. I'd never seen that in my part of town.

I parked in the driveway. Walking up four wooden steps, I pulled the screen then knocked on the door. We hadn't met since I'd last visited him behind bars.

"Coming."

I wasn't sure if I'd heard "coming" or "come in." I waited.

Nyle Carter opened the door. "Hey, good to see you. You look great."

"Good to see you're taking care of yourself."

The red fitted halter maxi dress I'd put on this morning was appropriate. Seventy degrees was the temperature an hour ago. Eighty had settled in and it wasn't noon. The projected high was ninety-seven.

"Just trying to decide what I want to pursue." He paused then added, "Legally."

"May I?" I said gesturing to enter.

Nyle stepped aside. "Whatever the reason, I know you didn't come all this way to stand on my porch. My apology. May I offer you something to drink? Water? Wine? Both?"

"A glass of chardonnay please. How's your son, Landry?"

"Thanks to the support from your nonprofit, he's settled into college. Doing great."

Sitting on his sofa, I noticed framed pictures of Nyle and his son. His wife was conspicuously absent. There were no photos of a woman, not even his mother. The hardwood floor could benefit from polishing but at least it was clean.

"Here you go," he said handing me a glass. He placed the bottle on the table, sat beside me, then raised his glass. "To freedom."

"To freedom." He was glad to have it. I never wanted to be without it.

Waking up, setting my schedule, not needing permission from anyone to deviate was what I considered living the American dream. Getting married, buying a home, and having children weren't things to aspire to if a person wasn't financially ready. All three components of the "dream" meant creating debt, not wealth.

"If you're here to ask me to do anything illegal," he adamantly said, "Forget about it."

"I changed my mind about your pursuing the

rumor of Granville attempting to kill Roosevelt. You took off everything you put on social media like I told you?"

Nyle exhaled. "Yes. Thank you. What about the video and pics I have of Sarah Lee Washington's grave? There was a gun in her coffin."

Why was I not surprised? "Where is it?"

He nodded toward a room I couldn't see.

"Give me everything you have."

Rushing into the room, Nyle returned with a small black laptop bag. "It's all there. I'm done with this?"

"Yes, you're done."

"What you want from me now? Is it legal?" he asked.

Quietly, he filled his mouth with wine, swished it around, then swallowed. He raised his brows, stared at me. His blond hair was neatly trimmed. Nails, well manicured. His white button-down shirt was crisp.

I nodded. "I need you to do this tomorrow."

His eyes remained fixed on mine. "What's in it for me?"

"After I tell you, you tell me."

"Fair." He took another swallow. This time he didn't swish. "I'm listening."

"I need you to purchase a property."

"What Realtor is it listed with?"

I'd trained Nyle well. He didn't ask why I needed this favor. "It's not. It's an all-cash transaction."

"How much cash?"

"Two million."

The wine in his mouth almost landed on me the way my father's blood splattered on Granville. He covered his mouth.

"And why can't you buy it yourself?"

"They won't sell to me direct. How much for you?"

"One hundred—"

"Twenty thousand?"

He nodded. That was the standard six percent commission for a listing between two real estate agents. I countered the split rate. "Sixty thousand."

"Ninety," he said.

"Deal. I'll have everything arranged by ten in the morning. I need your part complete by noon."

"What if they refuse?"

I stood, sat my glass on the table, then confidently said, "They won't."

It was time to make my next move.

CHAPTER 30

Madison

Pulling the sheet up to my neck, I asked, "What are you doing here?"

The last person I expected to see at the hospital was Vermont. A phone call would've sufficed. My new breasts were perfectly shaped. Higher. Fuller. Rounder. There was no way I could hide these twins. I wasn't going to burn my bras but I definitely didn't need them.

My attorney's eyes focused on my erect nipples. His dick grew longer. I ignored it. The doctor warned me it was natural for people, especially men, to become distracted by the attractiveness. I gave him a moment of silence.

Time up. To redirect his attention, I said, "I'd given thought to giving in and moving on." Being a single mom wasn't the worst thing that could happen. I'd rather parent alone than deal with Granville. Perhaps I should be strong and continue what I'd started with my husband.

Papa shouldn't have told Mama about the paternity test. I hadn't asked him to intervene. That man never did what was in anyone else's best interest. To take another test meant confessing to Roosevelt for a crime I did not commit. Nor was I an accomplice. My husband wouldn't believe me.

Vermont held my hand. "How are you feeling?"

Tears clouded my eyes. Was the settlement that bad he had to tell me in person? "The procedure went well. I'm in a lot of pain emotionally and physically."

"You focus on getting healthier," he said, then smiled. "I come bearing good news that will definitely cheer you up."

"Really?" Between the headache the medication had caused and the throbbing in my breasts, I couldn't smile.

The enthusiasm in his groin shifted. "The first twenty-four to forty-eight hours after any surgery are expected to be hard." Standing beside my bed, he covered my hand with his. "When are you going home?" he asked.

"If all goes well, day after tomorrow. I chose to stay an extra day. I'm in no hurry to deal with my situation. Was she there?" I had to know.

"Who's she?"

Exhaling, I stated, "Sindy."

Vermont shook his head. "Her being in the courtroom wouldn't have helped his case. I want you to take your time, dear. Your divorce is not final yet. I got you a thirty-day continuation. He should see what he's missing. If you want to subpoena Sindy, let's do it right now. You can't sue for alienation but you can make her uncomfortable if Roosevelt is pursuing her. And you're going to ask for half of everything, including that ten million dollars his grandfather gave him. Doesn't hurt to ask. All the cards are in your favor, Madison."

My eyes widened. I forced a smile. "We go to court before Christmas."

"Right before Christmas. Clever, huh?" He flicked his brows. "You can pay me later," he said as he kissed my forehead and released my hand. "I've got to go. Take care of yourself and Roosevelt's son."

Vermont was brilliant! I felt another continuance coming. Roosevelt would have to juggle being a father to Zach, his football schedule. I paused my thoughts, then continued thinking. *With Chaz as his assistant, Roosevelt's being able to take time off from work may not be a competing factor.* Obviously, Vermont had a plan. I should've asked him to fluff the pillow behind my head so I could relax. I reached for the remote to page the nurse.

Papa entered with a dozen white roses. "There's my sweetheart. How are you?" He kissed my forehead then placed the bouquet across my lap.

"Hold my flowers closer and let me smell them, Papa." I inhaled a healing fragrance.

One rose or a dozen—the number was not more important than the scent. Roses that had no smell were disappointing.

"I have the best news ever, Papa!"

This time Papa placed the bouquet on the stand in the corner. Though my words were a normal tone, in my heart I'd shouted from the top of the highest building in Houston, the JPMorgan Chase Tower.

Papa sat in the chair next to my bed. He didn't hold my hand the way Vermont had done. That would've been nice but Papa wasn't very affectionate. I imagined the young girls he'd had sex with were strictly for his pleasure, not theirs.

"I'm great now. Helen is keeping Zach until my release."

"What? Madison, you know that woman can't be trusted. Did she volunteer to keep the baby? Or did Roosevelt leave him with her? I'll have Rosalee go get him."

What difference did that make? "If she bonds with Zach, maybe she'll accept me too." I was not concerned with Helen. What could she do? Make Granville take . . . "Call Mama and tell her to get my baby."

Papa put his cell on speaker. It rang twice. Mama answered, "How's Madison doing?"

"She's fine, honeybunch."

Honeybunch? Haven't heard my father call Mom that in years. Did that mean Mama had forgiven him again?

"Look, we need you to pick Zach up from Helen's."

"Is she expecting me?" my mother asked.

"She will be," I said.

"Call back when she is. I'm not going to that woman's house unannounced. Steve Harvey is going off. Madison, I'll be by to visit in an hour."

Mom had really changed. Her voice. Her attitude. The old Rosalee would've picked Zach up without asking questions.

I looked at Papa. He was the one who couldn't be trusted. I didn't have the energy to argue. "I go home in two days. Mama can get Zach from Helen's then and bring him to me at the condo. How are you?"

Papa moved from the chair and sat on the side

of my bed. "I'm good. I've been taking your mother out more. I'd forgotten how much that woman means to me. I'm not fooling around with those young girls anymore. I owe you an apology for how I disrespected your mother."

Was that an apology or a confession? I wished I had the strength to push him off of my bed. "Move, Papa."

He inched closer. "I know it's hard for you to accept but I don't want to die mistreating the two women I love the most." He held my hand.

Maybe I should let him have this moment. "I'm glad you realized Mama is worthy of being treated like your woman and your wife. I'm fighting for my marriage too. The divorce isn't final. My being in the hospital and having the baby got me a thirty-day continuance."

Papa whispered, "Sweetheart. God is giving both of us another chance. You must never tell a soul that I'm responsible for influencing the test results. The three of us must take this secret to our graves."

Mama was the unpredictable one now. She'd probably intentionally waited to visit me alone. I knew she'd try to convince me to do the right thing. Stop contesting the divorce. Tell Roosevelt that Zach may not be his. Have another paternity test. When she arrived to visit, I'd have to ask her to side with Papa and me and keep our secret.

I said, "You did say you paid for the results but you weren't sure."

"I'm pretty sure that Granville is the biological father."

"Based on what, Papa?" I wanted to strangle him.

"I'd rather not say."

CHAPTER 31

Sindy

"**I** need to do a two million dollar transaction."
En route from Nyle's house to JPMorgan, I called my investment banker. She responded, "Let me guess, an all-cash property acquisition."

She was right but my business wasn't hers. "Make the cashier's check payable to Roosevelt DuBois."

"I stand corrected," she said. "Unless you're purchasing his place."

Her comments were distracting. "Make the cashier's check payable to Nyle Carter. I'll see you in a few," I said ending the call.

Normally, I'd chat a few minutes with her. Ask how her family was doing. I didn't have time for frivolous chatter. I'd accomplished a lot already today. I hoped Granville hadn't spent any of the money I'd given him, but I wouldn't be surprised if he had. Nyle would get his check as promised. With a few more stops to make after the bank, I decided to stop at Avalon for a jalapeno Swiss cheese-burger, fries, and a strawberry shake.

Sitting at the counter, I ordered lunch, then I called Numbiya.

"Hey, queen. Where are you?"

"Grabbing a bite at Avalon in River Oaks," I replied scanning through my e-mails.

"I could really enjoy a juicy bleu cheese bacon burger. Things are slow today. I can be there in fifteen minutes."

Hearing Numbiya's voice lightened my spirit. I could use her company. Waiting for my girlfriend meant I'd be here for at least an hour. I'd make it to the bank in time to get the check but I wasn't sure I'd be on time for my other appointments.

"Let's do dinner," I said while responding to a text message.

"Okay." The smile in her voice made me smile until she said, "Roosevelt's divorce isn't final."

My food arrived but I didn't have an appetite. "I'll see you tonight. Talk with you then. Bye." Ending the call, I placed twenty dollars on the counter and left.

Contemplating whether to follow through with my plans, I sat in my car. State Representative Harold V. Dutton Jr. parked his black Cadillac Escalade next to my Bentley.

I lowered my window. "Thanks for bills on education, inmates' right to vote, and blocking the abortion law."

"My pleasure." His voice was deep and sultry. I'd heard him speak on several occasions. He'd always spoken the same as I'd heard him on television. "That's why I'm in office. To serve the community," he said before heading into Avalon.

He was also an attorney. Practicing. I wondered if anything bothered him or as a politician, everything was rationalized. Seeing him was no accident. I had no idea why Roosevelt's divorce wasn't final but my decision to continue my journey was clear.

The bank was abnormally crowded. Thanksgiving. Black Friday. Both were a few days away. I'd imagined shoppers were preparing to spend money they didn't have. The line for business owners was longer than usual.

I waved to the president of the bank. She motioned for me to come to her.

"Let's go into my office?"

A teller buzzed us into a secured area. We took a private elevator to the fifteenth floor. Entered another secured area before arriving at her office.

"You look beautiful. Going anywhere special?" she asked sitting behind her desk. "Have a seat."

"How's your family?" I sat across from her.

I'd rather spend a few extra minutes here than to have sat eating a burger while chatting with my girlfriend. I made a mental note to make reservations for Numbiya and me tonight. Definitely not at Corner Table. The things I'd done with Roosevelt in the Lexington Room, fluttered my mind with orgasmic memories.

"What was that?" my banker asked.

What was what? If she'd mentioned anything about her husband and kids, I hadn't heard a word.

"Oh, nothing." I couldn't get Roosevelt out of my heart or my head. "You have the check?" I asked. Not that I needed to give her an explanation, but I told her, "It is for a real estate transaction."

"A lot of cash transactions are happening here

in Houston. You'd think a law was about to pass allowing homeowners to drill on their land for oil," she said handing me an envelope.

I opened it. "Pay to the order of: Nyle Carter." Everything was correct. "I'm going to have this person come by and see you tomorrow. He'll give you the cashier's check and have it reissued from his account to Roosevelt DuBois."

For a moment, she frowned, then replied, "Sure thing."

I put the check in my purse. The time was one o'clock. I had a few more stops to make. Getting into my car, I dropped the check off to Nyle, and explained to him what he had to do.

My next location was a familiar one. Entering the leasing office, I met with the manager. "I need to rent a two-bedroom unit for three months."

"We only have two units. We don't do longterm leases. And we only lease a few days at a time to homeowners for their family and guests. Have you tried—"

"I'm Sindy Singleton, daughter of Charles Singleton. He's one of the partners who own the company that manages and operates this building. I don't need to try. You do. Charge it to my card." I slid my black card across the desk. If the unit was for me, I'd request all new furniture. But it wasn't.

She made a few calls. I waited until she printed the agreement. I read it, signed, got the keys, and was en route to my next stop.

CHAPTER 32

Granville

"**P**ussy or food, dude? Whatever you want. I got you."

Beaux parked my truck in front of The Breakfast Klub. I was so hungry I could eat both at the same time. When a man's nuts were hanging low, he couldn't think straight. I wanted to chow down on every pussy we passed on the freeway, the street, and the ones in the sky. I had enough money to join the mile high club. Wonder how much that cost. Never been on a plane.

"What would you like?" the cashier asked. "Just so you'll know, we close in an hour."

Wasn't going to take us that long to finish our food. Give me a stack of pancakes, pussies, warm maple syrup was what I wanted to say. I was gonna eat asshole and all. "Yum. Yum, look at the ass on that," I said.

Beaux slapped the back of my head. "Shut up and order."

I frowned. That was kinda like when Mama used to say, "Shut up and be quiet."

"Excuse me," the cashier said placing her hand on her hip. She rolled her eyes.

What was up with her attitude? She thought I was hitting on her? I was talking about the woman by the beverages refilling her glass with tea. She was beautiful. Instantly I got hard wood. I adjusted myself.

"Give me the tallest rack of hotcakes you have and a side of crispy catfish and one of them iced teas. It's gotta be sweet since she got some. Maybe I'll ask her to stick her finger in me. I mean, mine. What you want?" I asked my brother.

Shaking his head, Beaux said, "Don't mind him."

The cashier commented, "Just got out, huh?"

Beaux laughed. I didn't see a damn thing funny.

"I'll have catfish, greens, yams, and mac and cheese and I'll have an iced tea too."

She tapped on a few keys. I pulled a hundred out my pocket. She shook her head.

I asked this broad, "What now?"

"We don't take hundreds and even if we did, I'm not touching your money." She looked at Beaux, then said, "It's twenty-seven fifty-two."

Bro handed her thirty. "Keep the change."

She handed us two large brown plastic cups. I rolled my eyes at her, then whispered, "The money you've been handling all day is dirtier than my dick." I started to give my cup back to her and ask someone else to wash their hands then give me one.

Beaux nudged me in my back. "Dude. Go on before you get us kicked out."

I sat across from my brother. We'd chosen a table at the window to keep an eye on my Super Duty. The suitcase of money was inside. I know Sindy had told me not to spend any of it until she called but I didn't see harm in padding my pocket with two g's. Technically, since old girl rejected my C-note, I hadn't spent a dime.

Beaux had enough cash to pay for the few things I needed. After we left here I had to stop at Walgreen's up the street and get toothpaste and a toothbrush. My old one had sat for a month. Wasn't putting either in my mouth.

I winked at the woman with the giraffe legs and stallion booty. She was eating alone. *Ride me, cowgirl!* "I want her, bro."

"Leave that lady alone. When we going to visit Mama's grave? We still have to take care of her business."

Aunt Wilma had probably emptied Mama's house by now. Any policy with our name on it was still there only because she couldn't cash it in. Mama's house was paid for. It wasn't going anywhere. Neither Beaux nor I wanted to live in it. Putting flowers on Mama's grave was more for us than for her. My mama lived in my mind, not some cemetery.

"We can go after Thanksgiving."

"When?" he asked.

Beaux was getting on my nerves. I noticed, "She ain't got no ring on her fingers. I could buy her one."

"Dude, if you just got to get it out, call Precious if you want to get laid. She's drama free and she still loves you."

How he knew that? "I don't want Precious anymore. I want her," I said pointing.

Precious was a nice girl. She was freaky and fun. The way she rode me was unbelievable but I wanted new pussy. I imagined sliding my salami between that girl right there's butt cheeks and cumming on her back. Didn't need another kid. Didn't want to use a condom.

What if old dude gave me something and I give it to her?

A waiter placed our food in front of us. I picked up my glass and headed to the self-serve beverage station. I filled it with ice then added sweetened tea. Beaux's sense of urgency to quench his thirst wasn't the same as mine. He'd never been locked up.

Pretending I was adding sugar to my drink, I stared at her. She was pretty. Dark skin, shiny legs. I wondered if she had big nipples. Would she let me bite them? I felt like howling like a dog. I should've gone back to my table. My cowboy boots traveled in her direction.

"Hi," I said inviting myself to a seat.

"Hello," was all she said.

"Why you sound sad? Where your man at?"

"Every woman isn't interested in having a man," she said. "Besides, men don't know what they want."

She hadn't answered my questions. Women were like that too. Didn't want to debate her. I wanted to eat her up.

"You into girls?"

"Maybe I should be."

Wow, some dude must've shattered her heart. "I can't stay." I pulled the bankroll out of my pocket, placed it on the table, then took out my cell phone. "Can I have your number?"

She picked up my stash, peeled off two hundreds, put them in her purse, then laid the rest of my cash back in front of me.

Now that I was rich, I didn't care about her taking a couple of bills. "Well?"

Her smile was still a little sad but friendlier. She said, "My name is Mahogany."

My dick started creeping down my thigh. I felt it widening. In a minute I'd have hard wood.

"You ready?" she asked looking between my legs. "Yeah, you're ready. My number is seven, seven, three, five . . ."

"Where you from?" I asked staring at her lips.

"Port Arthur, originally. Been to New Orleans, Lake Charles, made my way to Houston. Might move to LA," she said, sipping her drink.

"Really!" I gulped down my tea. "You sure move around a lot. I'm from Port Arthur too. And here. That's it. Why I ain't never seen you in PA? I would've remembered a face as pretty as yours."

Mahogany smiled. "Yeah, I would've remembered you too," she said. "I'ma order something to eat before they close. You want me to refresh your tea first?"

"Sure." What I really wanted was watch her walk away, then back. "Thanks."

"No problem," she said sitting next to me.

"Bro, we gotta go!" Beaux yelled.

"I'll call you in an hour, Mahogany." I left the other eighteen hundred where she'd put it, stood, and went back to the beverage stand. Didn't need any more sweetness from the tea. I got two to-go containers.

"You have to learn the hard way," Beaux said. "Why you give that woman money?"

Duh. Because I could. I didn't give a fuck what my brother thought at this moment. I handed him his container, then packed up my pancakes and catfish.

"Dude, her name is Mahogany and my dick is singing the blues. Take me home. Now so I can jack off."

CHAPTER 33

Sindy

"Where in hell were you?"
He should've been home. I'd waited an hour outside his apartment. Only an idiot would drive around with over a million dollars in his car. Obviously his brother wasn't that smart either.

Granville's eyes shifted to the side. "You didn't tell me to—"

Smack! I hit his jaw. "Where's the money?"

He tightened his mouth like a little kid who was guilty. "What you so mad about?"

Every damn thing at the moment, especially not knowing why Roosevelt's divorce wasn't finalized today. I had to complete my tasks before dinner with Numbiya.

"You spent the money after I told you not to?"

"Could you define spent?" he said hunching his shoulders. "It's mine, right?"

"Go upstairs, pack a bag, and get back down here fast as you can."

Beaux asked, "Why? Why are you trying to rule

my brother's life? He's done, right? The money is his, right? And what's up with this moving truck."

"I don't have time to answer any of his questions." I told Granville. "If you don't want to go back to jail, do what I said and hurry up before I take my father's money and leave."

I instructed the movers, "Go upstairs, start packing everything in his apartment. When you're done, take it to the storage unit. He might need it back later."

"You setting my brother up." Beaux raced upstairs to his brother's second-floor apartment. Good. I had a phone call to make. I dialed Helen.

"Where are you?" she answered.

"We'll be on our way in two hours top."

"The place closes at five, dear."

I'd made the appointment. Of course I knew that. Plus, I had other reasons to move fast if I didn't want to ruin my plans. Beaux and Granville were heading back toward me. Quickly, I told Helen, "I've got to go. Bye."

Granville had a suitcase. "Give me the keys to your place. The movers will store your things. You're going into witness protection," I lied.

Only a fool would smile after hearing that. He was the most ignorant man I knew but he wasn't stupid. I'd seen him represent himself in court.

"But I didn't witness anything."

"I'm going to get you out of this hit man situation with my father. We don't have time for this. Get in my car. Beaux, follow me."

A woman had to take charge of situations early and fast. By the time Granville figured out what was happening, I'd be done. "I'm going to assist you with setting up an account in your name. You can't keep that kind of money on your person."

He frowned.

On the drive, I told him, "If you do everything I tell you, by Christmas you'll be the happiest man in the world."

"Yes, dear." He squirmed in his seat. He rubbed his bald head with both hands. His brows stretched high. "You're going to marry me?"

"Not even if I were dead."

He frowned again. "Then why am I supposed to be happy and who am I hiding from?"

"You'll see." I turned into Helen's driveway then called her.

She answered, "I see you're here. We're on our way out."

A last-minute change of plans was necessary. "Give me thirty minutes leeway. We should be done and gone by the time you arrive. He doesn't know." I texted my next comment: Let's keep it that way. If he sees the baby, he is going to freak out.

"Know what?" Granville asked.

Helen texted: Who's in the car behind you?

I typed: His brother. See you there. Bye then drove away.

"What were you doing that took you so long to get home?" I asked him.

His eyes widened. "You just reminded me." He pulled his cell from his pocket. "Hello, Mahogany." He paused then continued, "I'm sorry I'm late calling you. I'll call you back tonight. Goodbye, dear."

Okay. I shouldn't take his saying "dear" personally. I didn't ask who Mahogany was. I didn't care. I parked in the lot outside a downtown building. Beaux parked in the space beside me.

"Don't sit there. Get out."

"Where we going?"

I waved Beaux in my direction. "I feel responsible for what happened to Granville at my father's house. I brought you here for a blood test to make sure you're not infected," I lied.

"You did this for me?"

"Of course." I wanted to shake my head the way he'd done.

Granville looked to his brother.

"This is a good thing. Is it confidential?" Beaux asked.

Helen would be here soon. I started walking. "Of course it is."

"Well, bro. If Mahogany is your girl, take this test for her."

Entering my doctor's office, I had to shake my head this time. *Take the test for her? Really?*

"Good to see you, Sindy," he greeted. "Which one needs testing?"

Granville volunteered, "I do."

"You're doing the smart thing, young man," my doctor told him. "I'm going to do a swab and she's"—he pointed at his assistant—"the phlebotomist is going to draw your blood for your test."

"Why both?" Granville asked rolling up his sleeve.

Quickly she tightened a rubber strap around his bicep, inserted the needle, filled three tubes, placed the cotton ball over the needle, removed the needle, and released the band. "You're all done."

"This way we'll make sure. Besides, the swab will give you faster results. Sindy, I'll text you."

Having watched Granville's blood flow into each tube, I'd already paid to make sure the results showed Madison's baby was for Granville. And I'd also paid for the real results. Hopefully, the two would match. Even if Roosevelt was the father, he shouldn't have to be held hostage to a woman like Madison.

Soon as the doctor was done, we left the office. "Granville you're riding with me. We have one more stop. Beaux, you can follow us if you'd like."

"Yeah, bro. I'ma need a ride back—" Granville stopped midsentence. "Follow us for sure."

By the time we'd get to his new residence, Helen should've been at my doctor's office with Zach to complete the paternity test. I'd come up with a brilliant reason why I'd tell Roosevelt the first test was false.

Granville was quiet for a while, then asked, "When will I get my results?"

A text message registered on my cell. It was Helen. She'd arrived with Zach.

"Oh, here it is. You're fine. Your results are negative."

"Let me see," he said reaching for my cell.

I pulled away. "It's confidential."

He frowned. "What about the blood test?"

"It'll be the same. Don't worry," I said.

I cruised into the driveway, parked in a Future Homeowner space, and motioned for Beaux to park beside me.

"This is where Chicago lives," Granville shouted. "Did you bring me here to kill him? Is a gun somewhere in that suitcase? I'm not doing it. I changed my mind. I'm not going back to jail. I—"

"Stop it!" I didn't mean to yell at him but what was wrong with this man? "You're not going to kill anyone. You're going to do everything I tell you starting with do not communicate with my father under any circumstances. He doesn't know where you are. Remember you're under witness protection. Be quiet and come with me."

We entered The Royalton. I introduced Granville and Beaux to the concierge on duty as the new residents in the rental unit.

"Welcome. If there's anything I can do to be of assistance, don't hesitate." He pressed a button and the double glass doors parted.

Granville laughed like a kid.

Something in his brain was seriously off balance. I gave them a quick tour of the wine cellar and tasting room, the mailroom, the theater, pool table, and entertainment room. After showing them the gym, outdoor patio, swimming pool, and Jacuzzi, we rode the elevator to the fifth floor. I handed him the key.

"This is your place until January thirty-first. Then you'll have to move out."

Beaux laughed. "Better not get rid of your things, bro."

When the door opened, Beaux wasn't laughing. His mouth hung open.

Granville said, "Wow!"

"Remember what I told you, Granville." He probably hadn't heard a word after he'd stepped inside but that was okay. I was not crossing that threshold. "I'll take care of setting up your account later."

My work for today was done. Now I had to get ready for dinner with Numbiya. All of my chess pieces would be in place before Madison was released from the hospital. It wouldn't matter which direction she'd move. I'd already won.

Checkmate, bitch!

CHAPTER 34

Madison

Day two into my hospital stay I was depressed. Madison Tyler-DuBois was my name for a solid twenty-nine days. Then what? *This is not my life.* I was supposed to be married happily ever after. What I had was a baby that wasn't my husband's and a husband who didn't want me. Even if he stayed, I wouldn't have his heart.

That man lied to me without any reservations. Then he told me the truth with no remorse. I told Papa not to visit me. I meant that for the duration of my hospital stay but there was no time frame. Our time apart could be months or years.

I was too hurt to cry. Too weak to push aside the pain pressing down on my implants. Inhaling deeply, I took shallow breaths; a side effect from the medication and my fucking Granville. That one night, I . . .

"Hey, Madison," my mother said entering my room.

"Hi, Mama." I forced back my tears.

She kissed me on the cheek. "I love these flowers Johnny brought you." She inhaled. "They smell exactly like the bouquet your father gave me."

All of sudden my mother was in love again. I should be happy for her but I wasn't. Papa had ruined my life and moved a step up with his. Mama sat in the chair where my father was seated during his last visit.

"How do you feel, Madison? You look amazing."

"I'm good, Rosalee." Since she'd either forgotten or refused to acknowledge me as sweetheart or honey, I could do the same. Bet she'd stop calling Papa Johnny.

"Madison, don't alienate me like you've done your father. He loves you."

"Are you serious, Mother? If that's his way of showing love, I don't need it!"

Rosalee sprang to her feet. "Don't you raise your voice at me, little girl!"

Pissing my mother off would leave me dependent upon Roosevelt's family for support. After Christmas, I'd have Tisha. "Mama, I don't get it. You act as though what Papa did was acceptable."

"Acceptable? No. Forgivable? Yes, Madison. He's done far more to hurt me and I've made peace with him," she said sitting in the chair.

There she went again calling me by my first name. Peace? With a liar. "For how long? Until he has sex with another woman. You know he's going to."

"Hush, Madison. I'ma let that one go because those meds must be messing with your mind."

No. But she was definitely aggravating me. If I didn't have my baby, I'd have a surgeon inviting me out before I was discharged. I was pleased with the results of my breast augmentation. My being quiet helped calm my mother.

"Madison, the only reason you see your father's faults is because you're exactly like him."

That was a lie! She needed medication. "What have I stolen, Mother? And you can't compare my cheating once to all the times he's taken money out of our pockets and put pussy on payroll. Where are your friends, Mama? Did you get rid of them because Papa was sexing them too?" I regretted what I'd said but like having my son, I couldn't take it back.

Rosalee leapt from her seat, grabbed her purse. "I don't want to be alone and I don't want to start over. That's why I'm staying with your father." Her voice escalated. "You have implants. I don't. What man is going to want me at my age with no breasts?"

My mother started crying. I should've consoled her but didn't. Were her reasons to stay good ones? She stood there waiting for a response that wasn't going to come. I was tired. Of listening. Tired of caring.

She'd calm down. "Madison, at least I never lied to Johnny the way you're lying to Chicago." Mother put her hand on the doorknob, then said, "If you don't tell Chicago the baby isn't his, I will."

The second the door closed, I exhaled. I wasn't telling anyone what my daddy had done. I called my husband.

Roosevelt answered, "Hey, Madison. How are you?" His tone was flat.

"Can you come visit me?"

"I don't have time. I'm preparing for an away game this upcoming weekend. You home yet?"

"No, in a lot of pain though."

"You should be better in a few days. Zach is doing great. I know you didn't ask."

"A few months," I reminded him.

"So you say. I've got to go. Take care of yourself."

"Roose—" He'd ended the call? "Hello." I looked at my caller ID. His name and number were gone.

Papa had ruined my hopes of convincing myself that Roosevelt was Zach's father. How was I to make certain this secret remained? Well, I had four weeks to figure something out.

Knock. Knock.

"Come in," I called from my bed. I could get up. I didn't want to. I wasn't expecting anyone.

"Hello, dear. How are you feeling?" Helen asked. "Forgive us for not calling first."

The light of my life was in her arms. I got out of bed, took Zach, and kissed his little face a dozen times. I wasn't surprised Helen hadn't called. Roosevelt had given her my cell number after he'd proposed but Helen hadn't called me once.

"These are for you," Martin said placing a red vase filled with white long-stemmed roses on a table in the corner. He placed a diaper bag next to the vase. "Chicago couldn't come but he wanted us to bring the baby."

I cuddled Zach to my new breasts then smelled the flowers. "Oh, thank you so much," I said.

Helen sat in a chair beside the bed. Martin dragged the other seat next to his wife. I stood in the middle of the floor. They looked at me. For a second, my guilty secret haunted me.

"How are you, dear?" Helen was dressed in a yellow tapered long-sleeved dress that stopped slightly below her knees. The pink and purple three-inch heels coordinated well with her pink diamond earrings.

Sitting on the side of the bed, I rocked Zach. "I'm much better now. Thanks for bringing my baby to visit. I miss him so much." I kissed him again then stared at him.

I unwrapped his blanket and placed it on the bed. Zach felt as though he'd gained a few ounces and grown almost a half inch. I pressed my lips to his foot. He smiled. "Mommy loves you."

Helen's eyes shifted to the corners toward Martin then back at me. "What do you want from our son?"

Zach laughed but her question wasn't funny to me. "What do you mean?"

"Dear, you're a smart girl. We know our son wants you out of his house."

"Our house," I retorted.

She looked at Zach, then at me. "I'm giving you one last chance to name your price. If you don't, once we walk out of that door," she said pointing, "You'll have to fight it out in court."

Martin said, "You don't love Chicago. Do the right thing and let our son go. We're prepared to make you comfortable, give you back your company, and take care of our grandson."

Helen focused on Zach, raised her brows, looked at her husband, then sighed heavily.

What would I do without Roosevelt? "I have to discuss this with Roosevelt."

"Your augmentation won you an extension, dear, but it's not going to win back your husband. Only love can do that and you're incapable."

"If the two of you came here to insult me, you can leave." I wasn't ready to end my time with Zach but I'd had enough of Roosevelt's parents.

Martin stood, reached for my baby. Helen touched his arm. "He's where he belongs. Let him stay with his mother. Let's go."

CHAPTER 35

Granville

Thanks to Sindy, I was ballin'!

For the first time in my life, I was going to have a personal banker. Next time I saw her I'd kiss her feet. That might not be a good idea. What if she kicked me? Her hand was better. Yeah, that was what I'd do.

I rolled around in the king-size bed. A two-bedroom fully furnished condo? For me? She'd called and said I didn't have to clean up after myself, a maid would come by and do it. The Jacuzzi tub was the biggest I'd seen and the first large enough for me to fit in without having to have my knees touch my chest.

Beaux had to go but he could come back tomorrow. He wanted to stay but I had plans to get me some pussy. Tonight, I had to fuck a woman or my balls were going to explode. Meeting Mahogany, she was meant for me. I'd invited her over for dinner. The table was already set with more plates and forks than I'd seen. Growing up we had

IF YOU DON'T KNOW ME

Pappadeaux's fried fish platter was in the oven but I hadn't heated it up. I'd wait until she got here. I hoped Mahogany didn't fake on me and not show up. I'd kept busy to keep from jacking off. I had to have her. The banana pudding was in the refrigerator. She could eat after I was done eating her.

"You are the man, dude!" I stared in the mirror. I was sexy as hell. Tomorrow I was going to a tailor to get fitted for some new rags. Folding my arms over my naked chest, I smiled swinging my big dick. It slapped one thigh then the other. Since I knew I didn't have HIV, she was going to get all of this raw meat.

For a moment I got sad thinking about Madison and our son. Maybe we'd never be a family. I dressed in blue jeans and a button-down shirt, put on one of the colognes that came with the condo, then stepped into my cowboy boots. Didn't want to scare my new girl away with my ugly feet.

The doorbell buzzed. I straightened my collar. Unfastened two more buttons so she could see my chest, then opened the door.

"Wow!" My tongue fell out of my mouth. I jerked it in. I started breathing heavy. "Whoa."

Mahogany had changed from blue jeans to a little black dress. Now I saw why they called it little.

"Yum, come in." I closed the door then stared at her. "I'm glad you made it. Welcome to my home."

"This is nice. What do you do?"

"I'm an investor." I had to say something. She couldn't prove that I wasn't. Relationships were supposed to be about trust anyway.

"That's cool. I figured you owned a company or something. Two thousand dollars was a lot to give a stranger. Thanks."

"Don't mention it."

I knew this condo was on lease but she didn't. She had on high red heels with gold ankle straps; that dress hugged her booty, and showed off her breasts. I hadn't noticed at the restaurant that her twins were fully grown. She opened her arms. "Thanks for your generosity. You are heaven sent."

Me?

Mahogany continued, "You don't know it but you saved me from getting evicted. I'd stopped by the Breakfast Klub, didn't have enough money to buy something to eat. I got tea because the refills are free. I sat there praying trying to figure out what to do . . . and then you came and . . ." She started crying.

I couldn't remember the last time a woman hugged me like she really appreciated me. I wrapped my arms around her waist. She smelled amazing. I got hard wood and didn't want to let go.

Mahogany held me like I was her man. Never letting me go, she gave me a light kiss on my lips. Opening my mouth, I covered hers. When she didn't pull away, I let my saliva pour into her mouth. Loretta hated my wet kisses.

My hands slid from her waist to her booty. My fingers were full of what cheerleaders called "spirit." Was this how women treated men with money? I could get used to this shit. But I was a one-woman man.

"Yum, yum," I growled. "I'm hungry."

"Me too," Mahogany said unbuckling my belt.

Oh, damn! I didn't have to ask. I hoped she wasn't doing this strictly 'cause of the money. I loved her. She kissed my chest, then slowly opened my shirt one button at a time. I held her hand, then led her to my master bedroom. I wanted to be what Mama called "a gentleman," but my dick was about to burst.

"This is sizzling," she said, easing her dress over her head.

Crossing my fingers, I thought, *Please let her have pussy hairs.*

The red bra and matching thong were like them porn stars' and strippers' kind. "You're fucking hot!" I told her, removing my boots, jeans, and shirt. I threw all of that on the floor. When I took off my boxers, her eyes got big.

"Whoa, big daddy!"

"It's not too much for you is it?" I didn't like when a woman complained about I was too much.

"I love it." She sat on the bed and motioned for me to come closer.

The second she touched me, my dick grew to at least nine inches. She licked my head and I swore another inch popped out. She put her mouth on me and I pushed my head in as far as I could. I didn't mean to be rude. I couldn't help myself.

"Aw, fuck!" My cum came one wave after another.

She drooled on my shaft then massaged me. "Lay down on your back."

"I'm sorry. I didn't mean to—"

Mahogany straddled then kissed me. "We've only begun. This big ol' thing can work hard and soft."

Squeezing my dick right above my nuts, she licked her fingers, wet her pussy, then said, "Oh my God! You feel amazing, big daddy, I hope you don't think I do this all the time but you were so nice to me."

Her hips rocked back and forth. She cupped her breasts, pinched her nipples, then touched herself down there.

"You got me. I got you. Your dick is so big and good, daddy, I can stay on top of you all night. At least you not like the other guys that want to sex me for free."

I held her hips. "Don't tell me you one of them street girls." Even if Mama was dead, I still had to have a woman I would've been able to take home to her.

She sat still. "What you call men that use women for sex? Or the ones that hit me? And raped me? Or the one that got me pregnant and said it wasn't his?"

Mahogany hadn't answered my question. "All that happened to you while you were on the street?"

Lifting her leg, she said, "No, when I was in a group home. I see you like all the rest. Only difference you don't mind paying for what you get."

When she lifted her hips, I held her. "No, I didn't mean it like that. Don't leave me."

"You sure you want me to stay, big daddy?"

She called me big daddy a lot. Wow! "Will you marry me?" I asked.

She nodded. Rocked. Circled her nipple with her fingernail while touching herself down there with her other hand. She might not be a street girl but she sure liked her body. Me too.

I came again. She kept rolling her hips.

Tomorrow, I was buying her an engagement ring.

CHAPTER 36

Chicago

Was I wrong for not visiting Madison?
I'd slept well in my bed the last two nights
without her being here. I woke up to a text: Thanks
for having your mother bring Zach by yesterday. She
left him with me. I thought she wasn't coming back.
A few hours later she picked him up. We'll be home
in two days. We love you.

I texted back: Do not come to my condo.

Let's not create a messy media affair. We're not
divorced yet. See you in two days.

There was no need to respond. Madison only
gave a damn about Madison. I went to the kitchen,
got a black garbage bag, and put it on the bed. I
opened all of my drawers and tossed padded bras,
panties, and nighties, in the bag. I dug deep underneath my underwear, then held up a garter.

"I'm glad she never wore this." I stuffed it in
with the rest of her things. Maybe she'd brought it
hoping Sindy would've found it.

Zach's clothes, playpen, diapers, and crib could

stay. All of his belongings could remain long as Madison didn't come by claiming she needed them. If she did that, I was packing all of his items and buying whatever he needed. That dude was my heart.

Some women were pathological liars. Madison ranked at the top. She couldn't tell the truth unless her life depended on it. The finale was her lying about the recovery period for her surgery. Closing the curtains on her circus act.

My doorbell buzzed. I closed the drawers. The concierge hadn't called. It was probably Chaz.

I opened the door. A tall white man with blond hair and blue eyes stood before me. Beside him was a young man almost his height. They must have the wrong unit.

"Can I help you?"

"Roosevelt 'Chicago' DuBois, I'm Nyle Carter," he said extending his hand.

Looking at his hand, I didn't offer mine. He was a stranger, knocking on my door unannounced. "I'm going to ask you one more time before I close my door. How can I help you?"

"Of course. This is my son, Landry." The young man didn't offer a greeting.

His father said, "I'd like to buy your condo for my son. He's going to Texas State and needs a place to live."

Standing on my side of the threshold, I leaned into the hallway expecting to see cameras. I laughed. People in Houston were doing more of this offering to buy properties from homeowners for cash when the properties weren't listed but this had to be a joke.

"Madison sent you?"

"I'm serious, sir."

"Me too. I have a meeting to go to," I said motioning to close the door.

Chaz walked up. "Who's this? You ready to roll?"

"Nyle and son Landry, meet my brother Chaz. Chaz, I don't know them."

"Then let's go," Chaz said. "I don't know them either."

Nyle extended his hand, "Thanks for your time. If you change your mind, I have a cashier's check here with your name on it for two million dollars."

Landry's face remained expressionless.

Chaz raised his brows. "For?"

"I'd like to buy your brother's condo for my son," Nyle explained.

He didn't seem desperate. His son hadn't spoken a word.

"Give us a moment," Chaz said closing the door. "This is perfect. Have your lawyer find out if it's legit. Sell the place. Stay with me."

We were not in college. I did not want to share a two-bedroom condo with my brother and his woman. I rubbed my hand over my mouth, then showed Chaz my text messages from Madison.

"Make sure it's not a scam. If it's not, I say let it go for the offered price."

"I'll think about it," I said opening the door.

"Nyle, right?"

I shook his hand. Locking my door, I told them, "Walk with me. How'd you get to my front door without being announced?" I asked getting on the elevator.

Before he answered, the door opened on the

fifth floor. A tall beautiful woman wearing a short dress that was more suited for the evening instead of morning got on. She said, "I'll meet you in the lobby, big daddy."

Chaz smiled. I shook my head. It was bad business to talk in front of strangers. I remained quiet until we got off on the first floor.

"I'll order the car. You talk to Nyle," Chaz said walking outside to the valet.

"Let's move to a private area," I said relocating to the corner of the lobby so we could get away from the attractive woman. She walked outside.

"Two million, huh?"

"All-cash transaction. We can get started today. It can be done by tomorrow."

"What do you do?" I asked him.

"I'm an attorney."

"Why my place?"

"I figured a man like you, being the GM of our football team, was a businessman first. And my boy has already started college. I want to move him out of the dorm." He took a few steps, shifted his back toward the entrance door, and stood beside me. "Here's my card."

Facing the entrance, I looked for Chaz's black BMW. A black Super Duty truck was parked in front. The beautiful girl who was on the elevator was in the passenger seat.

Probably a jump-off of one of the ballers living in the building but I hadn't seen that truck before. It wasn't unusual not to see most of the home-owners as many, like myself, didn't linger.

The double frosted doors parted and I couldn't

believe the man who had shot me three times exited through the lobby, got in the truck with the woman, and drove off.

Chaz raced inside. "Did you see that shit?"

I nodded.

"Sell your fucking unit, man."

CHAPTER 37

Sindy

Helen called yesterday ranting, "Madison is a worldly surly woman with one foot on earth and the other ball and chained to the devil. I left that baby with her and I'm not going back to get it. Hurry up and get proof that's not my grandson."

"This is what we want. You have to be patient," I told her.

She retorted, "Until we know the truth, I'm done babysitting!"

We hadn't received the results. Helen was over-reacting. Madison believing she had the DuBoises convinced Zach was Roosevelt's son was to our advantage. Hopefully, she wasn't right.

I insisted, "You have to go get the baby. If you don't, Madison wins. We have to present our test when she least expects it."

Opposition from Helen could've ruined my plan to reunite with Roosevelt. She'd coerced me into following through with getting Granville to take the test. I'd done that. I refused to allow Helen to quit on me. If we gave Madison reason to become suspicious, she'd come up with another lie to tell Roosevelt.

Helen would never have to thank me for what she'd never know. I doubt she would've agreed with my buying Roosevelt's condo or my having moved Granville into The Royalton.

Sitting in my car in the stadium's parking lot, I refreshed my perfume and retouched my ruby lipstick. I combed my hair with my fingers, then swept it over my left shoulder.

A text came in from Nyle: Sold!

I smiled. Each victory was essential. I replied to Nyle: Great job! Get the keys. Bring them to my house and pick up your check today. $120k!

He texted: Thanks!

A second text came from my contact at the laboratory: Confirmed, Granville Washington is *not* the biological father. Will proceed as agreed.

Holding my breath, I felt as though my heart had stopped beating. Was he serious? That bitch Madison Tyler was right and I was wrong! That baby looked exactly like Granville. Was Madison a step ahead of me? Was my contact hers too?

I'd paid to have the results changed if necessary to show Roosevelt wasn't the daddy. Dear God, now I had to follow through. Madison and I were alike in many ways but she was more of a match for me than I'd thought.

Taking care of Nyle was a priority. The 6 percent commission was Nyle's from the beginning but he had to earn it. The same held true for my employees. Bonuses were an incentive to work harder. The more my nonprofit made, the more I compensated my workers at the end of the fiscal year. Some believed not-for-profits didn't turn a profit. That was a myth and the reason a lot of successful people started their own organizations.

I responded to my lab contact: On my way to pick up both sealed results today.

An unexpected call registered on my phone. I answered, "I'm surprised to hear from you."

"I know. Can you stop by my office?" he asked.

"When?"

"Now, if you can."

"I'm on my way. Bye," I said. This was the confirmation I needed to continue my plan. He'd called asking to see me. I was already at his location to purchase game tickets. I'd prayed he see me. Maybe he had seen my car and that was why he called. It didn't matter. I was not going to stall and pretend our hearts weren't in sync. They were.

Heading into the stadium, I wondered what Roosevelt wanted to discuss. I prayed he didn't know the deed to his condo was being transferred from Nyle Carter to me first thing in the morning.

I'd parked in the reserved spot where I used to when attending the games. If all went well, soon I'd be the new Mrs. DuBois and this space would permanently become mine.

Flipping down the visor, I touched up all of my make-up, dabbed perfume behind each ear, then curled my hair into a bun. The lemon sunshine long-sleeved dress hugged my body. I remotely locked my car, then headed to the second floor.

"He's expecting you," the receptionist said.

Slowly, I opened the door. "Hi there."

Roosevelt looked up from his computer. His eyes caressed every inch of my body. "You look stunning," he said heading toward me.

I opened my arms. He stepped between them. We hugged. His embrace was strong. I rubbed his back.

"I miss that," he said.

"I miss you," I replied.

The unexpected happened when tears streamed down my face. I started crying. This was not supposed to be how I reacted. I couldn't stop. I loved this man so much.

"I love you too," he said as though he'd read my mind. Roosevelt took a step back. "Have a seat. Please. I need to ask a favor of you. If you say no, I'll understand." He scooted the chair at his conference table next to mine.

I inhaled deeply, then exhaled. I had no idea what was going to come out of his mouth but I knew I wanted my tongue between his lips.

"Call it foolish but I sold my condo. I have movers packing my things as we speak but—" He paused. I waited for him to say something but he became quiet.

I said, "But," praying he wasn't getting ready to say, "I'm moving in with Madison and I wanted you to know."

Men did say foolish things at the worst times. I closed my eyes, slowly inhaled, then stared at him in silence.

"I feel silly asking you this but I have an away game coming up. I don't want to stay with my parents. I could stay with Chaz but the dude that shot me . . ." His words trailed off. Tears flooded his eyes.

I dried them. I wanted him to ask. I needed him to ask me. But I didn't want to ruin the moment.

How would he feel if he knew I intentionally moved Granville in order to get Madison out? Not him.

"Granville moved into my building. This is all so strange but I can't go back there. I might kill that dude if I see him again."

"You're bigger than this. Don't let anyone push you to do anything that's out of your character." I'd avoided saying Granville's name. And while I'd love to say all he'd done for Madison was uncharacteristic, I didn't believe it was.

"You're right. That's what I miss about you. You have this amazingly calming effect on me."

A part of me wanted to ask him about his intentions with Madison. This wasn't the time. Gently, I rubbed his thigh.

"Sindy, is it okay if I stay at your house for a few weeks? It's just until my divorce is final. Then my Realtor can find me a home that I like. I'll pay rent. I can stay in one of your guest rooms, I—"

I pressed my lips to his. "Yes, you can stay with me." I didn't add, "As long as you'd like." I did let him know, "I'll leave a set of keys for you on the table in the foyer."

"How am I supposed to get in?"

"I'll text you the access code to the gate and the code to unlock my front door."

Roosevelt's mouth opened when his lips touched mine. He whispered, "I love you, Sindy."

I thought about showing him how much the sentiments were mutual by unzipping his pants and giving him an amazing blow job. There was no tablecloth to hide under. I didn't want to pretend. He had a mind-blowing fellatio session coming soon. Maybe. But not until I knew what his intentions were with Madison. What if he'd planned on moving her into his new home? I'd be the one who'd feel foolish. I couldn't assume I knew his intentions.

This moment was special. I didn't want to miss it thinking about things that hadn't and may never happen.

"I love you too, Roosevelt. See you tonight."

When I walked out, a man with a briefcase and a bodyguard entered his office.

Roosevelt called out, "Chaz, he's here," then said to the two men, "Perfect timing."

CHAPTER 38

Granville

*G*oing to the courthouse and we're going to get married.

I sang that from the second I opened my eyes. I was proud. Finally, I was going to have me a beautiful wife who loved me and wanted to have my babies. When two people loved one another and enjoyed the same things, getting hitched was a nobrainer. All that dating for years then breaking up made no sense to me. Mama would've loved my fiancée.

Mahogany was in the bed reading a book. Her twenty-five-years-young chocolate cupcakes made me crave squeezing her perky breasts. I was fortysix now. My birthday passed while I was locked up. That was okay. Celebrations at my age were silly. No friends. One brother. Who'd come to my party?

Sitting next to her I propped my feet up. "When I'm gon' meet your mom and dad?"

Both of her real parents were younger than me. Her foster folks were beyond my age. All those grown ups and my woman was starving. Not any more. Maybe she didn't talk much about them 'cause they wouldn't approve of me. Marrying Mahogany first was best. We were going to have what my parents had. One husband. One wife. No divorce.

Staring at the pages, she answered, "Soon. I guess. Our getting married on such short notice, my mom couldn't take time off from her job in Paris."

It didn't matter whom she was talking about. I said, "Bonjour." I raised my brows. "We can go visit her next week or whenever you're ready. I've never been to France."

"Me either. You have a passport? I don't."

"We can get one after the wedding."

"Okay," she said reading her book again. "But I meant Paris, Texas. We can still get those passports though."

We laughed. She had a sense of humor like mine.

I needed some attention. I pulled down the covers and buried my face in her sweet pussy hairs, then said, "Morning, dear."

All of my good qualities that annoyed Loretta made my woman crazy about me. If I didn't have that protective order looming over my head, I'd paint "Just Married" on the back window of my Super Duty, park in front of Loretta's house, then lean on my horn until she came outside. Mahogany wasn't annoyed with my raspy voice, juicy kisses, yellow teeth, or ugly feet.

"I love being your breakfast in bed, big daddy." She put her book on the nightstand then rubbed my bald head.

Her touch made me feel like a little boy. I thought about Zach and became sad. She fingered my ears. A funny feeling inside my stomach made me harder. My dick drooled on the sheet. It was sticky.

"Yum. Yum," I groaned lapping her up.

I slid my tongue from her asshole and stroked all the way up to her pubic hairs. I loved her pussy hairs. Madison could give her smooth hairless stuff to some other dude. No more rides for her. One day she'd see she missed out on a good man.

My tongue traded places with my dick. I rubbed my slippery precum with her wetness. "Will you have my baby?" I asked Mahogany.

"Of course, big daddy. I already told you I would. What woman wouldn't want to have your child? If it's a boy we're going to name him Granville Washington the second."

I preferred "junior" but "the second" was all right long as he was mine. If we got pregnant today, Zach and Granville could grow up together. "And if it's a girl."

"We gon' name her Sarah Lee Mahogany Washington."

I almost cried. "Really? You'd name our daughter after my mother?"

Kissing my tears, she said, "Yes, really."

My hardness softened with my heart. "Can we start working on it now?"

"With this rock you put on my finger, you'd better give me that dick and stop playing," she said holding up the ten-thousand-dollar rock I'd gladly given her,

It felt good to be a big baller. "Would you love me if I didn't have any money? Well, I don't mean broke. You know. Say, if I made two thousand."

"A what?" she asked.

"A year?"

Mahogany shook her head. "You wouldn't love yourself if you worked all year for only two g's."

She was right. I was at a hundred thou before Manny let me go. Twelve hundred equaled one hundred a month. I didn't want to do the math on that. But my mama could make twenty dollars last a week. Not from shopping off the back of the Mexican food truck that drove through our neighborhood. Mama would, when she had to, buy Camilla beans, a ten-pound bag of rice, and big packs of chicken—legs and thighs. They were cheaper. All that for less than fifteen dollars a week would keep our bellies full.

"Big daddy?"

"Yes."

"Since you have a lot of money, can I quit my job *after* we get married?"

"When?" I asked.

"Today."

Oh, she meant immediately.

I never wanted my wife to work. Her job was taking care of me. How did I get so lucky with her? I should thank Charles. If I hadn't gone to see him . . . wait. I should thank Sindy. She was the one who'd given me the dough.

"Okay." I told her, "Why not?" I could afford her.

I'd bought Loretta a ring and she refused to take it. I wanted to marry Madison so we could be a family and raise our son. But she rejected me and lied about Zach not being mine. Well, she can keep him. I was about to make another boy.

Mahogany spread her legs wide enough for me

to get close. I rubbed my dick on her clit, then I put my head in.

"Mmm," she moaned making my wood harder.

Pushing, I gave her some more dick. An inch at a time, I worked my head in so deep I couldn't go any farther. This was the best pussy I ever had. I could stay here until I died.

"Don't move," she said grinding her hips up to mine.

Her round butt felt like butter. Her pussy tasted like vanilla ice cream.

"How you do that?" I asked.

"Do what, big daddy?" she asked.

"Squeeze my dick like that?"

"Like this?" she asked squeezing tighter. She didn't let go until she said, "Or like this?"

This time her pussy rippled up and down my wood. I stared at her. She did it again.

"Fuck! Motherfucker!" I screamed like a bitch, then pulled back.

She grabbed my hips. Guided me into her. "Don't spill my seeds, big daddy. I am going to have your baby."

I didn't care why she was so in love with me. I was happy to have a woman treat me special.

Holding her legs over her head, she said, "Go take your shower and get dressed for our ceremony. I'ma need a few minutes before I get up." She wiggled her ring finger.

"I love you, Mahogany."

"I love you too, big daddy."

Big daddy. She called me big daddy!

"I'ma need some more of that dick when we get back and again tonight so don't play with my shit while you're in the shower."

Mahogany could sex me four to five times a day since she never had to go back to work. Hell, she might be pregnant with my baby already. On the way from the courthouse I was gonna buy her a pregnancy test.

Switching the water from warm to hot, I shouted, "Yahoo! I got me a wife!"

CHAPTER 39

Madison

"You sure you don't need me to pick you up?"

"I'm sure. Thanks for offering."

Tisha was a true friend. She'd come to visit a few times during my recovery. Brought me home-cooked vegetables, brown rice, and grilled chicken for dinner last night.

"I'll stop at Rice and get you groceries. Text me your list and I'll come by and help with Zach. Call me when you get settled. I love you."

"I'll be at the condo. I could use the company more than anything. I love you too. Bye."

Tears streamed down my face. When was the last time anyone had said "I love you" to me? Sitting on the side of my bed, I waited for my ride to arrive. The peach maxidress I wore had elbow-length sleeves and loosely draped my body. I didn't have on a bra but there was an extra built-in layer covering my protruding nipples.

Earlier, Roosevelt had said, "I can't pick you up. I have to fly out for a game today."

That, I understood. His not coming to see me the entire time hurt. Regardless of what he was doing with Sindy, he was still my husband and I needed him. We needed him. He didn't have to tell me, "Go home when you get out. To your house."

Every time my hospital room door opened, I'd hoped it was Roosevelt. Maybe he'd take a later flight and make time to come pick me up today.

The door opened. It wasn't my husband but I was happy to see the woman who'd walked in.

"Helen, thanks for coming to get me and bringing my baby."

The relationship with my parents was strained, since their last visit at the hospital. Seemed like Papa was trying to destroy me. The way he'd treated me was cruel. Mama thought I was mean-spirited. Papa would always be my father but there was no guarantee he'd stay married to Mama. He'd said what he had to because he needed my mother more than she needed him. Maybe that wasn't true but Tisha believed a person's core character didn't change. I didn't care much for either of my parents and had reason to feel that way. Helen was proving herself more of a caring mother-in-law than Roosevelt was a husband.

"My pleasure, dear. Zach is such a joy. Look at him." She held him closer to me.

There was something peculiar about the way she'd said, "Look at him."

I tickled his foot, then held him in my arms. "I don't know what I would've done without you guys. Thanks to you too, Martin."

He shook his head, picked up my suitcase. "I'll be out front in my car in the waiting area."

"Don't mind him, dear. He's in a hurry for us to

get to George Bush International to catch our flight to see our football team play. Roosevelt left this morning. Our flight isn't for another two hours. Our bags are packed and the driver is at our house waiting. Martin is excited. He's never missed a game since Chicago has been managing the team."

Helen had become nicer. I welcomed her attention and affection.

"The doctor did an amazing job. Would you like to see my new ones?" I asked her.

She stared at my breasts then looked at me. "No. Let's go."

I wasn't trying to make them miss their flight. Roosevelt hadn't invited me to any of the away games since we'd met. Maybe if I'd had this closeness with his mother sooner, I would've never had sex with Granville. My relationship with Roosevelt wouldn't have been tested. My father's tampering with the paternity came to mind.

"Dear, if you don't get moving, you'll have to call your parents to come get you."

"Oh, yeah. I apologize for asking you that," I said carrying Zach. I'd already signed my discharge papers.

My breasts were amazingly beautiful. I'd had my implants underneath the muscles. The incisions were underneath and barely visible. My doctor had done an impeccable job.

Leaving the room, I told Helen, "You can drop us off at The Royalton. My mother is on her way."

"Of course dear. I'll be glad to take you there."

I sat on the back next to Zach in his car seat. The drive from the hospital to the condo was quiet. Martin parked in front of the building. The valet hurried to him, handed him a ticket.

"That won't be necessary, young man. Just dropping her off," Martin said. "I'm not missing our flight, Helen, stay in the car. I'll be right back." He got my suitcase from the trunk.

Helen got out of the car, took Zach from the car seat. "I can help, Martin. I got the baby."

Entering the lobby, the concierge asked, "May I help you, Mrs. Tyler?"

I rolled my eyes at him, then said, "Mrs. DuBois." If my husband insisted on divorcing me, I was keeping the last name.

"Roosevelt is away, dear," Helen replied. "We're just seeing Madison to his front door."

The man shook his head.

"What's wrong with you? First you call me by the incorrect name. Now you're not speaking at all. I'm reporting you." I told him, "Say something."

My heart raced. Roosevelt told me he didn't want me here but he couldn't deny his son.

Staring at my breasts, the concierge finally said, "Roosevelt 'Chicago' DuBois?"

The double frosted doors parted. Someone I hadn't seen before exited.

While the doors were still open, Martin lamented, "I don't have time for this. Let's go up."

"To go where?" the concierge asked. His eyes lowered.

I wasn't offended by his staring, I was pissed off with his unprofessionalism. "I'm up here. What is wrong with you, little boy? To my husband's condo!" I shouted.

Zach started crying as my mother walked into the lobby. She took my baby from Helen. "Madison, what's the problem? I could hear you outside."

The little boy said, "Chicago sold his unit yesterday. He doesn't live here anymore."

"You're lying," I said moving closer to him. Between clenched teeth, I hissed, "I know he told you to say that so you wouldn't let us in. I'm going to pretend I didn't hear your last comment. For the last time, let me in." I was two seconds from slapping this guy.

"There must be an error in your system. My son didn't sell his place. If he had, we would've known. It's okay to let her and the baby go up," Helen said. "I'll see my son later and have him call to straighten this out."

"Helen, I don't have time for this. I'm going to call him now," Martin said stepping outside.

"I came here directly from the hospital." Since nothing else was working, I opened my bag and showed him my discharge papers. "Please let me up. We'll clear up this misunderstanding later," I told the concierge, trying to sound apologetic.

"No disrespect. I'm telling you. Roosevelt 'Chicago' DuBois sold his condominium."

Sarcastically, I asked, "What about Chaz?"

"What about him?"

"He sold his too?"

"That's confidential, ma'am."

Okay, now he was fucking with me.

"Fancy seeing you guys here."

I turned toward the familiar voice. Sindy Singleton stood dressed in a vibrant green dress. Martin reentered the lobby.

Sindy hugged Helen, then Martin. She scanned me from head to toe and back then smiled. "Good boob job, Madison. I'm sure those will come in handy."

Instantly, I felt underdressed. The first thing I was doing when I got upstairs was putting on my sexiest dress and heels.

"What are you doing here?" I asked her.

"I was going to ask you the same question. But, there's no need."

"I live here," I told her. I wanted to add the word bitch but not in front of Roosevelt's parents and my mother.

My mom said, "Madison, why don't you and the baby come home with me until you figure this situation out."

"And deal with Papa? No thanks, Mama."

"I have to go upstairs and pack for my flight," Sindy said winking at Helen. "Can't miss kickoff. See you guys at the game tonight."

Sindy looked at the concierge. He opened the double frosted doors. Sindy entered and Granville walked out with this gorgeous woman on his arm.

I overheard Sindy tell Granville, "Your son is here," before she disappeared behind the closing doors.

"Why in the hell are you here?" I asked him.

"He lives here," the concierge said.

"Oh, now you can talk? Shut up!" I told him. What in the fuck was going on?

Granville stared at Zach. "He is mine. I knew it."

The woman standing beside him cleared her throat. "Big daddy, who is she?"

He had that stupid grin on his face. Desperately I wanted to slap it off.

"Mahogany, this is Madison. The woman I told you about. Madison, this is my wife, Mahogany Washington."

"Your what? In your dreams." I laughed.

"Don't talk to big daddy that way." Mahogany stared at my baby. "He does look exactly like you. He has your cheeks. Your nose. And your hands."

Granville stuck out his chest. I wanted to push him away from me.

"Helen," Martin said, "He sold the condo to some guy named Nyle Carter." He stared at Granville. Granville stared back. "Helen, let's get the hell out of here before I kill that"—his voice escalated— "son of a bitch!"

Helen smiled at me. "That Sindy Singleton is a smart girl. Good seeing you, dear. Take care of yourself. Same to you, Mrs. Tyler. It is still Mrs., right?"

My mom narrowed her eyes at Helen's back, then mumbled, "I'm not Madison. Don't disrespect me again."

I shouted, "Mom, she didn't hear you."

Why couldn't my mother defend me? She was always passive. That was why I had to be aggressive all my life. I was tired of being the b-i-t-c-h.

Martin took Helen by the hand and escorted her out the door. I watched in disbelief as they sped off. This had to be a joke. I scanned the lobby; there had to be hidden cameras somewhere. "Okay, you can come out now!" Any moment I expected cameramen to appear.

"Mrs. Tyler, I'm going to have to ask you to leave," the concierge said.

"Shut the hell up!" I told him. No one asked for his opinion.

Zach screamed.

"Can I hold him?" Mahogany asked taking my baby out of my mother's arms. "Hush little baby," she sang and her voice sounded like an angel. "Look at his eyes, and his mouth and his big head." She gently touched my baby's head and he stopped crying. "Here, hold him," she said handing my baby to Granville.

Zach kicked and smiled. He started cooing baby talk. Granville's face lit up with the biggest smile ever. He stood tall, squared his shoulders.

"Hi, son. Daddy loves you, bro."

What the hell was going on? I was shocked.

The frosted doors parted. Sindy exited rolling a suitcase. "He's yours, Granville," she said handing him a note before strolling out the lobby door. The valet opened her car door; she got in her cute little Bentley and left.

"Can we keep him?" Mahogany asked.

My child was not up for adoption. Hmm. I took my baby from Granville. "Mama, let's go."

CHAPTER 40

Chicago

Selling my condo was the best decision I'd made. My stress level decreased significantly and I smiled more often. I was working on regaining my inner peace. Couldn't remember when I'd stopped my daily meditation and going to church on Sundays. Oh, yeah. It was after marriage, being shot, and a month-long recovery in the hospital that I'd stopped connecting with God regularly. I had to get back to sitting in silence and praying.

Couldn't say I understood why Adam bit the apple but I knew how a woman could be a major distraction. Didn't want to live without one in particular. Never wanted to be with the other.

Madison had called forty-two times earlier today. After I'd answered her first call and she yelled, "You moved that whore into our house!" I ignored the rest. Any person starting a conversation by screaming was not interested in what the other person had to say.

Wait until she found out where I was living. I

had to make sure that didn't happen before the divorce was final. I did not want a judge denying my parental rights because my ex-wife was angry at me for what she'd done. After our marriage was over, I did not care what Madison knew.

My soon-to-be ex had a house to go to. One that I'd paid off. She and Zach could stay with her parents if she needed someone to care for her. With her new breasts, Madison was going to have a lot more men to choose from. She'd best pray karma didn't bite her ass. I couldn't care less. If she wasn't desperately trying to win me back just to make me miserable, she could have another man. Hell, Madison could have another husband by Christmas.

The operations manager texted me. We're all set, baby! Let's get that W!

4sure I texted back.

Normally, I wouldn't claim a win until the game was over. I was turned up so high I felt like shouting and doing a praise dance. We were undefeated. I was about to become a free man. The woman I truly loved was back in my life. What could possibly go wrong? I wasn't asking. The question was rhetorical.

Ding-dong, ding-dong, the bell to my suite chimed. That could be one of the four people I was expecting. The second I opened the door and saw Sindy's angelic face, I said, "Thank you, Jesus," then told her, "You are so fine, woman."

Her red platform heels appeared higher. The sizzling red short-sleeved dress sparkling with blue rhinestones hugged all her curves. The scent of her cinnamon hair reminded me of a fresh ocean breeze. I wished I hadn't planned my honeymoon with Madison in Bora Bora. Taking Sindy there

after our wedding would be a honeymoon headache.

"It's good to see you too. I thought I'd come a
little early. Hope that's okay."

Inviting her in, gently I pulled her close to my
body. Inhaled her fragrances. We stood in a moment of oneness. Her energy penetrated my entire
body like a head-to-toe orgasm. Becoming sexually
aroused wasn't intentional. Slowly my shaft grew
longer, wider, and harder.

"I like," she whispered, then meshed her lips to
my ear. *Ah, the simple pleasures of life.*

Stepping back, there wasn't enough time to un-
fasten my pants. I pressed my fingers against the
base of my dick to keep from cumming. "Whew!
That was close. I have a bottle of champagne on
ice." A drink would help relax me and settle my
raging appetite. I'd had everything set up in the
living room. "Have a seat while I get you a drink."

I had to sex this woman. Hopefully, tonight. I
filled her flute, then mine.

Sindy whispered, "Roosevelt."

"Yes," I answered, turning to look at her. "Oh,
my God."

I placed the bottle on the table. Standing, be-
holding the most beautiful naked woman I'd ever
seen, I wished I were a painter and she was my
model. I swear I didn't know where to start. Her
nipples, clit, or her toes. Her feet looked amazing!
Red tips with blue stones. I could kiss every part of
her.

"Come here," she said softly.

I was drawn to her. If Eve were this alluring, I
got it. "What are you doing to me?"

She unbuckled my pants and unzipped them,

then held my erection in her soft palm. I inhaled as much air as I could. My abs were on the verge of exploding.

Ding-dong, ding dong, softly played. I wanted to say, "Go away!"

"Roosevelt honey it's your mother."

"And father."

"And brother."

Of all the days for them to be early too. Damn!

In a matter of a minute we were both presentable. Sindy fingered her hair, then stood beside me. I kissed her. "To be continued," I said before opening the door. She winked then smiled.

"Hi honey. Hi Sindy," my mother said walking in.

My dad said, "Son, you are not going to believe our day. You definitely did the right thing by selling your place. We have more than enough space if you want to come back home for a while. Your grandfather would love to see more of you. You too, Chaz. I don't know what's going on with that Madison woman but she's up to no good, again."

"Not now, Martin. Chicago has to mentally prepare for his game," my mother said. "And you need to practice your belly breathing."

Thankful, and not, for Mom's interruption, I did not want to have a conversation in front of Sindy about Madison. "I'd like to toast."

I filled three more flutes. "Hey, Mom and Dad. How was your flight?" Chaz and I had flown in on the team's plane.

The family jeweler had come by our office the day Sindy had come to visit me. Collectively, I'd say we invested a hundred and fifty thousand on engagement rings for Numbiya and Sindy.

"Not nearly as entertaining as seeing the expression on Madison's face when—"

I redirected my attention to Sindy when she started coughing. "You okay, babe?"

My father said, "You can't even take you own advice, Helen. Son, why didn't you tell me?"

Mom shifted her eyes in my dad's direction. Madison was going to be a topic of discussion for the next eighteen years. Sindy could handle hearing my response.

"I wasn't going to sell but when I found out that Granville had moved in, I had to go."

"Go where?" my mother asked.

I kissed Sindy on the lips. "This gorgeous woman is letting me stay at her place until I buy a home."

My mom looked at Sindy, then raised her brow. Scanning back and forth between them, I knew my mother. Something was up.

Handing a glass of champagne to each of them, I said, "A toast to the most loving and caring women in my life." I meant that.

"We have to find a way to move that continuance date," my mom said sipping her drink. "I want you divorced from Madison immediately before she does whatever she's scheming to do."

Sindy barely placed her lips on her glass as she glanced at me. Her eyes shifted toward my mom. They clicked their glasses and smiled. I scanned back and forth again.

"Son, don't ask," my dad said. "I don't even want to know."

"Roosevelt, I have a confession," Sindy said. "I—"

Mom interrupted, "Look at the time. We'll see you at the game, sweetheart." She took Sindy's glass, sat it on the coffee table next to hers. My dad swallowed his last sip, put his flute by theirs, then hunched his shoulders. Chaz had been unusually quiet.

"Sindy, dear. You're riding with us. Let's go."

I laughed as they left. "I'll see you there, babe."

My parents were too protective. Sindy wasn't scandalous like Madison. Sindy probably wanted to tell them how much we love one another.

CHAPTER 41

Sindy

The game was a big W for my man and getting him back was an important win for me.

Defeating Madison was gone-with-the-wind fabulous. The spooked expression on her face when I entered The Royalton was worth two million dollars. Looking pathetic, she stood beside her mother, who was holding precious little Zach. If Madison hadn't cheated she would've been 100 percent sure that Roosevelt was indeed Zach's father. She made my leaving her on that curb easy.

I bet she felt another punch in her gut when she saw Granville had a gorgeous wife who adored him. Guess there really was someone for everyone. The note I'd given Granville had Madison's cell number on it. I'd gotten it from Helen, knowing Madison would never give Granville her contact info. Madison had lost the battle. I did not feel sorry for her. She was sorry. She was also a sore loser not to be underestimated. Hopefully, she'd move forward with her life and not contest the divorce.

Roosevelt would never have to forgive me for what he'd never know. Zach was his biological son. The only persons who knew the truth were the laboratory tech and me. Being tied to Madison the rest of our lives was not going to happen. I would give Roosevelt as many babies as he wanted.

After we settled into our seats, the flight attendant handed us flutes of champagne. Holding my glass, I stared out the window, glad Martin and Helen weren't with us. Helen could speculate forever but there was no way I was going to tell Roosevelt, Helen, or Martin the things I'd done. My confession was more like a statement. I'd planned to have them over to my house during the Christmas holiday, before New Year's Eve. Timing had to coincide with the football games. My preplanned celebration was trifold: the belated birth of Christ, Kwanzaa, and Roosevelt's divorce.

First, I had to complete what I'd started. Instead of transferring Roosevelt's condo into my name, I had a different plan. Once Granville's lease expired, he'd move out, and I could close that chapter of my life and seal the record.

"Babe, I'm so glad I have you back in my life," Roosevelt said touching my leg.

This was the first time I'd flown on the team's plane. Every seat was like being in first class. Chaz and Numbiya were seated across the aisle.

"I feel the same," I said. My heart wanted to express, "I love you," but I'd wait for him to say it first.

Roosevelt's job was to ensure everything for game day was in place. He resumed his online preparation for our upcoming home game.

It was no longer a secret to the players and

coaches that Roosevelt was temporarily residing at my home. Having him there was wonderful. His sleeping in the guest room wasn't what he preferred but I insisted. His argument of my sleeping in his bed when he had his condo was valid but I wasn't at his place every night.

Temptation was not my friend. I refused to give up my virginity until after I was married. Soon as the plane touched down at Bush International, Roosevelt retrieved my carry-on from the overhead compartment. I powered on my cell and texted Nyle.

I need another favor.

Glad he responded right away with Okay I typed: I want you to sell the condo. I'm not transferring it into my name.

Madison had probably already done a property search to find out who'd bought Roosevelt's condo. If my name were associated with the transaction, she'd have her attorney use that information against Roosevelt. Strange things happened in court and Madison could potentially benefit from Roosevelt's cohabitation with his mistress. I hated referring to myself as a mistress. Thank God, alienation of affection was not a Texas law. If it were, I knew she'd sue me. I had no intentions of suppressing my feelings for Roosevelt.

Another commission for me?

Definitely. Or you can pay me for it.

Consider it sold. I can't afford that place.

"Babe, we gotta go," Roosevelt said standing over me.

I texted Nyle a sad face with a teardrop. I was not generous to give away seven figures to anyone.

"Sindy, we have get to the office for our two

o'clock meeting, girlfriend. Let's go," Numbiya cheerfully said.

Chaz was good for her and she was great for him. Numbiya was always upbeat. Before she'd met Chaz, she was a happy woman. Being with him made her happier. That was the way life was meant to be. Men were supposed to make women better, not bitter. My girlfriend's personality was unlike mine. I was the serious, loving type. She was the jovial, loving woman who brought sunshine to everybody's life.

As I stood, another text registered. Your father had a heart attack. Come to Methodist now. The text came from my father's number.

I fell into my seat. When had that happened? I texted: Who is this? Call me, please.

Roosevelt sat beside me. "You okay? I know you're not pregnant," he said jokingly.

His comment was untimely and definitely not funny. "My dad had a heart attack."

"What? Where is he?"

Softly, I said, "Methodist." Looking at my phone, I saw there was no response to my question.

Numbiya stepped into the row behind me, then leaned over the seat. "What is it?"

Roosevelt responded, "Charles had a heart attack."

"Move," Numbiya said to Roosevelt. She held my arm, then lifted me up from the seat. "We've got to go."

"Babe, I'll have my driver take us straight to the hospital," Roosevelt said.

Chaz commented, "Take your time, bro. I'll hold it down at the office."

"I'm going with Sindy," Numbiya said still holding me up.

"Of course," Chaz said. He kissed Numbiya, then told her, "I love you. Call and let me know how he's doing."

Based on my girlfriend's "I love you too," obviously this wasn't their first time exchanging those three words.

Did my dad love my mom? Did Roosevelt love me? Madison? Or both of us? I definitely believed it was possible to be in love with more than one person at the same time.

Exiting the plane, Roosevelt led the way to baggage claim. His driver was there waiting. "We have an emergency. Come back and get our bags. We need to go to Methodist."

Despite our differences, I loved my father. Daddy was a fighter. I convinced myself, saying out loud, "He'll be fine."

"Yes, he will," Roosevelt said, then prayed, "Heavenly Father, We ask you watch over and protect Charles Singleton. Restore his health, oh Lord, and with each moment we pray he gets stronger."

Roosevelt held one hand, Numbiya held my other. My dad was a complicated man. If he died today or lived another fifty years, I wouldn't understand what made him devalue people's lives.

Siara came to mind. If Daddy died, I didn't want to tell my sister via Skype. Regardless of how she felt about my not meeting her family, I'd have to go to Paris. We'd have to handle the details for our father's estate together. His trust was in order. I'd made sure of that. Everything he owned was divided equally between my sister and me.

The driver parked in front of the Emergency entrance. Numbiya took charge. She found out where my dad was. We arrived at the nurses' station on his floor and were directed to his private room. His two bodyguards stood on opposite sides of the door.

"I'll wait out here," Numbiya said. She didn't like seeing sick or dead people.

Roosevelt held my hand. I was glad he had. I didn't want to go in alone. Slowly, I opened the door. Softly, I said, "Hey, Daddy," then waited for the nurse to complete his vitals.

If he were well, I would've called him Charles. Why did I wait until my father might be dying to care enough to respect him? He had tubes in his nose, an IV in the back of his hand, and a monitor attached to his heart. "When did this happen?" I asked.

Faintly, my dad said, "Yesterday. If you're trying to kill me, Sindy, by being disobedient, congratulations."

"Yesterday?" I opened the drawer on the stand beside his bed. Shuffling pens and paper side to side, then front and back, I asked, "Where's your phone?" If he died, I had to have it.

"I don't know. Why do you care?"

"I'm not going to allow you to leave here making me feel guilty. Where is it?"

I was more concerned with how Roosevelt felt about what my father had said than my dad's intentions. I was at a game cheering for my man and our team while my dad was in the hospital. I could've been anyplace else on earth and my father's outcome would be the same. Understanding I had no control of his health, I couldn't change a thing.

Death sometimes happened when we least expected it. Charles could've died without my having a chance to say good-bye and that would've been okay. If it was his time, God had made that decision, not me. When Madison had taken Roosevelt off of life support and he lived, that was God's decision too.

Roosevelt looked at Charles and said, "Hang in there, man," then walked out of the room.

The nurse looked at my dad, then asked me, "Can you step in the hallway for a moment."

I kissed my dad's forehead. "I'll be right back and you'd better be right here watching that television. If you haven't done so already," I told him, "Repent."

"Sindy," he said. This time his tone was affectionate.

I told him to repent, not confess. If he'd killed my mother, I did not need to know that now. Jasmine's name had better not come out of his mouth. Looking in his eyes, I waited to hear what he had to say.

"Ask Roosevelt to come back in. Alone."

CHAPTER 42

Chicago

The moment I saw the tubes, heart monitor, and IV, I wanted to regurgitate. I had to get the hell out of there.

Charles Singleton's body was practically skin to bone. His face was sunken in. Maybe that was how he'd looked before being hospitalized. I had no images to compare. Standing in the hallway, I swallowed to keep from throwing up.

Seeing Charles flooded me with memories of my being on life support for thirty days. For a month, I fought to stay alive. Loretta was by my side every day. I knew how it felt to do nine things right, one thing wrong, and have the people you helped the most turn against you. Long as my team was undefeated, I was the best. Whenever the inevitable happened, and my losing season came, I'd be one paycheck away from being replaced.

Loretta had betrayed Madison, not me. But I, like most spouses, found it easier not to blame my wife. Truth was, the person who stood at the altar, had taken a for-better-or-for-worse vow, and had signed her name to take me off of the respirator believing, or hoping, I'd take my last breath, should be held accountable.

I didn't need any more surprises. I said to Sindy, "I'll go in only if you agree to enter the room with me."

She lowered her head, then nodded.

Reluctantly, I'd gone into Charles's hospital room. Being with Sindy made me believe if she were my wife, and I were ever in a life-or-death situation, she'd do the opposite of what Madison had done. Married or single, I wasn't taking that chance again. My mother would have power of attorney. I knew she'd do what was right.

What could her father possibly have to tell me? We stood at his bedside.

"Sindy, leave," he said in a demanding tone.

"If she goes, I go too," I told Charles.

He shifted his eyes to the corners and stared in silence at Sindy. I not only saw but also felt his hatred toward her. Maybe it was resentment. Whatever it was, I'd only witnessed that from my opponents while playing college football.

Some of the dads yelled and called their sons obscene names during a game. Those were the ones who thought they'd go pro, didn't, and now their kid had to make it into the league for both of them. Whatever Charles had to say, I didn't want to hear it. I had to.

"Babe, wait for me outside. Please. Don't leave me," I said. Kissing her lips, I stroked her hair. I wanted Charles to see how much I loved his daughter.

Sindy had done right by me. If being in this room

with her father meant I had to overrule my desire to curse him out and hear what he had to say, I would do that. Seeing him stare at her that way made it harder for me to listen without judgment. But I had no respect for this man.

Soon as the door closed, Charles said, "I'll get straight to it. You may hate me after I tell you this but by the time you get over being angry, I'll be dead. My daughter loves you the way every man wants to be loved by a woman. Sindy loves you with every molecule in her body."

"I feel the same about her," I told him.

He shook his head, then said, "You don't get it. Men protect and provide. That has little to do with love."

I was not going to acknowledge him but that was why I'd stayed with Madison. I wanted to provide for my son. I couldn't do for Zach and not take care of the woman who had to care for him.

Charles said, "Men are incapable of loving deeply like women. We're not wired that way."

"Respectfully, I disagree."

"Doesn't matter. Let me explain why I said that. Sindy went against my plan to have you killed. I was the one who wanted you dead, not Granville. If I wasn't dying, there'd be a price on my head for fifty million dollars. And one on yours for two."

He couldn't be serious. Was that why Granville moved into my building? To kill me? This was the time for me to listen and not speak but I wanted to snatch Charles out of that bed and beat his ass.

"Sindy has a younger sister named Siara. I was paid ten million by one of the wealthiest Parisians alive in exchange for her. Siara was eighteen and a virgin at that time. Now she's twenty-eight."

I swear I wanted to pull his damn plug. I stepped closer to the head of his bed, then glanced toward the door.

"I have no regrets. I did the right thing. He's treated her well. She's given him three children. The fifty million I received was for Sindy. There's a man living in Dubai still waiting to marry Sindy. I don't care anymore if she goes or not. I'm dying."

Dirty bastard! I felt no sympathy for him. My jaw tightened. I wanted to ask, "Does the man in Dubai want me dead?" Sindy never spoke of her family—mother, sister, and seldom Charles. I had a lot of questions for her.

How selfish of me to frequently have her in the company of my family and not have asked about hers. That was going to change today. I wanted to meet her sister, her mother, and whomever she wanted to introduce me to.

"I may not have time to say what I'm going to tell you twice. Stay focused," Charles said. "The billionaire in Dubai requested Sindy because she's a Singleton and she's a virgin. We're descendants of the Singletons from Lancashire who settled in Texas."

I remained expressionless on the outside but thought, *Damn, for real?* Sindy has never had vaginal intercourse. That explained why she didn't want me to penetrate her. "I don't understand the significance of your family history."

Charles said, "What difference does it make? He's a nice guy but I couldn't deliver because Sindy is saving herself for . . . you. Can you say you've put my daughter first? Ever? You don't have to answer that. We both know you haven't. You still believe you love her the same? You don't have to answer that either."

When he'd said that, I felt like a fucking fool for letting Madison manipulate me.

"Ever since you became the youngest GM, all she talked about was one day meeting and marrying you. Before you became GM, she used to go to your college games just to watch you play. I know that you don't know any of this because I know my daughter. She was in love with you when you didn't even know she was alive."

A part of me was angry with this man I didn't know. What makes a father sell his daughters? I don't give a damn about where they came from. Everyone in America was from someplace else, including the Kennedys and the Rockefellers. Hearing Charles acknowledge the dirt he'd done, I loved and respected Sindy even more.

"Sindy is a jewel. I respect her for standing up to me but she put my life in jeopardy. She . . . here," he said handing me one large envelope. "When the time is right, after I'm six feet under, open this and give the letters to my daughters. One is for you. The fourth one is for, well, you'll see."

"Granville?" I asked taking the envelopes. Lifting my shirt, I shoved the envelope in the front of my pants, covered it with my wife-beater, and buttoned down and prayed Sindy didn't discover it was there. I knew she'd touch my back but I'd have to avoid hugging her until I could secretly hand the envelope to my driver.

Had Charles told Granville not to kill me? I was concerned, not afraid. God had me here for a purpose. It was time I start trusting in Him.

"I'm done talking. Do as I've said."

CHAPTER 43

Granville

"Where you going, big daddy?"

This young woman was going to give me a heart attack before I had a chance to enjoy my money. Mahogany was in the bed with her legs up in the air. We'd had sex for the past two hours.

"Why you like me?" I asked her.

"Why you keep asking? Get it right, big daddy. I love you."

"Why?" Mahogany couldn't take anything I wasn't willing to give. She was no scammer. Never caught her going through my stuff. She never asked me for money or things.

"What's there not to love about you? You a big ol' sexy teddy bear. And you treat me better than any of the men I've been with," she said. "I've told you that."

Wow. Me? I guess Mama did raise me right. But she also said, "If it sounds too good to be true, it probably is." Guess my mama could be wrong this time.

"I love you too. Take another pregnancy test when you get up." Buttoning up my shirt, I stepped into my cowboy boots. "Sindy wants me to meet her in the lobby," I lied.

"Okay, big daddy, I'll be right here letting your seeds swim upstream."

I'd never cheat on my wife. She made sure of that. I'd never had so much pussy in all my life. Three times a day. Hours at a time. Oral. Vaginal. Anal. Going in the back door on a regular was new. Felt different. Crazy good. But I'd never do that to a dude. The time I slipped inside of Madison's asshole was an accident. Mahogany started wanting to try anal sex out of curiosity. Found out she could cum harder, now I had to do that too. My wood was tired. I had to hurry up and get her knocked up so we could slow down.

Stepping off the elevator, I smelled the fresh scent of popcorn. I went to the concession room, got me a Sprite and some of that popcorn. The theater room was empty. Two guys were shooting pool. I'd watch but I really did have to meet Sindy. I chilled in the lobby waiting for her.

What was Sindy like in bed? Was she a freak, or conservative? I didn't want Sindy sexually but I was a man. What made Madison so crazy about Chicago? Was his dick bigger than mine? I doubted it.

Sindy had told me she was coming by to see me for something important. She'd asked me to stay inside my condo but if I'd done that, I'd be having sex again by now. Walking around the lobby, I needed to stretch all three of my legs. I was hoping she'd be with Chicago so I could apologize to that dude for what I'd done.

Sindy zipped up to valet in her Bentley like she

was in a hurry so I met her outside. She had on a dress with orange, green, pink, blue, and yellow. Why so many colors? Her high heels were red. Those didn't match her outfit. Women.

"Where did I ask you to wait?" she hissed entering the building.

That was rude. No "Hello, Granville" or nothing. Following her, I hissed back. "I'm not a little boy."

"I don't have time for this. Go to your condo right now. I'll be there in a moment," she said waiting for me to walk away.

Chaz parked his BMW behind Sindy's car, then handed the valet the keys. The beautiful dark-skinned woman with the red afro got out of the passenger side. I remembered her being in the courtroom during my trial.

Sindy rolled her eyes at me, walked outside, and greeted them. I followed her.

"What the fuck you hanging around for?" Chaz said to me.

"Look, bro. I don't want your problems and you don't want my troubles. Tell your brother I'm sorry."

Chaz swung at me. Shuffling backward, I dodged him, then threw up my fists. He was slow. Maybe he really didn't want to hit me. I dropped my hands. If I hit this dude in his head, I could kill him with one punch.

"What you sorry for?" Chaz asked. "That my brother didn't die or you're sorry you're not behind bars for shooting him? Stay the fuck away from my brother and me, dude!" He looked at Sindy. "How the fuck he move in here with his broke ass?"

Sindy rolled her eyes at me. I felt bad for not listening to her. Obviously, she was trying to protect me like she'd said.

Chaz didn't know she'd given me two million on top of the mil her dad gave me not to follow through with her father's request. I didn't care if he knew or not. I was happy I was off that hook. I was nobody's hit man. I was sad I'd messed up. Hope she didn't kick me out of the witness program.

The redhead said, "Baby, he's not worth it. We need to go upstairs." She paused, turned her back to me, then whispered, "And give Sindy Chicago's things so she can leave."

"What things?" I asked.

Mahogany ran to me, hugged me, then handed me a little stick. "We're pregnant, big daddy!" She smiled at Sindy. "We're going to have our own baby. Thank you for helping us out."

Sindy shook her head then walked away. That was rude. I called out to her, "I'll see you upstairs."

"Let's go inside and make another baby while we're waiting for her, big daddy," Mahogany said waving the stick.

The frosted doors closed behind Sindy, the redhead, and Chaz. I was sad. I guess no matter how much money I had I'd never be in their circle.

I followed Mahogany back to our condo. She took off her clothes, removed her panties and bra, then pounced on the bed.

"All you can eat, big daddy! Save some for dessert though."

The doorbell buzzed and I exhaled with relief. I guess our being pregnant was not going to slow my wife down. "Stay right there. I'll be back."

Peeping through the hole, I saw it was Sindy. I

should leave her out there. She buzzed again. I opened the door, looked down at her.

She waved something in my face. "You need to move out of this building by Christmas."

"And go where?"

"You're free. I don't care where you go," she said. "My father passed away today. He'll never make demands of you again. I don't want to see your face again. Take your money and your wife and your son Zach and move outside of Texas."

I shook my head. "I love Texas."

"Remember the gun you used to shoot Chicago. The one you hid in your mother's coffin. That's only part of what's on here. Watch this video. I'm sure you'll learn to love living in another state. Make your arrangements today. I'll bring you your son tomorrow."

"How do you know for sure he's mine?"

"Your blood test was really a paternity test. Here are the results. He's yours. I'll bring Zach by at noon."

I tore open the sealed package. Staring at my name, I said, "Why would Madison lie?" I was sad again.

"In case you misplaced the note I gave you when you first moved in," she said handing me a piece of paper. "Here's Madison's cell number." She took the paper back, tore it in half. "Don't call her until after you move."

I still had the note. If Madison's number hadn't changed, I didn't need Sindy's permission.

Mahogany ran to the door jumping up and down. Sindy glanced at Mahogany's firm bouncing breasts and naked body, flipped me a thumb drive like she was tossing a coin, then walked away.

CHAPTER 44

Madison

*B*itch! If you're all that, get your own man and leave *mine alone!*

Sindy Singleton walked away from me the other day dragging her suitcase out of The Royalton. I knew where she was going. Roosevelt had never invited me to an away game. Maybe he had someone before Sindy. I couldn't worry about that. Sindy might've been done with me but I wasn't through with her ass yet.

My cell buzzed. I'd turned off the ringer so it wouldn't wake my baby. I answered, "Please stop calling me."

"I want to see my son," he said. "I've got proof he's mine," Granville said.

It was pointless for me to explain "He's not yours" again. I ended the call. Why oh why had I opened my legs for that idiot?

Knowing my father had paid to alter the paternity, I had realized that Sindy, being an attorney, had possibly done the same. If I could prove she'd tampered with the test, I could have Vermont have her disbarred. And I'd forever be in Roosevelt's life.

Zach was face down across my lap. No parts of my son resembled Granville. At first, I thought, maybe. Now I was sure Zach was a DuBois. That was my truth, regardless of what Sindy had planted in Granville's mind.

The battle to keep my husband had become a fight I refused to lose. My determination to win had little to do with Roosevelt's feelings or desires. Intimidation was not going to work in Sindy's favor. She needed to focus on burying her father.

"Your daddy is Roosevelt 'Chicago' DuBois and your mommy is never going to change our last name." Well, if Zach's brain was a sponge, I was planting more seeds than the gardener had buried in my soil.

There wasn't anyone around to hear me, except my child. I was at my house. My dad and I weren't speaking. My mother came by once a day. We didn't discuss my father or the paternity. She believed my child was a Washington. Why?

Untying my halter dress, I sat in the living room on the sofa admiring my breasts. The implants made me sexier than before, and my standout nipples commanded attention from men and women. I refused to wear a bra ever again. I'd earned these twins by default. If cancer plagued my body again, I had to make certain my baby was with the right man. Maybe I should ask Granville to take a test to prove to him he was not the father.

Worst case, if he were, I'd end up divorced. Best situation, with these twins, it would take me less than twenty-four hours to start dating a new man with lots of money.

My doorbell chimed. It was Tisha. Picking up Zach, I let her in.

Tisha took him from me immediately. "Came by to check on you guys. Had to make sure you haven't done anything irrational."

Me? Irrational? "I could use a friend and a drink," I said. "Take him in the family room."

Pouring two glasses of champagne, I joined my one remaining girlfriend. I placed her flute on the end table near her, then sat in the white leather rocking chair she'd bought me.

"Your breasts look amazing. After feeding both of my boys"—she jiggled her titties—"I'm considering having mine done. What do you think?"

I couldn't tell her not to. Hers looked perfect to me but most of the bras these days had built-in padding. I automatically deducted a half bra size for any woman wearing one.

"I absolutely love mine. Take your time and decide if it's what you really want. Consult with several doctors. I'll give you the information for my surgeon. I have to admit," I said lowering my halter, "I'm happier with these."

Tisha stared. "Dang, girl. That's hot. You know I'm not gay but seeing those tits got me aroused. That's how I want men to feel about me."

"Why do we care so much about what men think about us? You think they care more about our feelings or theirs?" I asked her.

"Good question," she said holding Zach. "I definitely believe men are self-centered. Women move on. Men move up. My first husband replaced me with a younger, prettier wife. Bought her a pink diamond from Austria. Decreased my child support from twenty grand a month to fifteen. Hell, if I hadn't divorced Darryl, I would've gotten less money all because Lance didn't like the fact that Darryl didn't have a job."

I couldn't disagree on that. Tisha knew I didn't care for Darryl's leeching ass. Tying my dress, I admitted, "My dad told me he had the paternity test fixed. That's how my mom found out Zach might not be Roosevelt's son. But I swear, I believe he is."

Tisha kissed my son. "Regardless, this little fella is going to be loved." She held him close. "Figure it out before he's old enough to understand," she said, then asked, "Does Roosevelt know?"

"No," I said, shaking my head.

"Don't tell him anything until you're sure. Men are unforgiving. Are you willing to have Granville take a test?"

I shook my head again. Didn't want to tell her I'd thought about doing that. It didn't feel right. Regardless of the results, I knew Granville would find a way to tell my husband.

"Well, it's your choice. But I think you should have an independent test done with Granville, Zach, and you before the hearing. Go to a different place. That way, it won't matter what your dad did, you'll know for sure. If the baby isn't for Roosevelt, tell him the truth. Either way, you need to grant Roosevelt the divorce. He's moved on, Madison. You need to do the same."

Tisha was right. It was time for me to start dating again. Tears streamed down my face. I did not want the results to be in Granville's favor. I'd rather believe my son was my husband's baby.

My cell buzzed. It was my attorney. Drying my eyes, I answered, "Give me some good news."

"We got her served," he said. "Get ready for your stellar performance when I put you on the stand."

"Thanks. Will do," I said ending the call.

My cell buzzed again. I answered, "Was there something else?"

"Madison, it's me. Granville."

I showed Tisha the caller ID. She raised her brows and mouthed, "Ask him."

Exhaling, I said, "I'll let you do a test. If it's your baby, I'll let you see him."

Granville laughed. What in the hell was funny? I wanted to hang up on him.

"I already had a test. I can show you the papers. I can prove he's mine."

My heart thumped against my chest. "You can't be serious. When did you take a test?" I asked. "How?"

The first person who came to mind was Loretta but she hadn't shared time with my son. The second person was Papa. Was he trying to make things right between us? Tisha stared at me.

"Sindy had me take one," he said.

"Sindy Singleton had you take a paternity test for *my* son?"

"Yep. I can bring the papers with," he paused, then said, "I forgot. I can't come near your house. I'm not going back to jail. Can you meet me?"

Things were making more sense. Helen was behind this.

"No. No, I can't meet you because those results you have are false."

"Prove it," he said sounding the way he had when he'd represented himself in court.

"There will be no test. He's not your son. Don't call me anymore. Good-bye." I ended the call and blocked his number.

That bitch Sindy!

CHAPTER 45

Chicago

I sat alone in the guest bedroom holding the envelope Charles had given me.

He was dead. I'd more than honored his request by waiting an extra day. Whatever was inside, I prayed, "Lord. Please let the messages uplift and enlighten the addressees. Amen."

Slowly, I inserted a pen into the opening at the top. Separating the edges, I removed all the envelopes. I hesitated. What if what was inside would destroy our lives? I placed the letters beside me and texted Sindy: Where are you babe?

Wherever she had to go after she'd left this morning, I shouldn't have allowed her to go alone. I'd left the office two hours early to check on Sindy. I'd taken a nap thinking she'd be home by the time I woke up. She wasn't. I'd skipped dinner hoping to take her out to eat.

Daylight faded to midnight. It didn't take all day to handle business. Her house was quiet. Too quiet. Was someone going to kill me? Charles could've arranged that before he died. This could be a setup. I pulled back the drape. Darkness surrounded her house. The closest lights, approximately three hundred feet away, lined the driveway.

Suddenly, one light beamed, then another. An animal raced across the lawn. I closed the curtain, picked up my phone. No response. I googled her surname. Was she royalty? To me, she was. Her father definitely didn't act refined. I locked the bedroom door, sat on the edge, then picked up each of the envelopes.

One, two, three, and four, as he'd said, were in my hands. The first was addressed: "From: Charles Singleton; To: Sindy Singleton." I moved it to the back. The second was from him to Siara Singleton (postage was already affixed). Tomorrow, I'd drop it in the mail. The third was from Charles to me. The fourth was addressed to Jasmine Singleton. Who was Jasmine? Charles hadn't mentioned her. There was no postage or physical address like Siara's letter. How was I supposed to find Jasmine without opening her letter?

Reflecting on my childhood, I was blessed to have both of my parents. I wondered how Sindy felt having neither. Was she close to her sister before their dad sent Siara to Paris? What was her relationship like with her mother before she passed? That was, if she'd passed. A cool breeze brushed through the room reminding me the air conditioning was on.

The day my grandmother departed, she'd told my mother, father, brother, and me, "Take care of your grandfather." Of course we'd do that. My mother moved our grandpa in with her and Dad. Grandpa Wally didn't socialize often. He was content coming to a few games, and occasionally he'd join us for dinner.

Did we worry more about the welfare of others on our way out? Did we do all that we could while we were here or did we take the easy way out and delegate our responsibilities to our survivors? I didn't want to be insensitive toward Sindy, Madison, or my son, Zach. Balancing the three would become a challenge not to piss off Sindy or Madison. I had to make each relationship work.

Sindy should've texted or been back by now. I didn't like sleeping in her guest room but I felt lonelier when she wasn't here. No one to talk or chill with in the family room was boring. Would I be happy with Sindy? Would my life be melancholy?

There was never a dull day with Madison. Zach, that dude made me think about what fatherhood meant. How would I rear him? Women thought about having babies and taking care of them. Most men, myself included, didn't. Not like women. How was I going to teach my son to do the right thing if I wasn't his example?

I was hungry but didn't want to eat by myself when I got in so I decided not to cook and grab a beer instead. I hadn't heard her come in. Life without sex until marriage, this was a first. What if we weren't compatible? Damn sure didn't want to be the first man to fuck it up for her. Having a virgin girlfriend in high school was great but that experience was fifteen years ago.

The thought of sex made my dick hard. Sindy had to be a good lover. The only thing we hadn't done was penetration. Sex without intercourse was like eating a cake with no frosting. It wasn't bad.

Maybe it was more like enjoying a brownie with no milk.

I had to release my urge to cum. I didn't want her to walk in on my masturbating to relieve my built-up orgasms. She may have thought that insensitive of me considering her dad had recently died, but my sex drive shouldn't be taken personally.

I removed my shoes, pants, and the boxer briefs Loretta had bought. I had to throw these away the same as Loretta had done with all of the underwear Madison had given me. Women.

I played music from my cell, then sat in the chair with my dick in my hand. Taking a few deep breaths, I stroked my shaft. At first it felt good. Then I realized I needed lubrication. Forget it. I wasn't enjoying this like I'd thought.

I put on my clothes, picked up my letter and my cell. No response from Sindy. I decided to send another text. ?RU. UOK? Usually I wouldn't enter her bedroom while she wasn't home. I opened her door, placed the letter from her father on her pillow. I'd mailed the other one, addressed to Siara, as originally planned. Hopefully Siara would have the option to attend his funeral.

Returning to my bedroom, tired of procrastinating, I locked the door, sat on the bed, then opened the letter. It was handwritten.

> *Dear Roosevelt,*
> *First, I'd like you to know I had nothing to do with Granville allegedly shooting you. I say "allegedly" because I wasn't at your reception and no one has found the weapon. Not the one he used.*
> *When a man loves a woman, he'll do irrational*

things. I didn't kill my daughters' mother but I am responsible for her disappearance. Jasmine had begged me not to send Siara to Paris. Said she'd do everything in her power to keep our daughter from going. She never knew about the millions I'd received. Jasmine is alive. Wish I could say she was well but I have no idea. I haven't visited her in the ten years she's been in the mental institution.

Her slip and fall down the stairs was an accident. I carried her up the stairs to our room, gave her an overdose of pain medication so she could sleep it off, then lied and said she tried to commit suicide. Sometimes it's just our time and sometimes not. For you, it wasn't your time. For me, my time is up.

The institution thought Jasmine tried to commit suicide. With her telling them what I'd done with Siara, it was more convenient for me to let Jasmine stay where she was. Financially, I made sure she was comfortable. I would say, "Give Jasmine my love," but I have none to offer her or anyone.

Granville won't bother you ever again. Sindy made sure of it. She moved Granville into The Royalton and accepted you into her house to protect you. She bought and sold your place without ever having her name on the deed. She had Granville take a blood test to prove to you Madison's baby isn't yours. The kid is yours. Hopefully you'll be a better father than you are a cheater. You're still a married man. You shouldn't be dating Sindy or any woman.

The way you've treated my daughter is unacceptable. When she needed you, you were not there for her. Sindy is royalty. I arranged marriages for my daughters to keep it that way. Siara is happily

married. Sindy would be too if she weren't so stub-
born. If you procreate with Sindy, you'll taint our
family's name. You don't deserve her. If you truly
love Sindy, let her go.

Respectfully, Charles Singleton

Digging into my pocket, I pulled out the engagement ring I bought Sindy. Size six. Fifty g's.
Worth every penny. Now some dead dude was
telling me I wasn't good enough for his daughter.
After all he'd said about how his daughter loved
me when I didn't know she was alive. I didn't believe Sindy had bought my place or went behind
my back and had a paternity test done. I knew her.
She wouldn't do that.

I put the ring back in my pocket. Sindy would
have to tell me no, because I was definitely going
to ask.

A call interrupted my trying to make sense of
the letter. "Hello."

"You all right?" my mother asked.

"Nah, Ma. I'm not." I couldn't lie. I was fucked up.

"Go get your son," she said. "And bring him
to me."

"Is he really mine, Ma?"

"Do what your mother told you. And have your
attorney subpoena Johnny Tyler."

Ending the call with my mother, I had to call
Madison.

She answered, "Hi, there," in the sweetest tone.

"I'm coming to get my son. I'm on my way."

CHAPTER 46

Sindy

Getting home sooner was my goal but business came first.

Although my cell hadn't rung, I'd checked every half hour hoping there'd be a text or voice message from Roosevelt. There wasn't. No calls from Helen. *What now?* I thought. Hopefully he hadn't discovered any of my secrets, especially the one about his son.

I responded to the last e-mail, then powered off my laptop. Numbiya had left hours ago for a dinner date with Chaz. A stack of legal documents couriered over by my father's attorney would have to wait until tomorrow. Exhausted, I exited the building then sat in my car. I looked behind the passenger seat. Fortunately, the fresh-cut flowers I had delivered earlier hadn't wilted. They'd been in here over twelve hours.

As expected, there was no after-midnight traffic or accidents. I really didn't want to go home, or stay at the office, or be anywhere all day. Work helped me get through my sorrow. I couldn't explain the pain in my heart. I missed my father. After all the bad things Charles Singleton had done, he'd gotten at least two of them right. I dried my tears praying I would not inherit my father's manipulative ways.

The drive to my place was quick.

"Roosevelt," I called out as soon as entered my home.

I placed my purse on the table in the foyer. My arms were filled with the two dozens of roses I'd gotten to show Roosevelt my appreciation for supporting me during my loss. Both bouquets were a combination of red and white for love and friendship.

Where was he? I placed the vases on a table in my family room, then searched the first floor. "Roosevelt?" This time my pitch was higher.

Two o'clock in the morning. It was too late for him to be out. Too early for him to be gone to his office. Trotting upstairs, I knocked on his bedroom door. "Roosevelt. Babe, you in there?"

There was no answer. I turned the knob. "Not this shit again," I thought scanning the room. I knew he hadn't abandoned me. My father just died.

Don't make any assumptions. How could I not? He hadn't contacted me all day. Not once. I started crying. I was hurt. Angry. Maybe I was grieving.

I screamed, "I hate you!" In this moment, that could've been meant for my father, for leaving me. Roosevelt, for his fading to black again. Or for myself.

The bed was neatly made. Two suitcases were near the door. I snatched the handles, dragged both bags to the top of the staircase, then pushed them over. I watched his luggage tumble down twenty-one steps then land upside down at the bottom. I was so disgusted I didn't bother throwing them out. I left them there, went into my room, and slammed the door.

I exhaled in disbelief. A letter neatly lay atop my pillow. Roosevelt wasn't man enough to tell me in person. The envelope was face down. Picking it up, I had every intention of ripping it in half until I saw: "From: Charles Singleton." Felt as though my heart paused then pounded.

Okay, this was why he needed to talk to Roosevelt alone. The man was stiff as wood and I still had to deal with his shit. The muscles in my legs weakened. I sat on the edge of my bed holding the letter.

"If I open this, I may have regrets. If I never open it, it won't matter."

What difference will it make?

> Dear Sindy,
> Take care of Siara. It's okay now for you to visit her and my grandkids. Tell her that I love her. Don't blame your sister for refusing to see you. I told her not to. At first I thought you'd be a bad influence. Try to convince Siara to come home. Maybe I was right. I did what I thought was best but as I got older, I realized I could've done better.
> I'm still hopeful you'll go to Dubai, marry the man that is waiting for you. We must keep the Singleton name associated with wealth. It is the only way you can inherit your riches. If you don't go to Dubai, your sister will get everything.
> Your sister and your mother. You'll find out

where your mother is when the time is right. I know this is shocking but if I'd told you in this letter, you'd overreact and go straight to her. You need to prepare yourself. I have no idea what your mother's mental or physical state is. I have no regrets. Just sorrow. The two are not the same.

"What?!"

I didn't care about Charles's feelings. He was right. I wanted to see my mom. I scanned through the letter hoping to find out more about my mother.

"Thanks for saving me a trip," Roosevelt shouted from downstairs. "You didn't have to toss my luggage down here!"

I shouted, "You are truly welcome!" then slammed my bedroom door hard enough to make a picture on the wall crash to the floor. I had more important matters to tend to. How could I tell Roosevelt about my mother when I'd never mentioned Jasmine to him? How could I ignore the fact that he'd left me, again? I sat on my bed staring at the letter.

Roosevelt entered my room without knocking. "Sindy, what's wrong?" he asked sitting beside me.

Was he serious? *Smack! Smack! Smack! Smack! Smack!* "I don't need this right now," I cried.

Roosevelt grabbed my wrists. "Whoa, I am not your enemy."

I jerked trying to free my arms so I could slap him again.

"Stop it, Sindy. I know you're dealing with a lot but don't hit me again." His arms pulled me to him. He held me close. "Sindy, I love you."

"You don't know what love is. Let me go!" I struggled to free myself from his embrace. I was angry. At my father, for not loving me. At Roosevelt, for leaving me for Madison.

Holding me tighter, he said, "Yes, I do."

I screamed loud as I could, "Why didn't you call me? Where were you? Get your hands off of me!"

"Fine," he said releasing me as though I'd done something wrong to him.

I shoved the letter into his hand. "Is this why my dad wanted to see you before he took his last breath? Is it your ownership papers of me? Did you cut a deal with that devil? Do you have his cell phone?"

Roosevelt's eyes filled with tears. He shook his head, dried his eyes. "I don't deserve this or you," he said handing me a letter addressed to him from my father. "I'll see myself out."

"Do that! And don't come back! Madison can have you! You've abandoned me for the last time!"

I didn't want him to go.

Click. I cried when I heard my front door close. Felt like someone had pulled the trigger and shot me in the head. I was going insane. I went to the staircase, leaned over hoping he'd be there. He was gone. His bags were gone.

I was alone. Again.

My cell rang. My purse was downstairs. I didn't bother. Instead of reading the letter my father gave to me, I unfolded the page Roosevelt had given me.

I swore when I got to the end, it felt as though my heart had stopped beating. If I went to the morgue this moment, I'd kill Charles Singleton if he weren't already dead.

CHAPTER 47

Granville

There wasn't much to pack from my condo. Well, it wasn't mine anyway. Sindy had leased it for me. That was nice of her. Watching the video on the thumb drive made me sad. I wasn't responsible for Charles Singleton's death. But it could look that way. The footage of Mama's funeral showed Beaux putting the gun in the coffin. I couldn't let my brother go to jail. I couldn't be retried but Beaux could be charged.

Who gave Sindy that info from Mama's funeral? I guess women had their way of getting what they wanted.

If anyone saw that I'd knocked an old man to the floor weeks before he suffered a heart attack, my black ass would have to get real comfortable being in a cell. Sindy knew that wasn't my fault. She was there. He coughed on me. Blood. Well, at least I wasn't crazy. The paternity test proved I was right. Madison didn't have to keep ignoring my calls. I didn't want her. I had a wife and another baby on the way.

"Big daddy, don't worry," Mahogany said kissing my bald head. "When she bring us your son, I'm going to take care of y'all like you've done for me. We'll be one big happy family. I'm going to shower," she said powering off my computer. "You don't need to see that again. Ain't nobody sending my husband or his brother to jail."

She left me sitting at the dining room table looking at a blank screen. All of her clothes, except the ones she was going to wear, were already in the suitcase I'd bought her. She didn't have much. I didn't care about that. Mahogany was the first woman who loved me. I'd buy her whatever she wanted, which wasn't much. Here and there she'd mention she liked something, but she still never asked me for anything.

I knew Sindy wasn't my friend but I thought she cared about me. All she'd done was the same as Loretta and Madison—use me.

Material things were nice. Mama had said, "People are more important than possessions." I was going to miss the simple stuff like the oversize fluffy towels, good-smelling men's body wash, the big bed and the firm king-size pillows. I had enough money to buy it all again. Just couldn't stay in Texas. My wife could do the shopping for us when we got to Los Angeles.

Guessed I'd better stop moping. I went into the bedroom. Mahogany was sliding lotion all over her body.

"Put some on my back, big daddy," she said handing me the bottle.

No matter how down I was, seeing her beautiful naked body and smiling face cheered me up. I rubbed her shoulders and her back.

She jiggled her booty. I squeezed lotion in my hand, slid my palms together, then rubbed her butt.

"That feels good," she moaned bending over.

Instantly, I got hard wood. "Lay down."

"Okay." She sprawled across the comforter.

I knew we shouldn't have sex on top of the good cover but we were leaving and they'd have to clean it anyway. I stared down at my wife. I had a wife. Still didn't seem real.

Mahogany never denied me. I'd already cleaned myself, didn't mind doing it again later. I removed my clothes. This time I put my dick in my wife without licking her pussy first. Soon as my head went inside her, all I could think about was how good she made me feel.

I didn't have to rush. She wasn't leaving me. This was my pussy. Stuffing all of my salami into her warm juices, quickly I pulled out.

"Do that again, big daddy," she moaned.

Easing my head in, I slid deep as I could, then pulled out again. By the third time, I stroked her deep without coming out. She grabbed her titties. Her hips moved toward me. Felt like her pussy was trying to swallow my dick again.

"You ready," she said.

I shook my head. "Fuck. Motherfucker!" I screamed.

The back of my thigh tightened right when I was cumming. I kept stroking. Didn't want to mess up either of our nuts. Her sex felt so good, the charley horse would have to wait until I was done making love to my wife.

"You always make me feel good, big daddy. We've got to get ready for the baby and our flight to LA." She kissed my bald head, slid out of bed, and stepped into the shower.

I got in with her this time. I stared at her face as she washed my chest. My bottom lip covered my top. I wanted to cry. I felt bad for having shot Chicago. What if some man tried to kill me because I was in love with his wife. Guess I'd have to live with what I'd done forever.

"What you thinking about?"

"Nothing," I lied.

How could this gorgeous girl be raised in foster care by a woman who was jealous of her? Mahogany didn't have to worry about making minimum wage or not being able to pay her bills ever again. Once upon a time I thought I needed a woman like Madison. A showpiece that every man would like to have on his arm. Even after seeing Madison's bigger boobs, I still didn't want her no more.

Mahogany was attractive inside and out and that made her my queen for life.

"I love you, big daddy," she said getting out of the shower. "What time did you say the baby is going to be dropped off?"

"Noon."

"It's one o'clock," she said.

I dried off, then texted Sindy: Where are you?

Getting dressed, I finished packing my things and put my suitcase at the door.

A text came from Beaux. I'm at the gate. Where are you guys?

Damn, my mind really was messed up. Beaux was at the airport. Our flight to Los Angeles was in two hours. I wasn't leaving without my son.

I texted my brother. Zach isn't here yet, dude. Don't miss your flight. If we miss ours, we'll catch the next one.

You sure?

Bro, I'm positive.

Sitting on the sofa with Mahogany, we watched two episodes of *Divorce Court*. Two more of *Judge Mathis*. Two more of *Judge Joe Brown*.

I texted Sindy again. Where the fuck are you? I wanted to add, "Bitch!" I was tired of doing what women told me. I was a grown man.

It was five o'clock. Beaux had already landed in LA and checked into our room at the Beverly Wilshire.

"We can come back for Zach. Let's just go," Mahogany said. "She's not coming, big daddy."

When I opened the door, Chicago's mother was standing there with my son in her arms.

"Hello, Granville. You have a moment?"

CHAPTER 48

Sindy

What was I to wear to court?

In the midst of dealing with my father's funeral arrangements, I shouldn't have had to be sandwiched in between Madison and Roosevelt's issues. What did Madison intend to prove by having me appear as a witness for her divorce? I had more important matters to attend to. The most important was I still hadn't found my mother.

How was I to find someone that was legally dead? Had my father changed her name? Had he sold my mother? Was Roosevelt withholding information that my father had given him?

I needed to look better than I felt. *I'm not dressing down today.* After oiling my entire body, I toweled off the excess. The form-fitting cream-colored sleeveless dress I'd worn the day I met Roosevelt was what I'd selected. The same leopard stilettos, Rolex watch, and diamond earrings were on my feet, wrist, and in my ears. Ordinarily, I wouldn't wear red lipstick to court but I didn't care about what others thought. Not even the judge.

I opened the door to the bedroom where Roosevelt had slept. His scent lingered. Where was he laying his head now? Madison's? His brother's? His mom's? Why should I care?

My doorbell rang. I grabbed my purse, made sure both letters from my father were inside. I took them everywhere with me. Didn't want to risk losing them by any means. I headed downstairs.

As I opened the door, we both laughed. Numbiya had on a red pantsuit, animal print fitted top, and high leopard heels.

"Guess it's going to be that kind of day," I said.

"Girlfriend, we're going to get through this morning, and move on with our day," she said getting into her red BMW convertible. "After this hearing, I'm dropping this top, we're popping the bottle of champagne that's on ice in my trunk. I'm taking you to our favorite spa for a mani-pedi and massage. Then, queen, I'm taking you to dinner."

Corner Table came to mind. I had no regrets about that evening shared with Roosevelt in the Lexington Room. I could feel his lips on mine. My pussy twitched.

No, bitch. Not today. "I have to make the finals for my dad—"

Numbiya glanced at me. "Honey, Charles is dead already. You're not. Maybe if he were a better father to you and Siara, I'd understand. But he wasn't. I say cremate him and get on with your life."

En route to the courthouse, I was glad we'd left early. Traffic was backed up on the freeway. Numbiya was right. Why should I feel obligated to give Charles a decent burial?

"There's so much you don't know," I said.

"Well, that's only because you haven't told me. What is it?" she said exiting the freeway.

"I think my mom is alive." Tears clouded my eyes. I blinked repeatedly, not wanting to stain my dress.

Numbiya slammed on her brakes. "Shut the hell up! Did your dad tell you that?" She parked in a red zone. Gave me a big affectionate hug. "If she is, don't you worry. We're going to find her," she said drying my tears.

We sat still for a moment. Everything around me seemed quiet but it wasn't. Numbiya merged into traffic.

"What do you think I should do about Roosevelt?" I felt bad for going off on him. Before I'd given him a chance to explain, I'd practically thrown him out of my house. I'd only be lying to myself if I said, "I don't want him back."

"If it were me, I'd fuck someone else and forget about Roosevelt. But I know you still have feelings for him."

Wow. A half smile was on my face. Numbiya was a lot like Chaz. I didn't say anything. I stared out the window. Silence made me feel worse.

"Charles gave Roosevelt a letter before he passed. In the letter—" I paused, removed the letter from my purse, then read, "The way you've treated my daughter is unacceptable. When she needed you, you were not there for her. You don't deserve her. If you truly love Sindy, let her go."

Numbiya pressed on her brakes. "What?! No disrespect, but fuck Charles. Now you should leave his ass wherever he's at," she said. "Queen, your father is saying that because he's obsessed with money.

Is your sister's husband going to sell her girls when they turn eighteen? Maybe he already has. You don't want to live not knowing what will happen if you marry that man in Dubai. Your father is dead, girlfriend. Love whomever you want."

I waved at the attendant. He ushered us into the parking lot for attorneys. Maybe all of this effort to be with a man wasn't worth it. I could be happy by myself. But I couldn't kiss my lips at night or feel the same when Roosevelt wrapped his arms around me. I couldn't lay my head on my own chest and feel safe.

"Since you've told me that, queen, I don't want you to feel any certain way about Chicago. Don't try to get back at him or hate on Madison. She's a bitch but she's doing what the average woman would to keep her man. Girlfriend, I want you to go into lawyer mode on their ass when you're sitting on the stand."

I'd have to do that to keep from perjuring myself. Maybe I could tell Numbiya what I'd done after I testified, but definitely not before. We entered the courtroom five minutes early, sat in the back row.

"Hopefully, the judge will call me first. That way I could leave prior to any ruling."

"No worries," Numbiya said holding my hand. "I've got your back."

Roosevelt, Chaz, Helen, Martin, and his grandfather, Wally, were seated on the right in the first two rows. Madison and her father, Johnny Tyler, were on the opposite side from the DuBoises. Obviously, Madison's mother was with the baby.

The judge announced, "DuBois versus DuBois."

The attorneys and their clients stood. Roosevelt's

eyes widened when he looked back and saw me. Madison smiled as she sat at the appropriate table before the judge. He had to have known I was subpoenaed. That was his lawyer's responsibility, to communicate those who had to appear.

Listening to the case, while staring at Madison, I began to understand Roosevelt's attraction. Now that she had her implants, she definitely wasn't the woman I'd seen in that hospital bed pushing out his baby. Madison's hair was a striking platinum blond. Her waist was small, ass big, not wide. She had the kind of butt that went front to back. Not side to side. The dress she'd worn was an alluring blue. Her red, red-bottom five-inch heels popped without clashing.

Okay, the colors made sense. She was supporting the football team her husband managed. The judge was probably a fan. Whatever. I just wanted to get this over with.

Madison and Roosevelt were sworn in.

When I heard my name, immediately I stood.

"Approach the bench, counsel," the judge said.

I raised my hand before she'd asked, waited until the oath was completed, then said, "I do." Glancing at Roosevelt, I'd never say those two words to him.

Madison's attorney, Vermont, proceeded with questioning. "How long have you known Mr. DuBois?"

I asked, "Which one?"

"The plaintiff," Vermont said seemingly annoyed. "Can you repeat the question?"

He did. This time he asked the question slower. This was no laughing matter but I wanted to. That would piss the judge off but this wasn't my proceeding.

Including the years I'd watched him play, I answered, "Twelve years."

"Years or months?" he asked.

"Years," I said avoiding contact with Roosevelt. "He was a standout running back in college."

"Did he know you?" Vermont asked.

"You'd have to ask him that question."

"How long have you been sexually engaged with Mr. Roosevelt 'Chicago' DuBois?"

I felt Madison's eyes fixed on me. Intentionally, I looked at her, then replied, "I'm a virgin. I haven't had sex with any man."

Vermont's brows raised a half an inch, as if to say, "Really?"

"Are you in love with Mr. Roosevelt 'Chicago' DuBois?"

Without hesitation, I told the truth. "Yes."

Numbiya flashed a quick smile. Roosevelt smiled with his eyes.

"Are you aware that Mr. Roosevelt 'Chicago' DuBois and his wife, Madison Tyler-DuBois," he said putting emphasis on the last names, "have a newborn son?"

"It's not his baby." Okay, that response could get me locked up.

Vermont moved closer to me. "And how would you know that?"

Roosevelt's attorney said, "Objection, Your Honor. The question is irrelevant."

"Overruled. Answer the question," the judge said.

Suddenly, I realized I'd given the paternity test to Granville. He wasn't subpoenaed. I looked at Helen. She hung her head toward her lap. Roosevelt's eyes were fixed on me.

"The baby has features similar to Granville Washington and we've seen the sex tape of Mrs. Madison Tyler-DuBois sexing Granville Washington." That was my turn to put emphasis on *Mrs. DuBois* and *Granville Washington.*

"So you have no proof."

"No."

Vermont said, "No further questions, Your Honor."

Roosevelt's attorney stood. "No questions, Your Honor."

"You may leave the stand, Ms. Singleton," the judge said.

I stood. My seat seemed a mile away and I felt like hurdling over the rail and doing a hundred-yard dash out the door.

As I passed her, Madison smirked as though she knew something that I did not.

CHAPTER 49

Granville

"**B**ig daddy, let me see the paper. You done made us late."

Last night, Helen brought me my son and served me papers to appear in court at the same time. I figured if I had my son with me, they couldn't lock me up. I had to feed him and learn how to change his diaper. Mahogany gave him a bath and dressed him. I was afraid to do that. Thought his little two-month-old body would slip through my gigantic hands like butter.

"You sure you not a witness?" my wife asked.

"To what? I don't think so. But I'm not sure. Maybe."

"Where your proof you the daddy, big daddy?"

"I told you, it's in my pocket." I made sure I hadn't packed the papers away.

We were not going to miss our flight to LA this afternoon. I'd gotten over leaving Texas. At first I was upset because Sindy was making me go. Now, I was excited about Hollywood.

Mahogany opened the paper, then asked the policeman, "Where this courtroom at?" He directed us upstairs.

Leading the way, my wife whispered, "Here it is," then opened the door.

I wished Beaux were here. Felt like Mama was in the room. I held Zach in my hands like he was a ten-pound bag of sugar. Sindy was seated in the back row with that woman with the red afro. Her eyes widened when she saw me. Mahogany, the baby, and I sat in the row across from them. Soon as I sat with Zach, my wife took him from me.

The attorney standing next to Chicago said, "I'd like to call Johnny Tyler to the stand."

What did he have to do with this case? *That old dude better not have nothing to say about me. I almost hit him the last time. Might knock him out if he say this kid ain't mine.* I thought Madison was getting a divorce and I was getting my rights to see my son.

Damn! Noticing Madison, I saw she was hot!

I watched Johnny slowly approach the stand like a kid on his first day of school. I remembered my first day like it was yesterday. Mama walked me to class, told me, "While you're in school, the teacher is your mama. Don't do anything around her that you wouldn't do in front of me." That was the same thing I was going to tell Zach on his first day of kindergarten.

Johnny was sworn in. I was so familiar with the procedure, I could've done that. Madison turned around. When she saw me, I smiled and gave her a half-raised wave. Her head snapped forward, then back again. Then forward. She leaned and whispered in her attorney's ear. He looked at me.

"Your Honor, I'd like to request a fifteen-minute recess."

The judge said, "Denied."

Chicago's attorney stood before Johnny. "Do you have knowledge," he said, then paused. "Of leveraging your daughter's house in exchange for cash?"

Johnny adjusted his tie, then looked at Madison. "No."

Madison shook her head a little bit. I saw her though. He must've done it. He looked guilty. Wish I could question him. I looked at my wife and my son. Zach had fallen asleep. That was all this boy did. Eat. Sleep. Shit. And pee. Now that I didn't have a job, my kid was just like me.

"Your Honor, I'd like to submit Exhibit A," Chicago's attorney said, handing a document to the judge.

She stared at the paper, flipped the pages, looked at Johnny. He adjusted his tie again. The judge placed the document on her desk. "You want to repeat the question counsel?" she said to Chicago's attorney.

"I wish I had a Sprite and some popcorn," I whispered to Mahogany.

"Me too, big daddy."

"Order in the court!" The judge banged her gavel, then stared at us. I have got to get me one of those.

Chicago's attorney repeated the question. This time Johnny answered, "Yes."

"Did you leverage her home with legal permission?"

Johnny started sweating.

"Objection," Vermont said. "The question is irrelevant."

"Overruled. Answer the question."

"Yes."

"So this power of attorney that you filed was with full knowledge and consent of your daughter, Madison Tyler-DuBois?"

"Not exactly," Johnny said. He started sliding down in his seat.

I wanted to tell him to sit up straight but that judge would bang her gavel again. I was no fool. I was not getting thrown out of court.

"Did you sell your daughter's Ferrari for cash?"

"No, it was legally mine."

"Did you pawn her eight engagement rings?" Chicago's attorney asked.

Vermont stood. "Objection, Your Honor."

Chicago's attorney said, "I withdraw the question, Your Honor."

Madison turned around, stared at me, then faced the judge.

"Mr. Johnny Tyler," Chicago's attorney said holding up an envelope. "Did you at any time pay a laboratory technician or anyone else to alter the outcome of the paternity test for Madison and Roosevelt DuBois's son, Zach DuBois."

My jaw dropped. The courtroom was so quiet I could hear myself breathing.

Johnny removed his tie, wrapped it around his fist.

I wanted to string it around his neck.

"Remember you're under oath," the judge said.

Johnny mumbled, "Yes."

"I didn't hear him, Your Honor. What'd he say? Can you have him repeat the answer?"

"One more outburst from whoever you are. Who are you?"

Mahogany handed me my son. "I'm Zach's real father and I have the paternity test to prove it."

Chicago's attorney said, "I have no further questions, Your Honor."

"Well, I do. Fifteen minute recess. Attorneys in my chamber now."

After the judge and the lawyers left the room, Madison headed in my direction. She took Zach. "Give me that," she said snatching the paper from my hand.

Madison handed the baby to her dad, then approached Roosevelt. "How dare you come to my house, take our child, give him to that, to that idiot . . . and use our child against me. You know this is your son."

Roosevelt remained silent. He never looked back. I looked at Sindy. She pretended she didn't see me but I know she did. I felt it.

The judge and attorneys entered the room. The bailiff said, "All rise. Court is now in session."

Man that must be the easiest job ever. I wondered how much he made.

Madison's attorney whispered in her ear. She whispered in his. I couldn't read their lips. Vermont stood. I glanced across the aisle at Sindy. Her fingers were crossed. What she do that for? I frowned. She caught me staring and winked. I smiled. She was on my side.

The judge said, "*I'm* going to order a paternity test for this child."

Vermont stood. "That won't be necessary, Your Honor. My client states Roosevelt DuBois is not the father ... and she's no longer contesting the divorce."

The judge asked, "Are you sure you know what you're saying, Mrs. DuBois?"

Madison leaned forward, glanced at Chicago, then answered, "Please call me Ms. Tyler."

What the hell just happened here?

CHAPTER 50

Chicago

I rushed out of the courtroom, not stopping until I was out of the courthouse.

I jumped in the air and clicked my heels together. Felt like a cement building was lifted from my shoulders. My brother hugged me.

"Free at last, dude," Chaz said.

My emotions were mixed. Something inside of me felt as though Zach was mine. I really did love that lil dude. Guess I was wrong. Best to detach myself from him now. Sindy was standing by Numbiya. I put my hand in my pocket. It was there. I was ready. For real this time.

"Mom, Dad, Grandpa, Chaz, Numbiya, Sindy, thank you for your support." The smile on my face was so wide my jaw hurt. I was genuinely relieved.

All of Madison's lies had finally caught up with her. Her father's too. I saw them walking out the doors. Her dad was carrying Zach. Guess Granville would have to fight for his custodial rights. He walked away with his wife. They both seemed sad.

I thought, *I wouldn't want his problems*. Glad he had no reason to be jealous of me.

I knelt before Sindy, held her hand. People outside the courthouse stopped and watched. This was not for them. "Sindy Singleton, I refuse to let another second go by without asking, will you marry me?" I had no proof her blood was pure but this woman was royalty to me.

Her eyes shined for me. Smile beamed for me. Sindy was beautiful. She nodded, then said, "Yes."

Madison turned away, then turned back. Before I stood, she was standing over me. She removed her wedding and engagement rings then shoved them in my hand. Madison and Sindy were face to face.

I got up, brushed off my pants.

Madison said, "If you can live with your mistakes, so can I. But one day, he'll know the truth and just like me, you'll regret what you've done."

Sindy looked at her ring. Looked at me. Then told Madison, "I think you have a baby to attend to."

I told Madison, "Hey, I have no regrets. You got back your father's company and I'll do right by you. I'm just glad this is all over. Good luck to you and your son."

"Chicago," my mom called.

When I looked in her direction, Chaz was holding Numbiya's hand. He was on one knee. "I can't miss this," I said. Walking away from Madison, I held Sindy's hand. "Come with me."

Was my brother serious? I knew he was going to ask but had no idea he'd do it today. Tears of joy filled my eyes as I heard him ask, "Will you marry me?"

Numbiya nodded, then said, "Yes."

That lucky dog. What man wouldn't want a sex-ologist for his wife? Dad seemed excited for them. Guess he could get free men's health sessions from Numbiya now. Naw, knowing my dad, he'd still pay.

"Celebration at our house," Mom said.

Sindy said, "Congratulations, girlfriend. Give me your keys. You ride with Chaz."

"Sindy, wait a minute," I said. "I want you to ride with me. We can come back and get Numbiya's car."

Life was finally feeling right. I know Sindy had a lot on her mind but I was glad she'd accepted my proposal. I parked behind Chaz's car, then escorted Sindy inside.

CHAPTER 51

Sindy

"I need to borrow your fiancée for a moment," Helen said to Roosevelt.

She escorted me upstairs. We entered a spacious room. Tea was already prepared. "Sit beside me, dear," she said patting the sofa.

How long would I have to live with my lie? I had no inclination of what she knew. Not prepared to confess, I waited for her to speak.

"I won't keep you long, dear. Welcome to the family," Helen said, handing me an envelope. It was already opened. "After your father died, Roosevelt left this at my house. With the exception of that Madison girl, there are no accidents. I take that back," she said, then told me, "I opened the letter."

The name on the outside was Jasmine Singleton. I looked at her. "This is addressed to my mother. Why didn't he give it to me?"

"I don't know the answer. You'll have to ask my son. Read it," she said.

I didn't want to. I had to. Unfolding the page, I prayed it would give me closure. The letter was addressed to me.

> *Dear Sindy,*
> *I knew eventually this letter would get to you. Hopefully, before the letter I mailed to your mother gets to her. By the time you read this, your mother should've contacted you and your sister. I hope each of you can forgive me.*
> *Charles Singleton*

"That's it?" I asked, searching Helen's eyes for answers.

"Not quite, dear," she said, handing me a different letter. It was sealed. "When the time is right, I'll let you know." She took the letter back then said, "When I give this letter back to you, you must immediately give it to my son so he/we can properly raise my grandson. Inside this envelope are the real results from the paternity test for Zach."

Speechless for a moment, I inhaled. "You knew?"

Staring at me for a moment, she said, "If you thought I didn't, then you don't know me. I'll hold on to this for about six months."

For the first time, Helen opened her arms and wrapped them around me. "You did good. You got Granville out of Texas. You gave Madison a dose of her own deceit."

Wow. "What if Roosevelt doesn't forgive me?" I did not want to end up hurting him like Madison.

"You're not hearing me, dear. I'll take care of my son. I'll accept full responsibility. He won't hold this against me. In six months, Madison will have a new man and—"

"What if she refuses to accept the result?"

Helen shook her head. "Madison knows the truth. She's hoping to give you a dose of her poison. That's not going to happen on Helen's watch."

"And how—"

She interrupted. "And now, it's time for you to reunite with your mother, sister, nieces, nephew, and brother-in-law. Come, dear. It's rude to keep your guests waiting."

I sprang from the sofa, ran down the stairs. I couldn't believe it. This was the best surprise gathering of my life. After over twelve years, there she was.

"Mother, I thought you—"

The words stuck in my throat. I was happy my mother was alive. I hugged her, then each of my family members.

Our mother said, "I don't want to live another day without you guys in my life. I love you. At least your father did something right before he died . . . that dirty bastard. I'm glad he's dead. I—"

"I'm glad everyone could make it on such short notice. Let's break bread and candidly share our thoughts," Helen said.

Some people really are better off dead, even if it's only for the ones who were alive. Reuniting with my mother, my sister, and family, I too was eternally grateful that my father was dead.

Sometimes doing the wrong thing was right. I shouldn't have lied about Roosevelt's being Zach's biological father but I believe Helen was right. By the time he discovers the truth, Madison would have another man and Granville would have a child of his own. There were some lies a person just had to die with. I was indeed my father's daughter.

I whispered in Roosevelt's ear, "Tonight I'm going to be the best you never had."

Life is Short. Love is Shorter.

Or is that the other way around
Every time I think I've found
That thing they call love

I find myself lost

In the most beautiful space
I believe God created
Inept
Innate
My heart dances with joy
My passion pulsates with pleasure

Longing for that which I cannot measure
But imagine it will last forever

Whatever that is . . .

Reincarnation of fornication

It makes me not want to die
At the same time I lie

To myself
About the reality of the possibility
That this will last
For who or whom

Love is short
Life is shorter
Or is it other way around

Whatever it is I've found
I pray it never ends

Even when it Ends

Mary B. Morrison's

If I Can't Have You series

If I Can't Have You
What really makes a man plunge headlong into
obsession? And what does he do once he's past
the point of no return? Find out in this seductive,
mesmerizing tale of "love" gone dangerously
wrong.

I'd Rather Be With You
With Madison's marriage on the rocks, Loretta
couldn't resist looking after Chicago's interests
and reigniting his passion for life. But now
Madison wants to take back what's no longer
hers . . .

If You Don't Know Me
The scandalous story of two women, a sizzling
wager, and the fallout that's turned lives upside
down. Now, with the only man they've ever
wanted at stake, who will go one step too far to
claim him?

Available wherever books and ebooks are sold.

DON'T MISS

Mary B. Morrison delves into the outrageous love
maze of one family in her newest novel

Baby, You're the Best

Book 1 of the Crystal Series

After successfully single-handedly rearing four
daughters, Blake Crystal is finally looking out for
her happiness. And for the first time in her life,
she's getting what she wants—until she's betrayed
by the people closest to her...

PROLOGUE

Alexis

"Thanks for everything. I enjoyed serving you."
Not this shit again! That bitch had waited
on us for two hours. I'd kept my mouth shut when
the *what would you like to drink* was directed toward
my man only. I'd had to interrupt with my request
for a mai tai.

We'd adhered to their protocol by writing our
orders on the restaurant's request forms, meaning
there was no need to ask what we wanted to eat.
The repeat for confirmation: *So you're having the
fried wings, rice and gravy, and steamed cabbage, and
the vegetable plate with double collard greens, and fried
okra?* was asked of my man as though he was going
to eat it all by himself.

Now that the check was here I was still invisible?
Aw, hell no! I pushed back my chair, stood tall on
the red-bottom stilettoes my man had bought. The
hem of my purple mini-halter dress was wedged in
the crack of my sweet chocolate ass but I didn't

give a damn. That working-for-tips trick was about
to come up short.

I leaned over the table, pointed at the waiter,
then said loud enough for all the people on our
side of the restaurant to hear, "My man is not interested in you!"

James held my hips, pulled me toward my seat.

Refusing to sit, I sprang to my feet, then told
him, "No, babe."

Nothing was holding me back from the inconsiderate asshole who obviously needed customer
service training. I stepped into the aisle. The only
thing separating us was air.

"Not today, Alexis. Please stop," James pleaded.

Extending my middle finger alongside my pointing finger, my nails stopped inches from the waiter's
face when my man reached over the table and
grabbed my wrist. I was about to put both of that
dude's eyes out.

He posed, one foot slightly in front the other,
tilted his head sideways, put his hand on his hip
with a *bitch, I dare you* attitude.

The room was cold. I was heated. The guests became quiet. A woman scrambled for her purse,
picked up her toddler, then rushed toward the
exit. I didn't give a damn if everybody got the hell
out!

"One of these days, sweetheart, I'm not going to
be around to intervene," James said. He handed
the waiter a hundred dollar bill.

I snatched it. "Give his ass whatever is on the bill
and not a penny more."

James handed that jerk another hundred. This
time the waiter got to the money before I did. He
stuffed the cash in his black apron pocket, rolled

his eyes at me, scanned my guy head to toe, then said, "Thanks. You can come anytime you'd like. Let me get your change."

He stepped back. I moved forward. I didn't have a problem slapping a bitch that deserved it. I swung to lay a palm to the left side of his face. His ass leaned back like he was auditioning for a role in the next *Matrix* movie.

"Don't duck bitch, you bold. If you feeling some type of way, express yourself." I shoved my hand into my purse.

He yelled, "Manager! Manager!"

I didn't care if he called Jesus. "Say something else to my man. I dare you." If I lifted my gun and put my finger on the trigger, I swear he wouldn't live to disrespect another woman.

James swiftly pulled my arm and purse to his side, then told the waiter, "Sorry, man. Keep the change."

The waiter stared at the guests. "Y'all excuse my sister, she forgot to take her meds." A few people laughed.

"Take your lame-ass jokes to Improv Comedy Club for open mic, bitch. You weren't trying to be center stage before my man tipped you."

"I got you, boo." He pulled out his cell, started pressing on the pad. "You so bad. Stay turnt up until the po-po comes." He turned, then switched his ass away.

James begged, "Sweetheart, let's go."

Some round short guy with a sagging gut who was dressed in a white button-down shirt and cheap black pants hurried in our direction. "Ma'am. Sir. You need to leave now."

The old lady seated next to our table said,

"Honey, you're outnumbered in this town. You gon' wear yourself out."

I told my guy, "Walk in front of me."

Shaking his head, James said, "You a trip," then laughed. "You go first. I have to keep an eye on you."

That was the other way around. Atlanta was a tough place to meet a straight man who cared about being faithful. The ugly guys had a solid five to fifteen females willing to do damn near anything to and for them. The attractive ones had triple those options. The successful good-looking men with big egos and small dicks were assholes not worth my fucking with. But these dudes boldly disrespecting me by hitting on my man, they were the worst.

"It's not funny, James. I'm sick of this shit."

I knew it wasn't my guy's fault that he was blessed eighty inches toward heaven, one-hundred and eighty pounds on the ground with a radiant cinnamon-chocolate complexion that attracted men and women.

James opened the door of his electric-blue Tesla Roadster and waited until I was settled in the passenger seat. He got in then drove west on Ponce de Leon.

As he merged onto the I-85, he said, "Just because you have the right to bear arms sweetheart, doesn't mean you should. I keep telling you to leave the forty at home," he said laughing. "I'm glad you like my ass."

"Nothing's funny. I don't understand how men hitting on you don't bother you."

"The way you be all up on my ass, what the hell I need a dude for? Soon as you finish your dissertation, I'm signing you up for an anger management course," he said. "You can't keep flashing on men because your father is the ultimate asshole. Let it go, sweetheart."

"That's easy for you to say. Your parents are still happily married. I bet if your dad abandoned you, you wouldn't say, 'Let it go.'"

I was still pissed at that waiter. I had to check his ass. I was fed up with dicks disrespecting females. I'd seen my mother give all she had to offer and the only engagement ring ever put on Blake Crystal's finger was the one she'd bought herself.

James held my hand. "You're right, sweetheart. I know how much he's hurt you."

My father, whoever and wherever the fuck he was, had been the first male disappointment in my life. Some kids cried because their daddy promised to show up but didn't. Mine never promised. Before I ever had a first boyfriend, my heart was already shattered into pieces by my dad. Staring out the window, I refused to shed another tear.

Continuing north on Interstate 85, James bypassed exit 86 to my house. "I know how to cheer you up. I'm taking you to Perimeter Mall."

"Thanks, babe," was all I said.

I was twenty-six years old and I'd never met my father. My birth certificate listed the father as unknown. Hell yeah, I was angry. My mama didn't fuck herself but in a way she had.

My way of coping with my daddy issues was to not allow any man to penetrate my heart or disrespect me. Every man I dated had to like me more. The second a woman liked a man more than he liked her, she was fucked and screwed.

"Sweetheart, I have a question."

"Don't start that shit with me today, James. Don't go there."

He let go of my hand. "If you answer, I promise no more questions."

I knew he was lying. He always said that shit and didn't mean it. "What, James?"

"Have you had any men in your house other than me?"

I could lie. Tell him what he wanted to hear. Or I could tell the truth. Either way it didn't fucking matter! My blood pressure escalated. "I'm not answering that."

He exited the freeway, parked by Maggiano's. "Cool, then I'm not paying your rent this month."

That's why a bitch kept backup.